BOUND FOR YOU

JAYNE RYLON

Copyright © 2016 by Jayne Rylon

All rights reserved. No part of this book may be used or reproduced in any manner whatsoever without written permission from the author, except in the case of brief quotations used in reviews.

This book is a work of fiction. The names, characters, places, and incidents are products of the writer's imagination or have been used fictitiously and are not to be construed as real. Any resemblance to persons, living or dead, actual events, locale or organizations is entirely coincidental.

eBook ISBN: 978-1-941785-17-1
Print ISBN: 978-1-941785-18-8

Edited By Mackenzie Walton
Cover Art By Angela Waters

Sign Up For The Naughty News!
Contests, sneak peeks, appearance info, and more.
www.jaynerylon.com/newsletter

Shop
Autographed books, reading-themed apparel and more.
www.jaynerylon.com/shop

Contact Jayne
Email: contact@jaynerylon.com
Website: www.jaynerylon.com
Facebook: Facebook.com/JayneRylon
Twitter: @JayneRylon

OTHER BOOKS BY JAYNE RYLON

Men in Blue
Night is Darkest
Razor's Edge
Mistress's Master
Spread Your Wings
Wounded Hearts
Bound For You

Divemasters
Going Down
Going Deep
Going Hard

Powertools
Kate's Crew
Morgan's Surprise
Kayla's Gift
Devon's Pair
Nailed to the Wall
Hammer it Home

Hotrods
King Cobra
Mustang Sally
Super Nova
Rebel on the Run
Swinger Style
Barracuda's Heart
Touch of Amber
Long Time Coming

Compass Brothers
Northern Exposure
Southern Comfort
Eastern Ambitions
Western Ties

Compass Girls
Winter's Thaw
Hope Springs
Summer Fling
Falling Softly

Play Doctor
Dream Machine
Healing Touch

Standalones
4-Ever Theirs
Nice & Naughty
Where There's Smoke
Report For Booty

Racing For Love
Driven
Shifting Gears

Red Light
Through My Window
Star
Can't Buy Love
Free For All

Paranormals
Picture Perfect
Reborn

Pick Your Pleasures

Pick Your Pleasure
Pick Your Pleasure 2

DEDICATION

For Mackenzie Walton, who has put up with my shenanigans while editing more than fifteen of my books. Though our days at Samhain may be over, I hope our journey is just beginning. Thank you for all that you've contributed to my work and the fun we've had while doing it. Your stick figure reenactments of the Hot Rods sex scenes are still my favorite.

ONE

Clank. Huff. Clank. Huff.

Ryan admitted it. The sound of his roommate working out in the spare bedroom across the hall acted like the world's most potent aphrodisiac on him. His cock hardened, as if Ben was pumping iron into it instead of his own already magazine-worthy build.

Sprawled in bed, Ryan had been paying half-attention to some late-night comedy host, unable to muster a single chuckle. Against his better judgment, he muted the TV, then dropped the remote. It bounced, utterly forgotten, on the mattress. He glanced at the screen of the baby monitor on his nightstand to double-check that Ben's eight-year-old niece Julie was knocked out in her room at the other end of the second floor in the better-days Victorian they rented, as she had been for hours. If one of her periodic nightmares roused her, he'd know long before she ventured this way.

Clank. Huff. Clank. Huff.

Ben now had his full attention.

Nothing new about that, though the other man would probably grimace—or maybe deck him—if he could read Ryan's thoughts.

From where he leaned his shoulders against his padded leather headboard, Ryan could make out the curve of sweaty muscles in the spare bedroom directly across the hall. A sheen highlighted them in the mirror propped against the wall of their makeshift gym. They flexed and bunched as Ben did about a million reps with his fully loaded weights. In between sets he rotated some CrossFit shit, pulling himself up on whatever handy contraption he could find, inadvertently flaunting his spectacular body and the amazing things it was capable of doing.

There was a reason Ryan swore his room had the best view in their shared apartment. Fascinated, he could hardly stand to blink.

Though he had plenty of ideas about more enjoyable ab exercises Ben could try, Ryan knew better than to suggest them. Instead, he settled for taking enough mental snapshots to get him through another lonely night.

As he had in the past, enough times to diagnose his Ben-infatuation for what it really was—*obsession*—Ryan spread his legs. His fingers unfurled from the fist they'd unconsciously made as they mustered weak resistance to the inevitable. Then they wandered toward the growing bulge in his cotton shorts as if they had a will of their own. Ignoring the diminishing protests of his mind, which called him a perv for stealth-jacking to the sight of his unsuspecting roommate's glory, he slipped his hand beneath his waistband and cupped his hard-on.

Despite his best attempt to remain silent, he couldn't repress a soft gasp at the first contact of his hand on his cock. In his mind, he imagined Ben commanding him to be silent. He would do anything to please the other guy, especially if Ben was the one in control of Ryan's pleasure.

He allowed his thoughts to wander, only for a moment, to the times they'd spent in captivity together. Of course the entire situation had been fucked up beyond belief. Chock full of danger, extreme emotions, and a very unhealthy heaping of terror. But he'd thought some of the ecstasy they'd indulged in had been real rather than forced.

The times they'd served Mistress Lily in tandem sprang to the front of his memory.

His dick twitched and thickened in his trembling grasp.

Lost in his remembrance, Ryan wasn't sure if the hesitation he'd imagined in the steady rhythm of Ben's workout was real. Had he heard? Was he affected? Had he ever truly been?

Ryan paused and grew still, though he knew the shadowed interior of his private space would make it nearly impossible for his roommate to discern what was happening inside.

Disaster averted. Ben kept on lifting, as if his cut frame wasn't already irresistible.

It was foolish to think anything had changed between them, anyway.

Hell, he was lucky the other guy hadn't kicked his ass or tossed him into the street with all his shit by now. It wasn't as if he bothered to hide his unrequited lust.

Ryan gritted his teeth and worked his temporarily wilted shaft back to full hardness, refusing to let his doubts or regrets steal what crumbs of relief he could scavenge. It might have been wrong, but he didn't care. If he didn't find something to soothe the anxiety shaking him to the core soon, he might not survive.

Sure, it sounded melodramatic, especially considering the true jeopardy they had endured. Others hadn't been lucky enough to escape and go on to pout over an unreciprocated crush—Ben's sister April included. Ryan prided himself on the fact that despite his sexual preferences as a submissive bisexual man, he hadn't depended on anyone to make it this far in life. To thrive against all odds. To do what had needed to be done in those dark moments he refused to dwell on. Lately, though, the foundation of his confidence had developed a network of widening cracks.

Not the least of which was due to the man across the hall and what felt like one hell of a rejection, even if it had never been voiced aloud.

Ryan groaned, then lifted his head and dropped it onto his pillow a few times in a lame attempt to smash thoughts of anything except Ben's utter hotness from his cluttered mind. If he couldn't even focus on that long enough to rub one out, he was definitely in trouble.

He relied on his training, enabling his psyche to play more pleasant tricks.

After drawing in a series of deep breaths, he locked away his negative thoughts. Compartmentalization had ensured that even in captivity he'd been able to perform on demand. That skill had saved others who weren't so...let's say, *willing*, from being violated in those dungeons. More than once, he'd gladly served men high on a vicious sexual stimulant—Sex Offender—in Ben's place, protecting the other man from crossing his own boundaries. On their first night free, after downing enough alcohol to supply a frat house on a rowdy Friday night, Ben had tearfully admitted that Ryan had saved his soul.

So he didn't think his friend would mind returning the favor now.

Ryan stuffed reality into some far corner of his brain. In its place, he imagined himself bound to the sturdy metal frame of Ben's home gym. Not with silk ties or soft restraints. No, in his mind he pictured coarse rope. Tied tight around his wrists, it would chafe, leaving lingering red marks he could smile over for days to come. He'd press them and savor the burn, knowing Ben's show of possession hadn't been some dumbass fantasy.

Ben would stalk closer so that Ryan could smell the effort his best friend had made in honing his body into the most perfect version of his already phenomenal self that his striking Turkish genes would allow. Dark stubble would rasp over Ryan's face as Ben rubbed against him, snarling and biting his lip so that he was forced to peer deep into those nearly golden eyes, which had the power to mesmerize him.

"I figured I'd give you a close up view of the action, since you seemed so intent on spying on me," Ben would goad with a gloating half-smirk that proved he knew just how impossible it would be for Ryan to look away from a sight as magnificent as him.

His arrogance would heighten Ryan's need, making his cock throb in his shorts.

Though Ryan was tall, Ben was even more so. The crick in his neck from looking up would enhance his arousal. He shivered at the thought alone.

His bare toes curled into the sheets as he shifted, placing his ankles at the corners of his mattress, envisioning himself spread for his roommate's wicked pleasure. No matter what that might entail, he was game. Any way in which he could thrill the other man, and probably a couple extra Ben would never dare think of himself, would be just fine by him.

Maybe Ben would leave him there, strung up on the equipment as he did endless crunches, push-ups, and squats. Oh God, *squats*. Taunting him with that perfect ass.

Ryan swallowed hard.

Only when Ben was good and ready—plenty sweaty, too—would he return. With his trademark grin, which lifted the left half of his sinful lips slightly higher than the right, he'd ask, "If I'm the one doing all the work here, why are you breathing so damn hard?"

Because the hammering of Ryan's heart demanded extra oxygen, that's why. Even in his dreams, he didn't dare admit that aloud, though.

Instead, he'd yank at his bonds, impatient and riled.

If the tugs resulted in additional abrasions to his wrists, well, wasn't that a shame?

In real life, one of his hands choked his cock hard enough to edge into discomfort. The other reached down and wrapped around his wrist, squeezing until he could drown himself in his bondage fantasy. If only he could swipe the length of rope he kept in his nightstand. Even he wasn't bold enough to push that far with Ben so close. So he pressed harder. It would feel just like that.

Fuck, yes.

Immersed in his mental movie, he shifted, allowing his palms to roam so that one cupped his balls while the other began to stroke.

Just a little. It wouldn't take much to set him off with such vivid desires burning through his imagination, and he'd prefer to savor the waves of rapture, which finally reached into the cold spaces inside him and brought him alive.

When Ben began to towel off in the room next door, Ryan bit his lip to keep from moaning at the sight. What if he had free rein to run his hands over that taut, glowing skin?

To lick and bite and savor.

He'd certainly make the most of it.

Ryan remembered falling asleep next to Ben as members of the temporary harem Lily had constructed within Morselli's dungeon. She'd protected them, sheltered them, as much as possible. Which was why he'd read more into Ben's clean scent and the slightly awkward way they'd woken up cuddled together in their shared bed than had obviously been there.

Especially in those circumstances, Ryan couldn't fault his roommate for needing to form a simple human connection with anyone who happened to be handy. That was part of the reason he'd never called Ben out on mornings where he had pretended to sleep after he'd clearly awoken, as reluctant to break their connection as Ryan had been. Or maybe Ben had endured those blissful moments to give Ryan the only comfort he could in their captivity.

Shit. Shit. Shit.

Ryan shook his head, refocusing on the apparition of fictional post-workout Ben instead of the ghosts of dungeons past.

Right. Right. Tied to the home gym. Ogling Ben's package and wishing like hell he could taste it.

"Something interesting down there?" Ben would ask when he caught Ryan's gaze locked on the front of his jersey shorts. His fingers would spear into Ryan's slightly shaggy blond hair, gripping tight enough to have him panting all over again.

"May I—?" he'd ask, his throat too dry at the mere thought to finish his request.

"Are you asking for permission to speak, or permission to suck?" Ben cocked his head, then grinned, as if there were any true doubt.

"That." Ryan nodded, increasing the sting Ben's grip imparted to his scalp, too fervent to be more specific.

Ben chuckled, then cut him loose with the bone-handled pocketknife he always had handy. If the blade pricked Ryan's skin, he wouldn't complain one bit.

Without wasting a single second, Ryan would drop to his knees and paw at Ben's shorts, tugging them to the tops of his thighs. More than that was unnecessary for his purpose.

In his fantasy, he nuzzled Ben's heavy balls, licking them with the flat of his tongue a few times before swallowing his best friend's cock inch by inch. His fingers dug into Ben's ass, drawing him closer. So close Ryan choked, but he didn't give a fuck.

A hum of approval and the tightening of the glutes in his hand were reward enough for the minor inconvenience. Who needed air anyway, when he could have this?

What could be better?

As they sometimes did, his waking dream shifted. Shari appeared, perched on the balance ball in the corner. Their mutual friend radiated approval as she beamed at the two of them, witnessing the power of the raw energy surging between them. In her most prim voice, she would ask, "Have I ever mentioned how much it turns me on to watch a man sucking another man's dick?"

Oh, fuck.

Back in his bedroom, Ryan's hips began to rock, jabbing upward to meet his hand when it plunged toward his body. His cock jabbed through his fist, long and proud.

"Do you want me to fuck you while she watches?" Ben asked. "Show her how you take me so deep inside your tight ass? I bet she'll like that show even more."

"Yes. Yes, please." Ryan would have done a better job of begging if he could have sucked more oxygen into his lungs at the thought.

"Fine. But no coming yet." Ben reached down and pinched Ryan's nipple, making his cock pulse. "When I'm finished with you, you're going to take care of her. However she likes. And if you do a good job, maybe then we'll reward you, you hear?"

"Yes, thank you." He meant it sincerely. The chance to please these two would bring him as much joy and delight as he imparted, maybe more. In fact, the idea alone was enough to nudge him toward climax. He tried to slow down. To muster some self-control, but it was no use.

Ryan hovered on the edge, desperate for his daydream to continue. Refusing to go over until his balls ached from holding back. Until even rapture became a special brand of torture.

Only then did he allow himself to imagine the impossible, though the seductive thoughts tumbled through his brain in fast-forward.

Ben would mount him, face-to-face, so there couldn't be any mistaking the lust in his stare. For Ryan. Without apology.

That was Ryan's greatest desire.

Sure, Ben's big fat cock would feel amazing plowing into him with enough force to shake the home gym and clank various metal parts together in a furiously escalating tempo. The pressure of his dickhead on Ryan's prostate would be divine. The eventual liquid heat of his come filling Ryan's ass when he lost control would grant some affirmation of their compatibility both in and out of bed. But unflinching acceptance of their attraction—hell, their bond—despite the fact that Ben identified as straight(ish) and Ryan was most definitely not a woman...

Well, *that* was what he craved above all else.

"Ben..." he whisper-gasped into the night.

To his horror, a soft grunt came in response.

Ryan's eyes flew open, yet his hand didn't stop its furious shuttling along his length.

Flesh and blood Ben turned and stared into the mirror, indirectly meeting Ryan's gaze. He had to know it was a monster erection clutched in Ryan's fist. The motion of his masturbation was unmistakable.

The dominant flare in those molten eyes was irresistible. Close enough to Ryan's vision.

He surrendered. Shattered, pumping his release from so deep in his balls he'd swear they were in danger of flipping inside out.

He hoped his roommate could see every bit of the longing, desire, and pure need etched onto his face as he allowed his orgasm to overtake him, possessing every molecule of his being. Ryan grunted as the first blast of his thick come shot from his dick and decorated his chest.

Ben inched closer, as if drawn by the pull of so much naked arousal. He approached until his toes teetered on the threshold to Ryan's room.

And went no farther.

As Ryan milked the final drops of fluid from his cock, his eyes rolled back for a moment before he could refocus on his best friend.

Ben offered a wan smile. "Felt that good, huh?"

"You should try it sometime," he rasped in a shredded whisper. Though he already knew how this would end, he had to try. "Like right now. Let me—"

"I can't. I'm sorry." Ben cut him off with a murmur that held steel despite being softly spoken. "I know I have no right, but can I ask just one thing?"

Ryan nodded, a lump in his throat.

"Were you imagining Shari just then?"

The complicated, detailed answer—about how he'd been imagining all three of them feeding off each other—didn't pop out of Ryan's lust-addled brain fast enough. The look on his face must have confirmed Ben's suspicions, though.

"You should go after her. You deserve each other. You'll be happy together." His roommate nodded solemnly.

"Ben—"

"Good night." Ben shut the door softly, as if the sight of Ryan—absolutely wrecked—was too much for him. Hell, maybe it was.

A clunk sounded from the other side of the solid oak, as if Ben let his forehead rest there for a moment before the thumps of his footsteps faded down the hall, toward his own private space.

Wrung out, exhausted—in so many ways—Ryan simply collapsed.

He stared at the ceiling for so long, infomercials for some off-the-wall invention flickered in the background by the time he had recovered enough to budge. It was shame that motivated him then. Not over his honest arousal or how he'd let Ben see it clearly. But because it wasn't enough to lure the other man to his side.

Not now, and—he was coming to believe—not ever again.

Ryan flicked off the TV. Then he snatched his discarded T-shirt from the floor beside his bed. He swiped it over his abs, wishing he could clean up the mess he'd made of things between him and Ben as easily. Rolling to his side, he punched his pillow several times in rapid succession.

The soft blows did absolutely nothing to alleviate the flood of uselessness that rushed into the space ecstasy had occupied for the briefest of moments. It formed in that hole clean through his center like pus filled an abscess.

Marching into Ben's room and demanding that his best friend use him to vent some of his pent-up rage might take care of both their problems. But he couldn't take the chance that Ben would reject him.

Again.

Ryan squeezed his eyes shut. He didn't consider himself a quitter, but what else could he do?

Maybe it was time to give Ben what he really seemed to want—distance. A life without Ryan lurking around to remind him of the past while jacking off to memories of his luscious mouth or the very current temptation of his gorgeous body... *Confusing* Ben, as Ben had so assholishly put it during one of the rare fight-discussions they'd had about the twisted vibe between them.

There was nothing to be uncertain about.

Ryan wanted Ben. Ben didn't feel the same. Not anymore.

That disinterest crushed Ryan in ways he hadn't realized possible. It broke him when nothing else—not even being captured and forced into sex slavery at the hands of a monster—had.

It was time to go.

Time to move on.

What a joke! That would never be entirely possible. But at least he might give Ben the chance to find something that made him happy. This—their living arrangement, their thorny relationship—certainly wasn't it.

Shari?

Hell, no. Although she was perfect for Ben—a*nd* Ryan—the dumbass had never made a move on the woman either, despite the hurt Ryan could see in her that mirrored his own. Fuck that, Ryan could at least alleviate some of the guilt adding to his own misery.

Floundering any longer would certainly mean going under. So he committed to a single goal.

Stop doing to Shari what Ben was doing to him. No one deserved this kind of cruelty.

With that resolved, he fell asleep quickly for the first time in months.

∽ TWO ∾

Julie scuffed the toe of her lime green sneaker in the dirt beneath her play set. The rut there grew bigger every day. A few orange leaves swirled then settled into the dip she'd dug, so she crunched them with her heel as if they were nasty bugs.

It didn't make her feel any better, though.

She clung to the chains of the swing she sat on, hard enough that they pinched her fingers in places, but the stinging hardly distracted her. Neither did the rust stains they probably left behind.

All she could think about was Uncle Ryan's face.

Julie had run outside after seeing it. His expression had been kind of mean and lots sad when he stared at the back of Uncle Ben's head across the kitchen. He didn't look anything like the fun person she had come to know since he'd moved in after...the bad stuff.

His silly grins at the rotten jokes he told her had come less and less often. Then stopped. And she sort of missed them, although she didn't need cheering up as much as she had a few months ago. Even when she'd tried out the worst knock-knock she'd heard at school this week on him, he hadn't cracked a real smile. At least not the kind that made his eyes seem even bluer than her friend Johanna's.

Uncle Ryan still made the yummiest pancakes ever for her before school each morning, but he'd stopped painting on smiley faces with the whipped cream and berries. He didn't wear the special chef's hat or apron Uncle Ben had given him for his birthday either.

It was kind of like that. The same, and different. Everything.

Julie's tummy flip-flopped like the fish Uncle Clint had caught at Uncle Lucas's pond last weekend, waiting for the worst part of this morning to start. Sure enough, angry shouts had her scrunching her eyes closed and flinching a few seconds later. The noise reminded her of those two mean dogs down the street, who snapped at her every time she walked too close to the beat-up fence that barely held them inside.

She wished she could make her uncles' fight go away just by crossing the street.

It was hard to breathe when their loud words mixed with blurry memories of other arguments. Her heart beat so fast she thought it might pop right out of her body and plop onto the ground.

Before it did, though, a truck pulled up at the curb out front, on the other side of the white wooden fence. Well, mostly white. The paint had started to peel in a few places. Last week, when Julie had played with her ponies in the mulched flowerbed next to it—making a jumping course for them—she had started to pick at the flipped up edges until the piles of flakes made it seem like her figurines were trotting through the snow.

Maybe she should see if any more had gotten loose since then.

Uncles Ben and Ryan took her to talk to a nice lady, Dr. Epstein, once a week. She was smart about feelings and had explained that Julie did stuff like that—and the dirt rut she realized she'd just widened some more, and the paper she ripped into itty bits at her desk in school sometimes—because of something she called nervous energy.

What Dr. Epstein really meant was that Julie did weird things because of the bad stuff that had happened. Only she was too polite to say it exactly that way.

Julie couldn't help it. Now she knew how terrible some grown-ups could be. To kids, and other adults, and even to themselves.

Uncle Ben was hurting Uncle Ryan. Or himself. Right now. Nothing she did could stop it. It was as if she'd found a time machine then jumped back to last year, when she hadn't been able to fix things for her mom either. Uncle Ryan seemed as grumpy as Uncle Ben had been when Julie's mom had started taking drugs. Uncle Ben wouldn't do that too, would he? Not after what happened to her mom, who had been his sister.

They'd said it was a disease that made her mommy act like that, do all those bad things. What if he'd caught it too? Could Julie have it?

She scrubbed her shoe over the dirt some more.

Until she thought of her Uncle Ben and how he tucked her in every night. The way he'd kept her safe and how brave he had been to make sure she escaped the bad stuff. He wouldn't hurt their family like that.

Not on purpose, she didn't think. But it seemed like whatever was wrong was getting worse. And she knew just how awful things could get.

Julie gnawed on her lip, biting off the chapped skin and maybe a little more. Busy trying not to cry at the thought of going back to those places, of losing more people she loved, she didn't realize someone had opened the gate and walked up the sidewalk until the visitor started talking.

"Hey, sweetie, what's going on?"

Julie's head snapped up at the familiar voice. "Aunt Shari!"

She hopped off her swing and charged their visitor, a friend of her uncles. The two that lived with her and all the other police uncles too. Uncle Ben told her the police uncles were Men in Blue and they'd met their wives, husbands, girlfriends, and boyfriends, while protecting them from danger. That's how Uncles Ryan and Ben had met all the police uncles too.

Except for Uncle Lucas, who was going to marry Aunt Ellie. Aunt Ellie was Uncle Ryan's sister and Uncle Lucas used to be a real life spy before he'd helped get her out of the bad stuff. Aunt Shari's brother had been a spy too, with Uncle Lucas, and somehow he knew Aunt Jambrea, who became really good friends with Aunt Shari. It was confusing, and some of it she couldn't remember. Once she'd tried to draw a family tree with all of them on it. The thing had looked more like a plate of spaghetti, so she gave up. Really, all Julie knew for sure was that she might not have a mommy or daddy, but she sure did have oodles of aunts and uncles who always told her how much they loved her.

Aunt Shari wasn't very tall. Still, her hugs were big and warm. Right then, it felt so good Julie wished she didn't have to let go until Christmas at least.

So she didn't.

Aunt Shari laughed until she realized something wasn't quite right. She held Julie out at arm's length and studied her.

"Are you okay? Have a tummy ache?" Aunt Shari squinted. Her head tilted kind of sideways as she looked at Julie even more closely.

She realized she'd been rubbing her stomach, trying to stop what felt like rocks tumbling around in there. Before she could stop it, the truth exploded from her. "I don't want him to leave us!"

"Huh? *Who*, honey?"

"Uncle Ryan."

"Oh." Aunt Shari might have said more, except all the things Julie had been keeping inside started to bubble up and she spilled her guts.

"I don't want to move to a new house, start another new school, have to find new friends. Or a new mommy. Or new uncles. Or be on my own—"

"Hey, now." Aunt Shari drew Julie close again, then squeezed her tighter. "Slow down. I promise, your Uncle Ben isn't going to abandon you for anything. I'm here too. All of the Men in Blue and their wives adore you. They would do anything you needed. You have lots of people who care for you, remember? You will *never* be alone. I know I'm not as important as your uncles, who are really like daddies. Or your Aunt Ellie or Uncle Lucas. But I swear—"

Julie stopped listening as each of the people Aunt Shari talked about flashed through her mind. Their smiling faces blocked out her ugly thoughts and started to calm her. When she could think, something Aunt Shari had said stuck out in her brain. She thought she didn't count as much as the other grown-ups? Julie hated when she felt that way.

"Aunt Shari, don't tell, okay?" Julie whispered.

"Umm... If it's something that puts you in danger, I can't promise that, sweetie. I'm sorry."

"Nothing like that." Julie shook her head where it rested against Shari's shoulder. "You're important. You're my favorite aunt."

"I am?" Aunt Shari blinked a few times then grinned and let her arms loosen enough to do a funny dance. "Yes!"

Julie giggled.

"See, you always make me feel better. You listen good, and tell me things that make me less..." What was the word Dr. Epstein used? "Anxious."

"I'm so glad I can help." Aunt Shari scrubbed her knuckles over the corners of her eyes, which were shinier than before.

"Did I say something wrong?" Julie chewed her lip again, tasting blood this time.

"No. You made me really happy, that's all." Unafraid to tell Julie the truth unlike most grown-ups, Aunt Shari continued, "Sometimes I feel kind of useless. After my brother died, and some boys I liked didn't like me back, I don't know... I started to wonder what I'm good for."

"You're great at being my friend, and you do the best braids." Julie hugged Aunt Shari this time. Then she peeked up and asked, "Were Uncle Ben and Uncle Ryan the dumb boys?"

Aunt Shari laughed extra loud and flung her hand over her mouth. "Oops. Maybe I shouldn't have said that part."

"It's okay. I won't tell. They *are* being jerks today." Julie wriggled until she could stand back and cross her arms. It felt kind of like she was hugging herself and also like she was protecting herself from the yelling she could still hear a little from all the way at the edge of their yard.

"Is that why you're out here by yourself?" Aunt Shari angled her head and cupped a hand around her ear. "Are they fighting?"

"Yep." She could hardly get the word past the knot in her chest.

"Oh, honey, don't let that scare you. Sometimes adults lose their tempers. It doesn't mean Uncle Ryan is leaving. I mean, it could—I won't lie to you—but it doesn't have to. I, uh, *shit*..."

Julie stared wide-eyed at Aunt Shari. She hardly ever said bad words. Not like Uncle Razor, who hardly ever said anything *except* curses.

"Okay. How about this? I'm going in there. I'll find out what's happening. Then I'll tell you as best as I can." Aunt Shari bent down to kiss her forehead. "And no matter what happens, I'm here for you, remember? I'm sure that Uncle Ryan would say the same thing, even if he didn't live in your house anymore. You are *so* special. We all love you very much. Nothing will change that. Ever."

Julie nodded, trying to swallow. If she said anything, she would start to cry. She hated acting like a big baby. Ever since the bad stuff, she had tried her best never to do that. Except for when she'd dropped her mom's favorite glass and it smashed on the kitchen floor. That time she couldn't help it until Uncles Ben and Ryan had glued it back together. Extra crooked. They'd agreed it wasn't as pretty, and after she'd cut her finger on its jagged edges twice, they'd convinced her to throw it away.

Another thing gone forever. Like Uncle Ryan might be if he was so mad at Uncle Ben that he was actually yelling, which he never did. Or both of them if they were angry because of her and she didn't know it.

"Can you hurry, Aunt Shari?" Julie rocked back and forth, but it didn't help get rid of quite as much *nervous energy* as she'd hoped.

Aunt Shari nodded, her mouth pressing into a frown.

Then she marched toward the house, letting her shoes clomp and bang on each step.

With one foot on the porch, she turned around to say over her shoulder, "If you hear me shouting too, don't get scared. I'm tough. I have a tattoo and everything."

"You do?"

"Yep." Aunt Shari lifted up the edge of her shirt and tugged the waistband of her jeans down a little so Julie could see the American flag and the name *John* written in pretty script above her hipbone. "See? So if I have to raise my voice, it's just because I'm trying to get through their big, thick skulls."

"Okay," Julie agreed, though she didn't really mean it. Maybe she could cover her ears for a while. Someone would probably come find her when it was safe to go inside again.

With that, Aunt Shari fixed her clothes then disappeared, letting the door bang behind her. A few seconds passed, and then...

"Keep it down, you idiots." She scolded Julie's uncles as if they'd been caught eating too many cookies. She hissed it like that black and white stray cat who got all cranky when Julie tried to hug him, invading his personal space, as Uncle Ryan liked to say. "You're frightening Julie."

Not a peep more came from the open window of their house.

That didn't mean things were better, though. They hadn't been for a while, and Julie was starting to think they wouldn't ever be again.

She ground her fists over her prickling eyes.

"Hey, kid. You okay?" a gruff, unfamiliar voice called.

Julie jumped, her spine straight enough to hurt. She frantically looked around until her gaze locked on a stranger who was strolling along the sidewalk outside the fence with a teddy bear in his hand. Without thinking, she dashed to the nearest tree and climbed up to the fort Uncles Ben and Ryan had built for her. Although she slipped a little, her palms sweaty, she made it to the shelter in record time.

Flashes of memories, almost like ghosts, passed before her eyes. Nothing specific. Still, the fuzziness scared her even more. That made it seem like a nightmare she was having while she was awake. Uncle Lucas had told her that happened to Aunt Ellie—who had also gone through the bad stuff—sometimes too.

That was the thing about the bad stuff. She didn't remember much about it, during the day. Enough to know it was *really* bad, though. If she tried to think hard when something seemed sort of like she might be able to make it out, that's when her nervous energy got stirred up.

Uncles Ben and Ryan had their own funny habits like that too.

Because of what had happened, they were extra super careful around strangers. They never let her out of their sight, even though the rest of her friends were allowed to play anywhere in the neighborhood. One reason she knew their fighting was awful today was because they hadn't stopped her from going outside alone.

Still, they'd hammered stranger danger into her so often, she might as well have seen a fire-breathing dragon out on that sidewalk. So she didn't answer the man, ducking behind the thickest tree trunk holding up her hideout instead. Maybe he would forget she was there and go away.

"I just moved in down the street, in that blue house over there." The man pointed, and she couldn't help but steal a peek. A moving truck *had* been parked near there a couple days ago. He put the teddy bear on the ground. "Anyway, I found this in one of the bedrooms and I don't have a need for it myself. You can come get it whenever you want after I leave. You're a real smart girl not to trust people you don't know. I'm sorry, kid. I didn't mean to scare you. But you know, if you need help, maybe I could call someone for you?"

Julie shook her head as hard as she could. She refused to speak to him, even though he seemed less scary than he had a minute ago. She even noticed he had a cute puppy on a red leash that she would have liked to pet if her uncles or Aunt Shari were around.

"Okay. Well, it was good to meet you." He shrugged, then waved kind of uncomfortably. "Sorry. Again."

As the man began to back away, Julie wanted to kick herself. Why was she so afraid of dumb things? He had been kind of nice, not really scary at all. Now he was gone, and all she had to do to pass the time was think of the horrible things that could be happening inside her house.

Julie wondered how old she'd have to be before Uncle Ben would let her get a tattoo. She wanted to be just like Aunt Shari when she grew up. Not afraid of anything or anyone…not a stranger, not nightmares, and not even two big, strong uncles like hers when they were yelling.

She spent the rest of the time it took for the grown-ups to stop fighting drawing designs on the floor of her fort with a stick. Maybe Uncle Ryan would take a picture of her art to show Aunt Ellie so they could make them prettier together. She was the best artist Julie knew and she had tattoos too.

Now that she thought about it, all the bravest women she knew did.

They could be her armor.

Maybe she could ask Uncle Ben for a tattoo for her birthday next week. She would turn nine then. Could that be old enough? He kept asking her what present she wanted. She hadn't answered because before all she'd really hoped for was for things to go back to normal and she thought telling him that might make him sadder.

Julie closed her eyes and wished again for that.

Or a tattoo.

Then she scampered down the tree, grabbed the teddy bear, and hauled it up to her fort to wait.

↶ THREE ↷

Inside, Shari was freaking the fuck out.

She had no clue how she was going to force these two overgrown knuckleheads to behave themselves long enough to convince them they were screwing everything up royally. Before she could devise a semblance of a plan, something they were shouting stole any power of concentration she might have had and threw her headlong into their fracas.

"You said it yourself, Ry. You were thinking about *Shari* while you were jerking off last night!" Ben roared.

What? She stumbled, leaning against the wall of the entryway. Giant gulps of air weren't enough to fill her lungs, and she swore her eyes nearly popped out of her head and bounced down the hall like rubber balls.

Goodbye logic, hello emotions.

Though she desperately wished her morals would permit her to lurk in the shadows and eavesdrop, she couldn't spy on them when they were discussing her. When they had the rest of this conversation—and she fully intended to make sure they did—they would know she was listening intently to whatever convoluted bullshit they'd concocted while she pictured, in great detail, the aforementioned stroke session.

But would they be as honest then?

Visions of hard male flesh wrapped in long, hastily shuttling fingers dissipated. Her fists balled at her sides as she charged into the kitchen and warned them, "Keep it down, you idiots. You're frightening Julie."

Not to mention how inappropriate their accusations had turned. They probably didn't want the little girl outside, not to mention the whole rest of the neighborhood, knowing about what went on up here in the midnight hours.

In an instant, their growly shouts muted.

Step One achieved, anyway. Shut them up, check.

Stunned, they turned to her in unison.

"Shari?" Ryan flashed her a wan smile. Was it relief that momentarily relaxed his tensed jaw and uncreased his forehead? Or something else entirely? Guilt? Embarrassment? They had to realize she'd overheard that last juicy bit of their argument.

She honestly had no idea what they were thinking, not even after months of rehashing each of their conversations, encounters, and non-events in her mind over and over.

Hell, they would always be a mystery to her in a lot of ways. One that fascinated her, like Bermuda Triangle disappearances or trying to figure out who shot JFK enthralled other people. How could two men be so amazing, loving, funny, and kind when it came to the little girl they both adored, strong enough to have willingly endured captivity and abuse to save their families, and yet be so hurtful to each other? And her.

It didn't make any sense.

Worse yet, she had no clue how to fix things, though she sensed the potential arcing between the two men. If she could be included in their bond, even sort of tangentially, all the better.

"Hey." She lifted her hand then let it drop, limp, at her side.

Awkward much?

"Shit," Ben snarled. "Just what I needed now. As if this wasn't bad e-*fucking*-nough—"

Ryan shuffled closer, as if to come between her and Ben's harsh words. She didn't need him to protect her. Not today. Not from this man they both cared for, even when he was being an utter dumbass, crashing around, stomping on their feelings like an ogre on the loose, unintentionally squashing some nearby village.

"Look." Tired of being trampled into the dust, she snapped. Damn his foul mood. Instead of recoiling as she'd done in the past, she struck. She tossed the package she'd offered to deliver for Ellie onto the kitchen table, then said, "I didn't come here intending to hash this shit out, but hey, why not now? I think maybe it's time you two started being honest with each other about what's between you...or not. It's obviously stressful trying to pretend that whatever happened to you during the Sex Offender scandal hasn't influenced who you are today and what you mean to each other."

"We should leave the past behind for good," Ben said solemnly. His face devoid of life. The flat tone of his voice and the lack of luster in his eyes made her want to hug him. She might have if he hadn't started walking backward, away from them. "She's right. It's time to let that shit go and focus on what you can have in the future."

Ryan's wide-eyed stare whipped between Ben and Shari.

Why did she feel like they were having a whole conversation she couldn't hear?

"I'm not sure what I meant came out right." She tried again. "I'm trying to say that lately it seems like you're tearing each other apart instead of supporting each other. Worse, you're not the only ones being jerked around by this pointless tug-of-war."

Ryan reached for her hand. She dodged.

Shari hadn't been speaking of herself. That was a lost cause, she was pretty sure. They'd never seemed to reciprocate her interest. Or maybe it'd be more accurate to say they'd never acted on the chemistry she could swear they had in every possible combination between them. Especially if Ryan had spent last night...you know, doing what Ben had said earlier.

Resigned, she decided she could at least yank the sticks out of their asses and force them to see what they could offer each other, or what they stood to lose.

"Julie needs you. Both of you. She also needs a *stable* environment. If you can't support her together, then maybe it's time to stop making the people around you miserable. Even if you don't have enough respect for each other to do the same for yourselves."

Except her plan backfired.

Big time.

Instead of rejecting that doomsday scenario, Ryan shocked the hell out of her.

"You know what?" He stood taller, drawing himself up to the impressive height he often masked behind a casual slouch. Grim determination made his warm face seem downright cold and craggy. His long limbs looked as powerful as she knew them to be in that moment. Not that she'd drooled over his tight ass when she'd passed him jogging down the street, or the smooth cut of his arms through the water when he'd swum in the lake at Lucas and Ellie's place. Though his nature made him defer to others more often than not, it wasn't because he was weak. No, she thought it made him strong, and generous, that he often put the needs of others so far above his own. Today he showed them a different side of himself. One she found made her breath hitch in her chest. "She's right. That's what I was so stupidly trying to hint at before. So I'll just come out and say it. Do this clean."

Ben's eyes narrowed to slits, as if daring his roommate to cross a line.

Which he did, like a marathon runner smashing through the finish ribbon, exhausted yet proud of having the endurance to do what was needed to win in the long run.

"I'm moving out." Ryan's gravelly declaration bruised Shari's heart. She bet it was ten times worse for him to give up on his friend, though. They all knew that was what it came down to. He'd been struggling to reach his roommate.

He'd failed.

So much for her playing matchmaker when it came to the two guys.

She expected Ben to argue. Maybe even to break and plead, finally admitting how much Ryan meant to him in the new life they'd built together. But he didn't.

He stood there, arms hanging at his sides, hands dangling open and empty as he drew in ragged breath after breath.

"If it's okay, I want to tell Julie myself. Maybe I can set up a schedule to still hang out with her before school, take her to the bus stop and stuff, and visit in the mornings on weekends before the restaurant opens." The requests sounded reasonable but lifeless. There was nothing left, no passion, to keep him fighting. After this moment, nothing would be the same again.

Ben surrendered a single terse nod. His golden eyes flared while his dark skin flushed. Still, he didn't utter a single objection. To any of it.

With nothing to stop him from doing so, Ryan turned and walked away.

It was as if she'd watched them negotiate a divorce and custody agreement in ten seconds flat. After all they'd been through together, it disgusted her to see their connection reduced to so little.

Shari still couldn't figure out how to make things right between them.

Maybe it wasn't her place, but she would have tried if she knew how.

The utter devastation on Ben's face when he clutched his chest, turned around, then punched the wall hard enough to leave a hole in the sheetrock had her rushing to his side. When she looped her arms around his waist, too short to attempt to reach for his shoulders, he broke free.

Sometimes you had to admit you couldn't help someone who didn't want assistance.

"You go get Julie. I'll handle Ryan," Shari ordered as she pointed toward the yard.

Ben gave her another curt nod. "Thanks. It's for the best, you know?"

"I don't." She had some ideas about that. Now wasn't the time to discuss them. There was only one thing she needed to know at the moment. "Do you really want him to leave?"

"What I want isn't the most important thing."

Shari nodded, hope fizzling to life in her guts again. Maybe she had a chance—however tiny—to fix this after all. Eventually. "Go."

He did.

And so did she.

In opposite directions.

FOUR

Ryan stalked to his bedroom, trying to act like he wasn't slinking away with his extremely limp dick tucked between his legs. Having Shari witness him quitting like that had only made a lowlight of his life that much shittier.

Fuck. How could she ever see him as anything except the pathetic loser he was when he hadn't even fought for what he really wanted? Both her *and* Ben.

He preferred submission in the bedroom. That didn't mean he wasn't a cocky son of a bitch. There was no doubt he was plenty capable of singlehandedly pleasing them both—in bed and out. If only he'd had the chance to prove it to them before things got so twisted around that both of the people he was in lust with doubted how desperately he wanted them.

It had caught him off guard when he'd turned and spotted Shari right there in the kitchen, as if summoned by his dirty thoughts. So he hadn't said any of the things he wished he had.

Like, *yeah, I was thinking of her watching you fuck my ass.*

Or, *I've imagined sucking you off while you eat her pussy so many times I'm pretty sure I can taste it by now.*

Instead, he'd stood there like an idiot and choked on anything productive he could have argued.

Ryan pounded the heel of his hand against the solid wood doorway a few times, scowling at the dents the detailed historic trim made in his flesh. At least he hadn't broken anything. Nothing physical, anyway.

A huge portion of his world had just shattered into a billion pieces he could never imagine putting back together again properly. Hadn't everything already been broken before this morning, though? Today, he'd simply acknowledged it. Forced his roommate—*ex-roomy*—to do the same.

Maybe his goal shouldn't have been reconstructing their dysfunction. No, he needed to move on from it. Create something better, stronger, even more amazing. Something that could last a lifetime.

As if the universe was sending him a message in the form of a compact, smoking-hot woman, Shari cleared her throat and knocked delicately on the door he'd so recently abused. "Can I come in?"

For a moment, all he could do was allow himself to stare, devouring the very sight of her like the patrons at the restaurant he worked for did when they gobbled up his desserts. Petite yet lush, her dark hair fell loose past her shoulders. Warm eyes contrasted with her pale skin. Light pink gloss was enough to make her mouth remarkable. She was tiny but mighty. The way she stood there, her mouth opening and closing as if she couldn't decide what to say first, pissed him off.

They'd done this to her—made her uncertain of herself around them. He planned to fix that, at least. If she would let him.

Was she going to ask him about that whole jerking-off thing she had to have gotten an earful of? He kind of hoped so. If she took the lead, he definitely knew how to follow. Wasn't that the whole problem he'd been having with Ben? He'd been waiting not-so-patiently for the other guy to take charge. Ben never had.

Shari seemed like she might have more balls than Ben at the moment.

Though Ryan hadn't invited her in, she didn't wait for his permission. Thank God.

Instead, she stretched out her arms and stood there, presenting an open offer.

Unwilling to shun her as he had been rejected so many times by Ben, Ryan rushed to close the gap between them and practically smothered her in his grasp. It was so easy to wrap her up and tuck her against him. She settled perfectly against his chest, her ear pressed near to—if slightly below—his heart. Could she hear it pounding against his ribcage?

Why the hell had he waited so long to do this?

The heat and weight of another human being against his body instantly soothed him. Somewhat. If they stood there too much longer, though, it might rile him instead. Her wandering hands, which skimmed the top of his ass, and the way she rubbed against the full length of him, made him think she might not object to taking their comforting caresses to the next level. Briefly, he imagined lifting her so she could wrap her legs around his hips, shoving down their jeans just far enough to fit his cock into her pussy, and nailing her against the wall until neither of them could feel anything except pleasure.

It would serve Ben right to walk in on them finally hooking up. Let him believe Ryan wasn't devastated by the enormous fireball things between them had ended in.

Shit, maybe the other guy wouldn't give a damn, other than having to explain what was going on to Julie.

For that reason alone—okay, and because Ryan suspected Shari would knee him in the balls for using her so crudely—he'd never act on the revenge-fuck fantasies that zapped through the primitive portion of his brain.

"I'm sorry," he mumbled against the softness of her hair, which smelled like something sweet. Strawberries. He thought of a thousand recipes he could whip up with the fresh fruit, though none would be as delectable as her. "Shit, seriously. I'm *so* sorry. For everything. I just want you to know that even if you hadn't shown up here today, right when I needed you the most, I was coming for you. Okay?"

Shari sighed. She nodded and melted into his embrace. She rubbed his back in languid circles, then whispered, "I won't ask if you're okay. I'm not *that* dumb."

"It's been a long time coming," he admitted.

"Doesn't mean it hurts any less." She hugged him tight. "I'm sorry too, Ryan. It was never my intention to make you choose between us."

"That's not what happened." He separated them enough so that she could read the truth in his stare. Of course, that meant she could see the shredded bits of his soul practically seeping from his pores.

Who cared? Ryan vowed never to hide his emotions from her again.

Look where that had landed them.

"So tell me what did?" She ran her hands down his arms, then linked their fingers. Walking backward, she tugged him with her until they reached the bed. He gladly went where she led.

Together they sank, side-by-side, onto the edge of the mattress.

After months of keeping everything inside, she made it easy to say the stuff he'd been worrying about, over and over, without changing any of it. The time for progress was now. "I guess it's more that I realized Ben's never going to take what I'm trying to give him. You can only put yourself out there like that for so long before it's too tiring to keep it up."

That sounded like a reference to dick drama, and that was not what he meant at all. No Viagra needed here, thanks. He glared at his already half-stiff cock, which had been stuck in a near-perpetual boner for the past six months. Being near Shari did that to him, had from the first time he'd met her, in a fucking hospital room crammed full of cops, friends, and even his little sister. Shit.

"Uh, yeah. I totally get that." She frowned.

Fuck, of course she did. She didn't have it in her to artfully conceal the attraction she had to Ben—what living, breathing woman, or man, wouldn't find him irresistible?—and, he thought, to him too. "I've been fucking this all up, Shari. I'm trying to make it right. It's just...really hard for me. Goes against the grain, you know?"

"You mean because you like to let your partners take initiative?" she asked. The sincere curiosity in her almond eyes softened the question, made him less defensive.

"That's the nicest way anyone's ever said it." He grinned. "Yeah, that's what I mean. Because I'm not a typical guy."

"Hey, what's that bullshit?" She puffed up, propping one hand on her hip. Adorable, even when pissed. "Since when is there some standard way to be for a person of any gender? Don't be stupid. You are how you are...and I *like* who you are, Ryan. A hell of a lot."

It'd been nearly forever since he'd felt this good about himself, sure of his appeal. He'd forgotten how it encouraged him. Damn, things had gotten worse than he'd realized. It was time he reclaimed his self-confidence.

As fucked up as it was, when he'd been part of Morselli's stable of fuck boys, he'd known precisely how often he was requested to service his abusers. The fact that they hadn't killed him—or worse—meant he'd been pretty terrific at it, too. But when it came to the outside, the only guy he'd been interested in since then had seemed unaffected for so long...

It was like getting his superpowers back.

"I want to help," Shari said, snuggling close to his side. "I just don't know how to do it best. There are some deep issues in play here and I'm no relationship expert. I mean, I've never even had a real boyfriend before. Would you consider talking to Lily and Jeremy about how you're feeling, or is that too weird considering...?"

Considering how he'd knelt at Mistress Lily's feet? How they were friends in the real world now, instead of some elaborate fantasyland? Or how Lily and Jeremy were open yet still human, with the same jealous tendencies as any couple even if they were better at stifling them?

"Yeah, it's kind of uncomfortable." He shrugged. No sense in lying. "I try to think of her as plain old Lily, now that she's married to JRad. In my mind...the other stuff...that was a different person. Mistress Lily. It's stupid, I know. But keeps me from popping a stiffy in the middle of a family BBQ. I'd never want to come between them. It's probably more my discomfort than theirs, but I don't think I can do that."

"Hey, I understand. I'm happy to listen even if I'm not qualified." Shari smiled up at him without a hint of judgment.

How could she be so perfect?

She reached out, her soft hand covering his as her thumb caressed his knuckles.

He sighed.

"You know, if it's about more than talking that's the problem, Lily could at least recommend someone who tops. I'm sure Jeremy would understand if you went to her in that capacity. He gets it. That bond she has with her slaves. What it does for the men who submit and trust her. We all do..."

"Nah." Ryan shook his head. "It doesn't feel right anymore. I did go to Gunther's Playground a couple times since we came home, when I needed to blow off some steam, but...uh..."

He cleared his throat as he recalled the club where Lily worked, run by her husband's mentor. It should have been perfect for him. It wasn't.

"Something's missing?" she speculated.

Ryan nodded, his lips pressed into a thin line. "It's too clinical. Impersonal. Again, I think because *I'm different*, not because they are. I couldn't connect like I used to."

In his mind he added, *because I'm already interested in someone...someones...else.*

He'd felt like he was cheating. Disgusted, he'd sworn off returning.

Unless it was with Ben, or Shari in tow. Hopefully both.

"It must be frustrating to have that outlet stolen from you." Shari's brows drew together, causing fine lines to appear there.

Without thinking, he leaned in and kissed them away. "Thanks, but I can handle it. I'll figure this out."

Could he, though? Today had demonstrated he was closer to the edge of disaster than he'd realized.

The way she looked at him, with that *oh-really* stare, proved she saw right through his reflexive bravado. Damn.

She simultaneously freaked him out and turned him on. How could she be so intuitive and so attuned to him already? They'd never been anything but platonic in the months they'd hung out together. Maybe she had what it took to top and she didn't even know it.

If she started talking to Lily, who knew what might happen…

He shifted beside her, rearranging his package and glancing away for a moment to get himself under control.

Out the window, he watched Ben clamber up to the fort they'd built Julie in the elm tree, making the entire trunk bend and sway somewhat precariously. He hoped she was okay, and that their fight hadn't scared her too bad. Almost certainly, she'd have nightmares tonight.

He wouldn't be there to chase them away for her.

Ben would have to be enough. He was her real uncle anyway. Ryan had only been blessed enough to play the part for a little while. He rubbed his chest, but it didn't diminish the ache there.

When it came to Julie, there was no doubt Ben would get the job done. He'd given up everything for her, including part of his own sanity. It had been easier for Ryan to submit to the sex-drug addicts who'd stolen both Julie and her mother, April. Ryan's own sister, Ellie, too.

Ben had never been with a man before then. Never been told what to do in bed. And certainly had never liked either, though Ryan knew—for sure—that had changed.

Was that part of why they were struggling now?

Could Ben ever separate his new desires from the place they'd been born?

It seemed like the answer to that was a big fat fucking *no*.

"Can I ask you one thing? Something really personal?" Shari drew his attention back to her. She was picking at the comforter and tapping her foot. "This might not be the right time, but I have to know..."

Ryan couldn't help himself. He hated seeing her so apprehensive. He reached down and cupped her jaw in his trembling hand and lifted her face to his. "You never have to wonder that again. Anything you want to know about me, I'll tell you. You have a right to ask me anything because I don't intend to keep playing stupid games. Everything is on the table from this moment on. Okay?"

She blinked at him once, then again, before a gorgeous smile blossomed on her face. For once he'd managed to do something right by her. He planned to keep that streak going.

Shari nodded, then came right out with it. "Can you be attracted to a woman? *Only* a woman? Like, romantically? Is that something separate from your ability to submit? I know you were with Lily in a group situation, with Ben...and whoever else in that hellhole..."

"Quit worrying. That's an easy question." He smiled right back, equally intense, long ago having accepted this part of his nature. "I'm bi, Shari. Technically, probably pansexual. Whatever you want to call it is fine. I like men. I like women. I like androgynous people. Transgender or cisgender folks, too. Anybody who is capable of a consensual relationship, really, has the potential to turn me on. For me, it's more about who the person is than what equipment they're packing. When I take someone to bed, I love them for who they are."

"Oh." She swallowed so hard her delicate throat flexed. "That's really beautiful, Ryan."

"In case I haven't been obvious enough these past months, I'm *extremely* attracted to you. Have been ever since the moment you stepped into Izzy's hospital room. I sensed your loneliness, along with all that fire you tried to hide behind your shyness. No, it was more than that. Like you were afraid no one could see it burning in you as you stuck to the perimeter of the room, never interrupting or talking over anyone in the chaos, hoping you'd found a group you could belong to. Well, I did notice, Shari. In that way, I think we're kind of alike. I get you."

He went with his gut, choosing then as the moment to steal his first kiss with her.

∽ FIVE ∾

Ryan leaned in until their lips brushed ever-so-slightly. He stared into her eyes, giving her the final call. She pressed forward. Their mouths grazed over each other in the most affectionate kiss he'd ever received. It was part flames, sure. Sparks heated the parts of him that had seemed frozen for ages. More than that, it was comfort. Reassurance. Acceptance. A soft, snuggly blanket.

With potential for so much more.

Though he could have kissed her for as long as it took to age some excellent whiskey, he decided instead that it was better not to get lost until they'd wrapped up business here. So he settled for a tiny appetizer compared to the banquet he was sure was to come.

Shari hummed as they drifted apart. Her unfocused eyes did a lot to boost his ego after months of rejection.

"To be perfectly clear," he whispered. "The reason I haven't acted on what I felt wasn't because I needed a guy in the equation to get off, or in order to feel totally satisfied. I didn't hold out this long because I preferred Ben to you. It's more that I was aiming too high. Thinking of how good it could be with the three of us together. For each of us. If he doesn't get that by now, he's an idiot. I'm tired of going without while I try to show him what he could have if he was bold enough to take it."

"I know this is where we've all been heading. I've spent a lot of nights with my vibrator thinking about it—"

"Shari." He couldn't do more than rasp her name. The vision went straight to his cock.

"But…"

"No buts. Go back to the part about you and your toys."

She laughed, slapping his abs with the back of her hand. At least it broke the tension. "I guess I'm trying to say that I don't know if I'm the right woman for you. Solo, I mean. I want to be. Yesterday we were trying to pretend like there was nothing here, and suddenly today it's all real. There's a chance to have everything I've hoped for, and it's overwhelming. I just don't know if I have it in me to be the person you need. Or maybe that's who I could become with you. *For* you. It's one thing to think about, but…"

"Hey, I only want you to be yourself." He tried to reassure her. "Because that woman is pretty damn amazing. Shari?"

Ryan gathered as much courage as he could muster.

"Yeah?" she peered up at him, her eyes wide and innocent.

"How about we forget all the complicated shit? I won't lie. This shit with Ben fucked me up. You're right. It doesn't seem real. It hasn't sunk in yet that it's actually over. That I'm moving out and he won't be there in my life every day anymore." As quick as that, the knots in his guts retied themselves.

"Of course." She hugged him, laying her head on his shoulder this time as she peered up at him.

"Can we start simple? With a date?" Ryan smiled as best he could. He didn't recall it having ever been this nerve-wracking to ask someone out—for dinner or more—before. "I know for sure I can satisfy you in the kitchen. So take me home with you. Let me make you a fancy dinner tonight."

"Seriously?" She rubbed her gently curved stomach. He couldn't explain how much it turned him on to watch a woman enjoy his meals instead of picking at the rich courses he preferred to whip up. Serving her his creations would be a bonus.

"Please?" He tried not to let his cock harden as he begged her, but it was no use. So he shifted on the bed to keep her from noticing, he hoped.

"What am I, an idiot?" She grinned. "Hell, yes."

He couldn't help stealing a quick kiss against her mostly closed lips. At least that was what he'd intended, but after learning the true meaning of amuse bouche, he couldn't restrict himself to a single taste.

"And Ryan?" she said breathlessly.

"Yeah?"

"You're welcome to stay as long as you like."

"It helps knowing someone with a mountain resort, huh? Plenty of cabins to choose from when you need to bum a place to crash." He looked around his room in Ben's house, knowing it would never be home again.

"Sure, that works." The way she refused to meet his gaze and the softness of her reply made him wonder if she'd had other sleeping arrangements in mind. He didn't want to assume or overextend his welcome, though.

They'd figure that part out later.

The best way he knew to make his side of things apparent was to stick to action. It seemed a lot more effective than all this talking about their feelings, anyway. Who was he kidding? He simply needed a second helping of her sweetness.

Not only did she allow him seconds, but she also launched herself toward him hard enough that they knocked their foreheads together. Laughing, they crashed to the bed with him on his back and her straddling him. Her hands gripped his shoulders, using his body to support herself, hovering over him for only a fraction of a second before she descended and captured his mouth with hers.

Hunger.

He was an expert in the feeling. It was an empty sensation he made it his life's work to satisfy.

With Shari, he found they could do it so much more effectively through physical contact than with something as ordinary as food. The moment she slipped her tongue inside his mouth, he let his head fall back with a groan. His hands flew to her ass, kneading. Both to anchor her to him and to ground himself in her presence.

It was bizarre to be equal parts devastated and optimistic after the events of the past hour. Reeling, he reached for the good in his life and tried to block out the bad.

Her fingers speared into his hair and the light scratch of her nails on his scalp had him forgetting where they were along with his promises to himself to take things slowly so he didn't ruin another relationship he held dear.

Sometime after the point he'd forgotten to breathe for a while and the moment Shari's tongue had wandered between his lips to dance with his own, driving him insane, a noise at the doorway caused him to sit up, barely keeping Shari from tumbling to the floor.

Busted.

Ben examined their flushed faces, the way Shari immediately crossed her arms over her chest when they broke apart, and the unmistakable bulge in Ryan's pants. He cleared his throat, then nodded, one side of his lips curving up though the shadows in his eyes certainly weren't caused by elation.

"Uncle Ryan and Aunt Shari sitting in a tree..." Julie started up her favorite song, swinging her feet so they bounced off Ben's thigh—nearly thicker than the elm out back—without making a single dent. She clutched a teddy bear he hadn't seen before. Maybe Ben had given her an early birthday present to make up for the impact of their aggression, something that rightfully freaked her out after the shit she'd lived through.

Damn, he was going to miss her. Them.

When he patted the bed next to him, she squirmed so that Ben set her down then bounced onto the mattress beside him. Her exuberance didn't last when she caught sight of his face, though.

"Are you trying to figure out how to say goodbye?"

And that did it.

She'd managed to crush his heart with a single innocent question.

Shari put her hand on his and squeezed, lending him the strength he needed to do this properly.

"Yeah," he croaked.

"It's okay." Julie dangled from his neck in a chokehold hug. "Uncle Ben told me how much you love us and that sometimes people have to move on. You're still going to come to my birthday party next weekend, though, right?"

"I wouldn't miss it for anything." He made sure she could tell how serious he was. "And just because I won't live here anymore doesn't mean that I don't love you. Very much. You can call me whenever you want to talk, okay?"

"Even if it's the middle of the night when I have nightmares? You sing the best songs to help me go back to sleep." Her eyes couldn't possibly get any bigger.

"Especially then." He smooshed her in a bear hug when he couldn't find the words to express himself well enough.

She seemed to understand as best as an eight-year-old could. For now.

Ryan grinned when she motioned for him to come closer and put her hand up to block her secret from the other adults in the room. But he couldn't suppress a single snort when she glanced at Shari and then flashed him the world's most unsubtle thumbs-up.

He laid a giant smacking kiss on her cheek, then stood. It was now or never.

She was a smart girl, their Julie. He swallowed hard. Would he still have any claim to her after this? Ben wouldn't be cruel enough to take her away. Or worse, to let their bond fade into nothing as the days rolled by. Would he?

With his heart simultaneously broken and hopeful, Ryan packed a duffle. Then he called his boss and told the guy he needed to cash in some of that vacation he was always being lectured to take.

Shari held his hand as they strode out the door together. She never once complained, despite the fact that he nearly crushed her delicate fingers in his shaking grasp.

His stride hitched once, when he caught sight of Julie peering down at them from her window, tears on her cheeks. Ben stood behind her, stoic. One hand rested on her shoulder as they watched Ryan abandon them.

"Do you want to go back in?" Shari asked.

"Yes. Fuck, yes. But I can't."

Together, they blew Julie kisses. Then left.

It was the hardest thing he'd ever done to watch their old house fade to nothing in the side mirror of Shari's enormous pick-up. A thousand times more difficult than when he'd sacrificed himself to a sadistic madman in the slim hopes of reclaiming his sister alive. At least there'd been a purpose to that pain.

This he could hardly bear.

It didn't have to be this way.

Why was Ben such a fucking moron? Why hadn't Ryan been enough?

He needed a distraction, something familiar and soothing. "Do you mind stopping at the store so I can grab some ingredients for that dinner I'm going to make you?"

SIX

Shari sighed as she unlocked the gate, then pulled her beast of a truck inside before re-securing the entrance to the resort. Some of her habits were too ingrained to set aside. True, the risks she faced from run-of-the-mill crooks were nothing like those she had guarded against back in the days her superspy brother had incidentally made her a target for a whole host of professional baddies. Still, vigilance had become customary.

She couldn't suppress a groan as she climbed behind the wheel again.

It had been a long damn day.

"You okay? I could have driven, you know?" Ryan reached over and rubbed her thigh, loosening the knot that had formed there after the four-hour ride. It shocked her how...*not* weird things were between them after months of hesitation and false starts. Could it have been like this all along?

Maybe she should have taken her friends' advice and made a move on him months ago. His hand spanned her entire leg above her knee. Capable, deft fingers rubbed until she thought she might crash into the woods and kill them both. So she put her hand on his and knitted their fingers together.

"I'm used to making the trip alone." She shrugged one shoulder while the other hand stayed on the wheel, steering them through the forest toward the main cabin she lived in. Only recently had she begun to regret how far away from the nearest city—the one where all her friends lived—her mountain retreat was located.

Call it what it was: a fortress compound. Or had been.

These days she'd been working hard to lure folks looking for some quiet time out to her slice of rural heaven. All the landmines had even been deactivated lest they blow up a customer by accident. Bad for business, that. Still, it'd been eight months and she'd already gone through five managers. It was starting to look like she'd have to stay up here constantly if she wanted to make her resort a success.

With Ryan in tow, that didn't seem so terrible. She was pretty sure he'd keep her occupied after he got settled in. Mmmm. If she was lucky, anyway.

"I've never liked that."

"Huh?" She'd lost the thread of their conversation as she drooled over mental movies of him making love to her on a blanket beneath the riot of color made by the canopy of changing leaves. Or surprising her with a quickie in the outdoor shower she used to keep the worst of her ranch dirt from migrating into her cabin.

"You driving all this way by yourself. It's not safe. Especially when you leave late and it's dark. I bet at night you can't see shit around here." He frowned at her.

"You can't blame me for wanting to stay." She smiled. "It's not like I have a lot of friends up here and..." Why not be honest? "...you were right before. It gets lonely sometimes."

"I get that." Was he commiserating with her, or referring to himself?

Either way, she supposed, they knew something about seclusion. Maybe it was harder to feel isolation pressing in on you even when there were plenty of people around. Ones you were in love with, even. Because she never doubted for a second that Ryan was devoted to Ben, even if the idiot didn't realize it...or care.

Now it was her who could relate, although she didn't dare admit it.

"Well, you can put your feet up and rest while I make you dinner." Ryan seemed to perk up at the idea. "Take a quick nap if you want. It's only fair."

"I'll keep you company. It's the least I can do when you're slaving over a hot stove."

"I don't mind." Something in the way he said it—maybe it was how his voice got slower and deeper, sexier—made her sure there was more to it than that. Like it was a pleasure, not a chore. True, he had often told her how much he treasured his career as a chef at a five-star restaurant in the city, a place she'd never even dreamed about eating at before.

Still, she couldn't help but feel like there was more to it than that.

Her stomach growled softly while she thought of the cooler bursting with supplies, which they'd stashed in the bed of the truck. A handful of items she hadn't even recognized. The best food was like that. If you trusted the chef, you just shut up and ate it, knowing it would be delicious.

She had a feeling this was going to be one of those nights. Meals, she corrected herself. She'd definitely been thinking about dinner. Not anything after. Sure. She shook her head softly. What happened after they ate, well...that was going to be simple.

Bedtime. In separate rooms. All the way on opposite ends of the upstairs hallway, if he decided to stay in the main house. Otherwise, she'd keep the long yard between them.

No exploring allowed. Not when his emotions had gone through the wringer once today.

Shari didn't want to dredge up ugly shit. It had taken almost two counties for him to quit gripping the door handle as if he needed that connection to keep from flinging himself out of the moving vehicle and running the hundred miles back to Ben's place.

It took a lot of talent to endure a four-hour car ride without discussing the heavy issues sitting right there on the gray fabric seat between them, but they'd displayed excellent avoidance skills by talking about anything and everything else during their voyage.

She'd like to keep things light a little longer. Just for tonight.

Ryan would have to deal with the fallout in the coming days. It wasn't going to be easy, but she hoped she could usher him through his mourning period.

Pulling into her usual spot, she hopped from the truck, sending a cloud of dust up from beneath her boots. Home sweet home.

When she reached into the bed to grab the cooler, Ryan stopped her with gentle pressure on her forearm. It was a light touch, but she felt it all the way to her core. "May I?"

It wasn't really a question, though. The urgency in his aquamarine eyes told her it was more significant than a matter of politeness to him. Manners be damned, this was part of who he was. No lover of his would want for anything if he could help it. After prolonged periods of necessary independence, there was something seductive and indulgent about letting someone else do the heavy lifting for her.

Even if it made her a lazy bitch.

"I feel weird. You've already got your duffle." She shifted from boot to boot in the yard. "I'm used to taking care of myself, Ryan."

"When I'm around, you don't have to. I would like to do it for you. Please?" He increased the pressure of his palm on her skin slightly, encouraging her to relent. So she did.

The smile he rewarded her with was nearly enough to obliterate her misgivings.

"Okay. Thanks."

"Anytime." He scanned the mountains as he ambled toward her house, seeming right at home. The open flannel shirt he'd thrown over his white, sleeveless tee had her fingers twitching, wishing she could grab fistfuls and yank him straight upstairs. "This place really is awesome, Shari. It's so quiet and peaceful. Gorgeous."

He shot a look at her as he said that last part.

It was enough to threaten to melt her panties, even though she didn't think he meant it like she imagined. Damn, did he have to have the most provocative eyes? Or such a hot body? Wasn't it enough that he was kind and so very easy to hang around with?

"My parents picked well. I just inherited the place."

"And kept it running all those years your brother was away saving the planet." They got to the door and Shari scanned her palm on the reader. "Do you like it here? Or is it a habit?"

"Good question." She sighed as she shepherded him inside and gestured to the kitchen, letting him know he should make himself at home. "I've always felt like this is my place. Lately, though..."

"The Men in Blue and their wives have sucked you in too, huh?" Ryan chuckled. "They're a pretty great group of friends."

Shari nodded. "Yeah. I didn't realize how much I was missing until they took me in, you know?"

"Yep." Ryan paused his unpacking, leaning one hip against the refrigerator with his hands full of some kind of alien vegetable that certainly did not grow in her garden. "For me it was the same. I spent so long trying to keep a roof over our heads—Ellie and me, I mean. I worked three jobs sometimes, so I didn't exactly have a social life. Then...well, you know. Now she's with Lucas. I'm happy she's happy. Proud that she's gone on after what happened. But I guess I got used to spending time with Ben and Julie, having someone to share simple stuff with and also someone to split the load with. It's going to be tough—"

He spun and plopped the groceries in the fridge, hiding behind the stainless steel.

That wasn't going to cut it anymore.

Shari approached slowly, certain he must still have triggers of his own even if they weren't as profound as his sister's. She wrapped her arms around his waist, letting her palms explore the flat expanse of his abs. "Hey. You're going to be all right."

"Eventually." He grunted, pulled free, then asked, "Would it be all right if I take a quick shower before I start this? I can't cook properly if I'm not clean."

Although she figured soap wasn't going to get rid of some of the stains he imagined on himself, she understood. To him, it was an art form. Frankly, she was dying to see him perform for her. Sure, he'd cooked at other Men in Blue functions, but...this was different. More intimate somehow.

Intended solely for her to ingest, it would be a gift straight from his hands to her stomach, and she loved the thought of having some part of him inside her.

"Of course not, go ahead." She lifted her chin toward the stairs. "First door on the left."

He bowed his head a bit and said smoothly, "Thank you."

The entire time the water ran, she couldn't stop imagining the way his chest had glistened with droplets that refracted the sunshine after his swim during one of their recent barbecues at Lucas and Ellie's house. Damn, she was going to miss the summer.

Winters up here were frigid. Though the tundra-esque landscape could be pretty at times, it had nothing on those afternoons and the masculine displays the Men in Blue unintentionally put on for their ladies.

Fortunately, when Ryan emerged in a cloud of steam and trotted down the stairs wearing only a thin pair of gray cotton shorts and a well-worn T-shirt advertising one of the pizza places he used to deliver for, she stored up plenty of memories to keep her toasty inside. No matter how low the temperatures dropped in the coming months.

Even better, she was starting to wonder if having him around might heat things up permanently.

Bring on global warming.

SEVEN

Shari thought Ryan looked good enough to eat with his blond hair slicked back and damp. Classic features, tan skin, brilliant eyes, and long limbs made him seem like he'd escaped from some fairytale princedom and wandered into her home. Remembering how he'd kissed her earlier, another blast of warmth flared within her.

It hadn't been her imagination. All this time, it was there. True chemistry.

Today they'd finally acknowledged it.

The possibilities seemed simultaneously astounding and terrifying.

She wondered how he'd feel if she ruined her appetite by devouring him instead of whatever culinary delights he planned to present her with. As she watched, he slipped a crisp black apron over his head and cinched it around his trim waist. It did magnificent things for his ass.

Whew, it was going to be harder than she thought to keep her hands to herself. Well, that wasn't entirely true. Some hands-on-self action might be required to fall asleep after spending an entire evening alone with him. She'd resorted to pleasing herself with her trusty vibrator more than once after their group outings. Solo, the lust he steeped her in was even more potent.

Shari forced herself to recall the disastrous parting they'd endured earlier and consider how raw Ryan must be after that informal breakup. "Are you sure you want to go to all this trouble? If you'd rather find something on Neflix and chill out..."

"Did you just proposition me?" A wicked grin lit up his face, making his eyes seem to sparkle like the aquamarine and diamond necklace in Izzy's jewelry collection.

"What? No!" She waved her hands in front of her, trying to think back. Had her desires spilled out of her mouth instead of what she thought she'd offered—comfort, relaxation?

"I don't think that means what you think it means, Shar." He winked. Laughing, he turned back to the stove and fiddled with some knobs she never used. Though he mumbled, she caught most of what he said with his back to her. "Too bad. I might have taken you up on it. I'm like a damn pressure cooker over here. Sooner or later...*kerpow*."

She tore her gaze off his spectacularly presented butt and whipped her phone out of the pocket of her jeans while he continued to ramble. Her fingers were a flurry of motion as she did a quick Internet search. Apparently some genius had decided "Netflix and chill" was secret code for a friends-to-lovers booty call.

Also known as knocking boots.
Also known as bumping uglies.
Also known as stuffing the turkey.
Also known as hiding the salami.
Also known as tickling the pickle.
Also known as making whoopee.
Also known as rumpy pumpy.
Or mostly known as plain old-fashioned *fucking*.

And she'd come right out and asked him to do it. With her. As if it was no bigger deal than taking a stroll to the lake after dinner.

"What the ever-loving hell is wrong with young people today?" She slapped her phone onto the table as she sank into a chair. Would she ever get things right with him?

"Like you're that old." Ryan glanced over his shoulder in time to catch her horrified expression and bugging eyes. He chuckled. "C'mon, Granny, don't freak out. I knew that's not what you meant."

"I'm an idiot. I mean, I would, you know. Like to do that sometime. But not tonight. I realize this is horrible timing. " Her head sank onto her crossed arms, hiding her smoldering face from him. Until she remembered what he'd said... *Too bad, I might have taken you up on it.*

"It is?" He didn't look at her when he asked, softer, "Why?"

"Because you had your heart broken today, for starters." Behind his back, she rolled her eyes. Was he going to pretend she couldn't tell?

"You know I can see your reflection in this vent hood, right?" He shook his head.

Refer to her earlier idiot status. "No. Obviously I'm not used to having people around."

That much was true.

"Hang on. Am I invading your turf? I can take you up on one of those spare guest houses if you want." For the first time, he paused as he gathered his ingredients and laid everything out just so. His hand hovered over the pull for a drawer where he had been about to start rummaging around for who knew what, she figured.

"No." Even if he hadn't already been booted out of one home today, she wouldn't turn this into a repeat performance. It was unequivocally true. Some people might grate on her in close quarters after spending so much time by herself, but not Ryan. Or Ben. Probably.

Unless he was acting like an idiot as he had been earlier today.

"Despite what you saw before, I'm not the kind of person to get my feelings hurt easily." Ryan stopped what he was doing and crossed to her, crouching at her feet. "If you need some space, I'll go."

"No, don't." She reached out and held his face in hers. "You're always welcome here."

"Just not for Netflix and chill?" He raised a single brow, making her want to launch herself at him and prove him wrong right there on the kitchen floor.

"*Not today* is what I said." She rubbed her thumbs over his lightly stubbled cheeks, tougher than they looked.

"What happened this morning was a result of months of shit piling up. This afternoon wasn't the part that caused the hurt—it was the day that stopped the pain. The day I finally quit letting other people dictate how I feel and when I act on that." Ryan swallowed hard. "I'm not saying I'm not screwed up inside, but that's really not anything new. It's been this way for months. I hate that I might have done the same to you by not pursuing the potential I felt between us. I don't want to keep being stupid, Shari."

"Oh."

"Yeah. I think I should rectify my mistakes as soon as *fucking* possible." He leaned forward and captured her mouth in another kiss. It sizzled. Despite their earlier performance, it caught her by surprise.

Could it be like this every time—shocking and brilliant?

She hoped so and was willing to try it a hell of a lot more to be positive.

Shari lifted her hands to bury her fingers in his sun-bleached hair. When she inadvertently tugged on it some as she tried to worm even closer, he groaned into her mouth. The intensity of his kiss ramped up as if he'd put her gas range on full blast. A flurry of his tongue, lips, and teeth, showed her exactly what she did to him. His enthusiasm had a similar effect on her.

If they didn't stop soon, they'd escalate this straight to table-smashing proportions.

The only reason she didn't shout *whoopee* and go for it, the hell with dinner first, was because her brother had meticulously handcrafted the furniture. She couldn't stand to lose another piece of her family when so few remained.

Damn.

As if Ryan felt her slight hesitation, he pulled back enough to separate them. Barely. His eyes opened slowly, showcasing the gorgeous cerulean glow of his sleepy stare, drenched in lust. Framed by golden lashes, his gaze—hell, all of him—took her breath away.

Or maybe they'd been kissing so long she was about to pass out.

Either way, she wasn't prepared for what he said next.

"So...if you have some objection to getting naked with me other than how you think I should feel right now, you should probably mention it before we finish dessert." He grinned before rising, staying bent over only long enough to kiss the tip of her nose. "Because I'm about to pump you full of energy that I will gladly help you burn off later. Sound like a plan?"

"Uh huh." She blinked up at him a few times. A grin threatened to split her face.

"I'm glad you're onboard." He caressed her hair a few times then glanced at the section of his apron distorted by his obvious erection with a wry grimace. He must have been going commando beneath those soft gym shorts, which rode impossibly low on his hips. "I'd better get back to work."

As he left her proximity, having utterly transformed her forever, she wondered aloud, "I thought you were submissive. Damn, Ryan."

An answering smile seemed to have taken up residence on his face. "That can mean a wide range of things, depending on the person. Besides, every situation is different. Just because mangoes are my favorite fruit doesn't mean I don't eat strawberries too."

Huh. Well, when he put it like that, it seemed simple.
Maybe it was.

He was adaptable, flexible, ellusive, and so damn sexy she couldn't imagine being more fascinated with someone for the rest of her life. Maybe she'd had it wrong all this time. Had her infatuation with the roommates been driven by her cravings for this man? Ryan could be enough for anyone. He amazed her.

"What's that look for?" He briefly met her stare in the range hood as he began to slice and dice vegetables with an impressive amount of skill and speed. She'd have chopped her fingers off already if she'd attempted that.

"Just thinking how incredible you are. Special," she admitted.

"A freak of nature, you mean?" He shrugged.

"Only in the best sense." Shari stood and crossed the kitchen. She couldn't help repeating her earlier gesture. Wrapping her arms around him, she slid her hands beneath the apron. Of their own volition, they stroked down his sleek torso and over the ridges of his cut abdomen. It was a luxury to touch him, finally, like she'd dreamed of so often. Molesting him while he cooked could quickly become her new favorite pastime. "I've never met anyone like you before. Someone who interests me as much as you."

"Keep that up and I might cut off something important." He sighed and his steady motions hitched.

She couldn't help herself. Shari allowed her hand to brush over his package, testing the weight of his goods for a moment before teasing him verbally to go along with her brief caress. "It feels pretty big, Ryan, but I don't think it'll reach up onto the countertop."

He cracked up at that. Then spun slowly enough to keep from whacking her with his elbow or stabbing her, but fast enough to dislodge her.

Ryan pointed with the handle of the knife. "Go. Sit. Let me cook for you, woman."

"How can I say no to that?" She left him with one last peck on the side of his neck, since she couldn't quite reach his mouth without him accommodating her. A hiss of air left him in a rush. It didn't turn her off to hear him give in to arousal. In some ways, that thrilled her more. Knowing she finally had a right to do what she had felt for a while now flooded her with glee.

She hoped he cooked fast.

From her outpost at the kitchen table, she studied his every move. Watching him became a feast for her senses. Confident and competent, he never hesitated in his preparations. Meticulous, he never rushed. Not even when flames were shooting from a pan or three different buzzers were ringing. The kitchen was his bitch.

So she didn't realize he'd finished until he had already started carrying armfuls of dishes to the table.

Shari rose. "Here, let me get some of those."

"No, please. Sit." For a man who liked to take orders, it seemed like a command. "I want to do this. For you."

Oh.

Servitude.

Shari remembered Lily talking about all the ways her submissives showed their affection for her. The concept of service hadn't quite made sense when they'd discussed it. How could it help partners communicate their dedication to one another? How did someone find it enjoyable to wait on another human being?

Here, in the moment, the feeling made perfect sense to her. And she was honored.

It wasn't sexual, necessarily. Though his graciousness made her shift a bit in her seat, uncrossing and re-crossing her legs to ease some of the ache he inspired in her pussy by showing her exactly how much he cared. It erased months of doubt with a single action. Far more than hashing things through could have.

If it made her guest content to do this, she certainly wasn't about to stop him. "I'd like that. Thank you."

He smiled his signature slow, wide grin. The one she hadn't seen on his handsome face in far too long.

Ryan placed things in front of her in a very precise pattern and order. The pomp and regulation of it all intimidated her. The last thing she wanted to do was screw up after he'd gone to so much effort.

"I can't wait to dig in. I have no clue what this stuff is, but it smells divine." She peeked up at him. "I hope you don't expect me to eat with my pinky out and take tiny nibbles. I only have one kind of fork and I'm starving."

He didn't laugh. Didn't answer right away, either.

Oh no, had she offended him? Her stomach wobbled, and not because of the scrumptious smells that left her salivating.

"Would you let me feed this to you?" He held a tray with yet more dishes and a decanter of aerated wine out on one hand, a towel draped over his forearm. "Or is that too...weird?"

Shari felt a flame as bright as the one he'd seared their dinner with fly along her nerve endings. She squirmed in her chair, wet at the thought alone.

"No." She shook her head when his smile dimmed. "I mean, it's not too strange. Sure, I'd like to try it, if that's what you want."

"I do." He stared at her with such awe and reverence, she would have thought she rescued someone from a burning building or discovered the cure for cancer instead of granting a simple, if unconventional, request.

While she absorbed his visual praise, he set down the tray, then plucked her from the chair just as quickly. Ignoring her surprised yelp, he settled her in his lap. "Here, sit on me. Get comfortable."

Shari found it was easier than she thought. She wiggled around until they fit together, her back to his chest. His legs cradled hers. If there was something long and hard pressing against the small of her back, she opted to pretend that it was his clothes bunching up instead of his very respectable hard-on.

Otherwise, she'd never make it through the first course without turning to gorge on him.

"Here, start with this." He held out a single mouthful of something frilly on a large serving spoon. "I had to improvise a little."

So busy staring at the colors and textures of whatever the hell it was he brought to her lips, she didn't open fast enough.

"Should I tell you what everything is, and what it's got in it, to make sure you like it?" He cleared his throat. "I should have asked first, I guess."

"No, this is the kind of food you just shut up and eat." She grinned. "I trust the chef. I hear he's fantastic. It's just that it's so pretty. It seems a shame to wreck it."

Ryan hugged her to him with his free arm. "Thank you. Seriously, though, it's meant to be enjoyed. Go ahead. Eat it."

Shari hummed. It did smell amazing.

It was right about then that she realized she hadn't even had a snack since breakfast. Suddenly, it seemed like she could snarf every last morsel piled on the table before her. She opened her mouth and Ryan slipped the spoon between her lips. Somehow, the simple act fed more than her body. When had anyone bothered to take care of her?

Since she had turned sixteen, she'd lived up on this mountain, alone, guarding their house and tending to the sanctuary the ranch had been for her brother, when he could find his way home. This was true decadence.

Shari gladly accepted the offering—the appetizer coupled with Ryan's care—and began to chew. Crunchy, tangy, and all-around delectable. A soft moan escaped her, inspiring his chuckle.

"I'll take that as a compliment."

He should, and she would have told him so if her mouth wasn't full of the beginnings of what was sure to be the best meal of her life.

By the time Shari swallowed, Ryan had prepared another incredible treat. Something containing scallops and a rich cream sauce this time. The flavors that burst over her tongue were nearly enough to distract her from the heat of him, the press of his muscles along her body, and the perfection of their fit. Almost, but not quite.

It did take her a while to realize that he wasn't eating, however.

When she did, the realization embarrassed her. The first plate was nearly cleaned already. He shouldn't have to sacrifice for her or anyone. Not anymore. "Ryan, where's yours?"

"I'm not very hungry," he said softly. "Honestly, my stomach's been in knots since we left."

She had no doubt that without intervention, he would suffer.

"Take some for yourself." It wasn't a suggestion. Without question, he did as she'd told. When he'd chewed and swallowed, she performed her best Mistress Lily impression, trying to muster up some serious sternness. "More."

"I don't want to take anything away from you." He shook his head behind her, nuzzling her hair in the process.

"You're not. You're giving to me by allowing us to share this experience," she promised. Angling her head, she stared up at him. "As phenomenal as your meal is, I can't enjoy it if you're sitting there going hungry, or too upset to eat. You mean more to me than that, Ryan. Don't piss me off by assuming otherwise. What kind of shitty friend would that make me?"

He kissed her cheek ever so softly, then nodded. Silently, he dug in as if those first few tastes had reminded his insides that he was ravenous...for more than simple food. She hoped their connection nourished him as much as it had her. He'd been putting himself last for entirely too long.

While he ate, she trailed her fingertips along his forearm. The muscles there bunched. He clutched her to him as if afraid she might slip away while he attended to his own needs. So she murmured reassuring nonsense to him as he took his fill.

After several bites, he relaxed and his stomach gurgled softly beneath her.

"Better?" she asked as he dipped his face to rest his forehead against hers.

"Yes. Thank you." His fingers trembled on the fork before her. She didn't really know how else to comfort him, besides maybe relying on distraction.

"I'm ready for more. Maybe some of that..." She lifted her chin toward the main entrée, which looked like steak in a thick pan sauce. Notes of wine and truffles, maybe, reached her a moment before she took the meat off the fork Ryan held for her, his hand cupped beneath her chin in case she dropped something. She didn't.

They went on like that for a while, her sampling and him providing. It got easier and easier to ask for what she wanted each time she did it. Maybe the problem all along had been his nature...and hers.

Shari had been searching for some sign that what she felt for him and Ben was mutual. Had Ryan been waiting for either Shari or Ben to take the first step before laying it out there? Probably. Well, she was done making this harder on them both than it had to be. As for Ben...he was going to have to catch up or miss out.

She wasn't so greedy that she had to have both of them or nothing.

This was plenty. Or at least it could be.

Lost in thought, they ate together, enjoying every crumb Ryan had prepared for them. Especially dessert. He fed her mango mousse off his fingers, letting her lick them clean after each mouthful. If she lingered, sucking on him, no one could blame her.

Shari and Ryan sighed in unison when he wiped them both clean with a linen napkin, then settled her across his lap so she could cuddle against his chest, damn near knocked into a food—and testosterone—coma.

"Wow. That was...spectacular," she murmured against his neck, loving the smell of seared meat and herbs that perfumed his skin.

"You gonna fall asleep on me?" He didn't seem disturbed by the idea.

"Bed does sound amazing right now," she admitted, then realized how it might have sounded.

"You didn't come up with any objections, and dessert is probably half digested by now," he reminded her.

"I don't want to rush you. I know today was a hard day." She kissed him gently, letting her lips linger. It was enough to taste him, to soak in his warmth and the smell of caramelized sugar that remained on his mouth.

It went on for a while, their careful exchange. Her fingers twined in his hair, thrilled by how it tickled her knuckles with silky softness. Dazed, she blinked hard when he pulled away long enough to whisper to her.

"It *was* awful. You're helping make it so much better." He stole another sample of her before confessing against her lips, "I would love to sleep with you, but I never imagined tonight would be my chance. I'm not prepared. I don't have any protection with me. That doesn't mean I can't take care of you, though. I would *kill* to do that."

"Oh, Ryan, Ryan, Ryan. While you were comparing the not-fancy-enough fungi they had in stock at the SuperDuper Mart, I was being somewhat more practical." Shari grinned, then reached around to where she'd hung her purse on the back of the chair. She dipped her hand inside and withdrew the jumbo box of condoms she'd purchased.

Just in case.

"I could kiss you right now." He nuzzled her neck and did one better, licking her right beneath her ear, sending shivers along her spine. "Oh wait, I already did. I'm going to again, too. Until you're begging me to undress you...and more."

"Why don't we go upstairs first?"

EIGHT

Shari prepared to lead Ryan to her room. Otherwise, they might never make it out of the kitchen. The hardwood floors weren't exactly the stage she had in mind for the slow explorations she'd love to indulge in for the rest of the evening. After waiting an eternity to be intimate with him, or any man she truly cared for, she didn't want to be rushed.

She climbed from his lap, groaning at the loss of contact. Before she could take two steps, Ryan swooped in behind her. He lifted her off her feet and cradled her in his arms. "Is it okay if I carry you?"

"Kind of late to ask, isn't it?" She laughed as she looped her arms around his neck.

"I'd rather you gave me permission," he rasped, "to attend to you like this. Better still if you want to order me around. Be direct so I know what will please you the most and can do exactly that. I hate guessing or assuming that if I take what I want, you'll get what you need too."

When he said it like that, she could totally understand the appeal. How many times had she wished for things to be simple between them? Now he offered her the opportunity to eliminate any misunderstandings or speculation.

Hell, yes.

"Take me to my bedroom, Ryan." Shari didn't think about it. She didn't have to manufacture some demand to suit his fancy. It was what she genuinely wanted, and her patience had just about run out. The freedom to get bossy with him after months of hoping for action was freeing. Maybe she'd been going about this all wrong from the start. "Don't forget the condoms, either, or I'll make you crawl back down here buckass naked and get them for making me wait a moment longer than necessary to have you inside me."

"Jesus." He shook the box so she could hear it before tightening his grasp and picking up speed. She swore he took the stairs three at a time after that. "You're awfully good at this, Shari. Have you been talking to Lily?"

"Nope. I'm pretty sure this is what you do to me." She laughed and buried her face in his chest, slightly embarrassed, but mostly relieved that they were turning out to be half as compatible as she had imagined.

The reassuring thump of his racing heart made her sure he was as affected as she was by their nearness-with-intent-to-be-intimate. Premeditated seduction. Finally!

When he entered her room, he set her on the comforter as softly as if she had floated down like the eagle feathers that sometimes caused delicate rings to skate across the surface of the lake on a calm day. With her stare locked on his, she absorbed the full impact of his gaze. His eyes seemed to change colors the more aroused he got, going from sky blue to something that reminded her of the water that had starred in the Caribbean ocean special she'd watched last week.

Maybe someday she'd get to see it herself, finally fulfilling her fantasy of having sex on a white sandy beach with the love of her life. For now, this was an amazing substitute.

Was that what she was to him? Plan B?

"I know I'm not Ben—"

Ryan burst out laughing at that. "Damn straight you're not. Not with all this smooth, soft skin and these absolutely beautiful curves."

For a moment, she lost her train of thought, worries scattering before his skilled fingers, which had her half naked before she realized what he intended.

"Hang on, I'm being serious." She worried her lip between her teeth, crossing her arms as if they could hide her boobs from him. Proportionally, they were impressive. Probably her best physical attribute.

The back of his knuckles brushed repeatedly across the exposed swells above her hands, making her shiver.

"I know." Ryan drew in a deep breath then let it out slowly. "It's no secret that I have a thing for him. You know we've fucked around and I loved it. Would do it again—or more—in a second if he was willing. But I'm not like other people. Or maybe I am. I actually believe most humans aren't designed to be monogamous. Does that bother you?"

She swallowed hard. This was not the time to lose her courage. She had to be honest.

"A little, maybe." Shari winced. "But probably not for the reasons you assume."

"Good, because I want you, Shari. I always have. I'm sorry I let you think otherwise for even a single second. I'm not talking about as some consolation prize, either. I want you as much as I want...*wanted* him." Ryan paused, sitting beside her, though never halting his caresses along her collarbone, then down her arms. Eventually, he held her hands.

"That's great." She gulped, hating how lame she sounded. Still, it *was* a relief. "It's not that, though. I'm more afraid that we'll do this and I'll feel things for you that aren't smart, knowing that you're going to want to be with other people. Besides me. When I'm not around. Yeah, I don't think I can do that."

Shari reached for her discarded shirt.

"No, wait." Rather than use force, Ryan distracted her by peeling his T-shirt over his head and tossing it to the floor, baring himself equally. It may have been a tactical maneuver, but it worked.

Suddenly she felt less vulnerable.

"Why?" What was the point of getting in deeper with him when she knew herself? She couldn't be his sidepiece, or even his mainpiece, if he had other pieces scattered about like a sexy god in some kind of fancy board game. Jealous, she'd never be able to stay sane wondering where he was and who he was doing, without her.

"I think I didn't explain right." He scrunched his eyes and stared at the ceiling for a moment before returning his focus to her. "I want to be in a committed relationship. If that's you and me, I'll be so damn happy. I care for you, Shari. This isn't only about fucking to me."

"Me either," she promised.

"But I love Ben." He said it with a quiet steel that impressed her. "No matter what he feels, or doesn't for me. Our time in the dungeons..."

"It's never going to go away. And I'm never going to replace him or the things you overcame with each other. I understand that. Truly." Somehow the knowledge didn't hurt either. How could it when she'd seen how they were together? Though she only had a vague idea of the awful stuff that had bonded them, as close as brothers-in-arms.

"If I could have figured out a way to have you both, that would have been my dream. I'm just saying that there was room in my heart for two very specific people." He tucked a strand of hair behind her ear.

She turned her head and kissed his hand.

He might not have declared his feelings outright—they didn't know each other well enough for that yet—but he'd eased one of her worst fears. Stinging eyes made her blink rapidly.

"What did I say? I thought I did a decent job there."

When she snorted a laugh, he leaned in and surprised her by gathering her to his chest as he reclined on the quilt she'd sewn last winter. It had been a never-ending season, giving her plenty of time to hone her craft. The intricate design she'd come up with made her proud looking at the finished product.

Shari pushed up a bit, her palms on his solid chest, until she could kiss him softly, gently, returning the gift he might not even realize he'd given her.

"Seriously, you okay now?" he asked between kisses.

"Yeah." She cleared her throat. "My worst fear...since my brother died, you know?"

"What is it? You can tell me." He cupped her face in his strong hands, rubbing her cheeks with his thumbs.

"Is dying alone. Unloved. Or maybe in love, but unable to act on it. Like John. Or my mom and dad. He was in the military. Killed in action overseas. She died of cancer while he was away. The three of them were so...*alone*." She couldn't help it. Her voice increased in pitch as she trailed off. Her secret hovered there, in the room with them, and she'd never been more ashamed or afraid.

"First, that's not going to happen." He sipped the tear she hadn't realized she'd shed from the corner of her eye. "I'm here. Unless you kick my ass out, I'm not planning to leave you by yourself for very long."

The future couldn't be certain, but she figured that was as good a reassurance as she would get. A tentative smile drove away her sadness.

"And second, your brother was insanely loved. Didn't Jambi hold out for like a *decade* for him? He might not have been able to be with her, but that doesn't make what they shared any less powerful, does it?" Ryan rolled over so that he was above her, bracketing her with his strong arms. His blond hair feathered over his forehead as he made absolutely sure she was looking at him. "I'm sure it was the same for your parents. Distance doesn't obscure what's in your soul. No matter where we end up after tonight, you've got a part of me that I'm never going to take back. It's yours for keeps. I will always be with you. Okay?"

"Yeah." It was all she could manage to say, though she desperately hoped he knew the same was true for her. Had been for months already. Him, Ben, and the rest of the Men in Blue family had become an important part of her fabric, like the floral print she ran her fingers over was inextricably woven into her quilt. She looked up, unflinching when she met his stare. "So come here and give me that piece of you."

He laughed, melting her further with the boom of happiness that was loud enough to rattle her windows along with her insides. "If you insist. But that wasn't the part of my anatomy I had in mind."

"I do. Insist, I mean." Shari squirmed beneath him, shucking her jeans and kicking them over the end of the bed before toeing her socks off.

Ryan was right there, skimming his hands along the length of her body, taking her panties with them before deftly unclasping her bra faster than she would have been able to do it herself. Impressive.

"Can I taste you?" He licked his lips, as if she would be every bit as delectable as the dinner he'd fed her.

"You'd better." A hiss escaped her when he dove forward, suckling her bared breast while one hand massaged the other. "Ah, yes. Right there. A little harder."

He did as she directed.

Shari drew her feet up beside his hips and tucked her toes into his waistband. It took a few tries, but eventually she was able to shove his shorts down enough that she had a great view of his tight ass while he made her feel things she'd never dreamed possible.

Who knew it could feel that good to have a man's mouth on her breasts?

Damn.

When he settled deeper into the V of her thighs, his abs pressed against her mound, inspiring her gasp.

Ryan lifted his head only long enough to grin and rotate his hips, grinding against her until he stroked her clit with his pelvis. Why did she have a feeling he was full of sly tricks designed to maximize his partner's pleasure?

It was like having her own personal sex slave. Which, come to think of it…

He'd been *trained* to produce pleasure.

And she was reaping the benefits.

No match for his experience, she quit trying to act rationally and instead gave herself over to pure sensation. What she lacked in skills, she made up for in passion. Or at least that was her goal. Shari buried one hand in his hair, and latched onto his shoulder with the other. If her nails rasped against his back and scalp, it was entirely unintentional.

Though it seemed to have a pronounced effect on the man making a meal of her.

"Fuck, yes," he groaned. "Tell me what you want."

Coherent thoughts? Nope, not going to happen.

Instead, she applied pressure, pushing him downward.

He went.

Right where she needed him.

Ryan kissed his way from her breasts, along her belly, to the juncture of her thighs. He teased then delivered on the promises his body was making for him. Toes curled, fingers balled in the sheets, and head thrown back, Shari was afraid she wasn't even going to last long enough for him to get to the good stuff before she flew apart.

"Hurry," she urged.

"Love knowing I can do this to you, make you feel so good," he admitted between licks and nibbles around her clit, his fingers swirling and probing the opening of her pussy.

She should have been self-conscious. But she wasn't. How could she be when it was obvious that her bliss sustained him? Though he went down on her, did as she asked, brought her ecstasy without so much as slipping a hand between himself and the sheets to rub his stiff cock, it was clear that worshiping her somehow gave him authority of his own.

If she'd ever had the misconception that submission made a lover—especially a man—weak, it disintegrated with deliberate swipes of his tongue and the steady advance of his fingers, which breached her opening.

"Ryan! More!"

He granted her request, inserting two digits within her so she had something to hold as her pussy clenched.

"Let me taste you, Shari. Please. Will you come on my face?" he growled against her flesh, redoubling his efforts, as if desperate to draw pleasure from her very core.

It didn't take many plunges of his fingers, combined with gentle suction on her clit, to ensure she was unable to resist. Not that she wanted to. Their needs aligned perfectly.

So she gave him his wish.

Shari screamed his name, her leg hooking around his back to draw him in tight as she bucked, riding his face. An orgasm of epic proportions stole her breath then slammed it back into her in a rush that left her gasping and moaning. Each of her primal vocalizations seemed to thrill Ryan, who released a victorious roar of his own without slowing in the least.

When she thought he'd wrung every last drop of rapture from her, he glanced up with a slick grin, then hummed. "I could do this all night."

"Huh?" She blinked a few times, trying to bring him back into focus.

"Eat you." He blew a warm stream of air across her clit, reigniting the pulses of pleasure that had begun to fade. "You're not going to make me stop, are you?"

"Um... I..." Oh! He could do that again? Sure. "Nope. Go right ahead."

Ryan smirked at her obvious confusion and her quick amendment.

The ease with which wonder flowed between them, an endless gift from one to the other, astounded her. More than the physical pleasure he was once again busy delivering, she relished that intimacy. Reaching down, she entwined their fingers. He squeezed them tight.

As promised, he never let go.

"How can I make this good for you?" she wondered.

"You already are." He smiled against her flesh when she shuddered beneath the impact of his words, which buffeted her sensitized nerve endings. "I like making you come. A lot."

"That's good." Because she was only a few seconds from shattering again from the incessant massage of his fingers within her and the slight impact of his breath on her clit.

This time he moaned loud enough to register in her sex-hazed mind when she flooded his mouth with her release. He made her believe it was true, that her gratification became his, with his unwavering enthusiasm. Time after time, he brought her to climax then helped her recover so she could experience it not only once or twice, but as often as possible.

On a couple occasions, she tried to scoot down, arranging their bodies so that he could fuck her if he wanted. He resisted, holding her still, content to bury his face in the juncture of her thighs and teach her the true meaning of gluttony.

Shari had lost count of the number of orgasms he'd given her. All she knew was that they'd done their best to make up for lost time. Her limbs had been reduced to jelly, perspiration made wisps of her hair stick to her temples, and she needed a damn break or she would spontaneously combust. "Ryan. Come here."

She patted the pillow beside her and sighed when he wrapped her in his arms, snuggling near to her. The position left no doubt that his cock was rock solid. It nearly branded her leg with its heat and hardness.

Though she tried to reach for him, he held her too close for that. "Let me…"

"You don't have to."

"Ryan, I want to." Shari mustered some determination despite her lethargy. "In fact, remember what you said before? I'm being direct. I *need* to take care of you too."

NINE

"Check that off your list, Shari. This is all I need to be content." Ryan nuzzled her hair, drunk on the sweet scent and the softness against his skin. "Knowing that I satisfied you is enough for tonight. Believe me, it's not the first time I've gone to bed eager. It'll make tomorrow even more spectacular. *If* that's still what you want in the morning."

She paused as if confused.

"Tell me whatever it is you're thinking. We'll figure it out," he coached.

"Are you sure? I have no idea what I'm doing. Saying the wrong thing now would devastate me. After everything you've given me, the last thing I could stand is to demean you in some unintentional way." She hugged him, nearly making him forget what they were talking about.

Nothing could be as important as the genuine emotion she demonstrated with every sizzling contact. After months of deprivation, it had him dizzy.

"I appreciate you trying to understand." He kissed her again and again, completely addicted to the flavor of his cooking lingering on her lips. "It means a lot to me that you would try to fulfill my needs, even if you don't really know what they are yet. Go ahead, ask me your questions."

"Okay." She took her time, gathering her thoughts.

Ryan couldn't help himself. He pressed another kiss to her mouth and wished they could spend the rest of the night making out. She was too damn adorable to resist when she was putting so much effort into being perfect for him, something she already was naturally.

What a stark contrast to the past few months with Ben, who had spent every minute desperate to ignore what was right there between them. Or worse, to snuff it out instead of nurturing it.

Eventually, though, the slight yet steady pressure of Shari's palms on his chest cut through his euphoria. She needed to talk. That was a pleasant change too.

"Sorry." He deposited one last peck on her cheek.

Her flush and the deep breath she released promised she didn't mind too much.

"Is this what it's like?" She considered before elaborating, "Being a bottom, I mean? Servitude—which you clearly excel at—doesn't seem like it would be enough to satisfy someone. When Lily took me on a tour of Gunther's, I remember the majority of the guests really dressed up. You know, like in latex and leather and stuff. Almost to the point of theatrics. There were whole rooms of whips and chains and implements I wouldn't even know how to name. Handcuffs. Black equipment. Moody lighting. It seemed a little over the top, I guess. I hate to say this, but...stereotypical, at least the parts I saw. There were these elaborate displays of how much pain a couple of the participants would take, like a badge of courage or something. If that's what makes them happy, cool. It's just that...I'm not into punishment or big productions, really. I prefer this, something personal and private. Unscripted. Feeling more than behaving according to a rigid set of rules. Unless those are things you need. I don't want to deprive you, though it would be unnatural for me. I'll try. I...it's confusing."

"Hey, slow down a minute." Ryan cuddled with her, wishing she hadn't lost some of that utter relaxation he'd never seen on her before he'd put his skills to the test and finally loosened her up some. "Don't make it so complex. What are you really trying to ask?"

"Can I be enough for you? Can this? Am I doing it right?"

"Of course you are. You're approaching things with an open mind and being honest about how what we're doing makes you feel. Those are the only real requirements for this—or any other relationship, as far as I'm concerned. It can be anything you want. Whatever we make it and both enjoy. Subtle or not." Ryan leaned into her touch when she stroked his shoulders. It was clear, because she hadn't had opportunity, and also by her shy seduction attempts, that she didn't have a ton of experience. He had to keep reminding himself that not many people had undertaken as many sexual escapades as he had. Scaring her off was not an option. "A lot of the things I fantasize about aren't probably what you'd imagine."

The entire time they talked, they touched. Their hands wandered everywhere, soothing and enflaming all at once. It easily surpassed the session where Mistress Lily had ordered him to jerk Ben off for the first time as the most intimate moment of his life. Because tonight he was being sincere about how he felt and what he craved. Even better, so was Shari.

Her affectionate caresses left no doubt about how much she desired him. For who and what he was. Relief softened him to her requests.

"Tell me about one of them." Whether she knew it or not, she coerced him by using that confident tone when she made her demand.

"What if it turns you off?" He swallowed hard as a million different scenarios rushed through his mind. Some too extreme to share just yet, but a few...tempting.

She leaned down and smothered his doubts when her lips possessed his once more. There was sugar there, sure. Spice, too. Something edgier than the languorous meeting of mouths they'd shared before. "I think you're sexy, Ryan. Even if it's not something I'd like to try, knowing what you visualize when you're aroused is not going to affect that. I swear."

When he saw the way her eyes had turned sleepy and dilated, he believed her.

"Okay." He cleared his throat. "I've had a lot of practice lately, dreaming of filthy things while I masturbate. One of the things that really gets me hard is…uh…being objectified. Used to bring women pleasure."

"How?" She paused, waiting for him to elaborate. "Can you give me an example so I can picture it better?"

"Like…" It was harder than he thought to explain what made him tick. No one had ever cared enough to ask before, to really want to know. The fact that she was interested in him beyond the surface helped him focus. "Jesus. Don't say anything to the Men in Blue or they'd kill me—"

"Hey, I'd never violate your confidence." She bristled.

"Because it's not really about the *who,* but just… Well, you asked for an example, and sometimes I've thought about this." He angled his head first one way, then the other, trying to stretch out some of the tension there that began to steal his arousal.

Shari had excellent instincts. Her hand meandered down his torso until she cupped his cock and toyed with him. As he grew in her grasp, the only thing he could think about was his illicit desire.

"Why don't you close your eyes and imagine it? Tell me exactly what you're picturing," Shari insisted.

Fuck.

He groaned and followed her instructions.

"It sounds shallow, but I work hard to keep my body like this because it thrills me when people appreciate it. When it can bring my partners satisfaction." He cursed as she tugged on him, rewarding his candidness. "I enjoy it when men and women look at me and think of what I could do for them in bed. And when it's my dick they're obsessed with, even better."

"It *is* pretty impressive," Shari practically purred as she massaged his cock from root to tip, making it nearly impossible to concentrate on anything but giving her what she wanted so she'd continue to manipulate him like this forever. "I'm pretty fond of it myself."

"Yeah?" he panted.

"Mmm hmmm. And I've hardly played with it at all so far. I think I need a closer look at this magnificent hard-on." She slithered out of his reach and down his body until warm puffs of her breath on his balls made it clear her face was level with his crotch.

When she murmured praise in conjunction with her admiring massage, he nearly lost control.

"Keep going, or I'm going to think you're not as affected by my awe as you claim to be." Shari teased him with the barest of brushes of her lips across the head, maybe sipping the fluid that surely decorated the tip by now. He didn't dare open his eyes against her wishes to find out, though. "Ryan, I'm waiting."

Her schoolmarm inflection had his cock pulsing in her light grip.

"Uh... Right. It's not vanity so much. I just like it when people assume I could please them even if—*especially* if—they talk about me like I can't hear or don't matter except for what I could give them. In some totally fucked up way, it makes me feel good about myself. To be wanted obsessively like that. Before any of my personality or skills or charm is factored in." He changed his tone at that last part, hoping she knew he wasn't totally serious. He paused. "Shit, Shari, this sounds bad."

"No, it doesn't," she whispered. "You're making me so wet. Especially your dick. I'm looking at how stiff it is. How big. Long. I can see every single vein standing out from the shaft and it's getting darker, flushed. I bet it would feel so good inside me. This gorgeous hard-on of yours could fuck me so well. Come on, Ryan. Don't stop now."

She got it. Entirely.

Any doubts she might have had about her proclivity for pleasing him were utter bullshit. Usually reserved, she tapped into some hidden sex kitten side of herself and used it to blow his mind. Somehow, he had a feeling they were only getting started.

So he did as she asked and confessed, "I imagine my sister and Lucas calling it a night early at one of our friends' gatherings. They leave. For some reason, everyone else starts to joke around about me being bi or sub or something. Ben jumps in and tells them they could never resist me if they saw me naked. That I had been enough to bend his straightness, just a little. Enough that he'd enjoyed the hell out of the times we fooled around. That he hadn't done it because of circumstances. That no one else would have been able to deny themselves when they could have had me either. It's like a matter of pride for him, and you, if I'm being honest."

Hopefully she couldn't tell his blush from the excited heat that had to be staining his skin by now.

"That's good, Ryan. You know we would do that. We would never let anyone put you down, not even jokingly." Shari's grip tightened as if she were imagining protecting him. Still, the squeeze of her fingers on his shaft had him arching off the bed. "You *are* gorgeous, you know? I could never get tired of looking at you. And see how easy it was for you to get me in bed with you. How could I say no to this?"

He groaned, not only because she was working his cock so well, but also because her responses fed right into his desires.

"So what happens next?" she wondered before licking him as if his cock were the tastiest lollipop on the planet. Shari had a legendary sweet tooth.

"Ben stomps over to me and rips my clothes off, then forces me to lie down on something low and hard—maybe a coffee table—in the middle of the roomful of people. For some reason, when I think about it, I see the ladies kneeling around me ohhing and ahhing, giggling a little. The rest of their guys watch on while standing in a ring behind them.

You..." He shuddered as he realized how close to his dream she was coming right now, tugging him slowly yet firmly between nibbles, as if savoring the weight of his cock in her soft hand.

"What do I do?" she asked, her voice raspy.

Could she really get turned on by his wicked desires?

"You take my dick and show it off, telling our friends that their guys aren't half as hot as I am. You dare them to touch me all over, to lick me and use me. To see for themselves just how amazing I can make them feel. I'll work so hard to make every one of them sure you're the luckiest bitch in the room. To make Ben proud he changed who he is just for me. Even if it was only for a little while."

Shari's intake of breath washed cool air over his erection, though it did nothing to wilt it. He paused, in case she was going to say something about what he'd revealed or ask more questions, probably in regard to that last bit with Ben.

She didn't interrupt.

So he kept going.

"The girls bet each other that they'll be the one to break my reserve and drain me dry. They all still have their clothes on. Mostly, anyway. Maybe some are reaching inside to touch themselves. I'm definitely the only one naked and exposed, though." He had to stop for a second to catch his breath. His hands wandered to his chest and pinched his nipples, rolling them between the pad of his thumbs and the bony side of his index fingers.

Though he easily could have surrendered and shot his load, making a mess of himself, due to the combination of his hands, Shari's attention, and the sheer euphoria of being able to spill his guts, he held off. Just like in his fantasy, he'd never come before he was allowed. Before he'd finished the task at hand.

So he told Shari more.

"They make some of the guys hold me down so I can't cheat by touching them. Then they start using me, all of me, to get themselves off. Some of them ride me, some of them hump my legs, sit on my face. They fight over who gets my cock next, the whole time thinking that one of them is going to set me off and they'll win. But I look at Ben and at you and your evil smirks and the three of us know I'd never cave. I'm saving myself for you."

"Damn, Ryan." Shari sounded a little like she had when she'd warbled his name as she prepared to come earlier. He'd have loved to peek and see if she was touching herself too. He bet she was.

The thought made him grit his teeth to keep from taking himself in hand and finishing before they were truly done here. It would only take a few quick swipes of his fingers to seal the deal.

Shari tortured him with light, uneven strokes that had him toeing the line without passing the point of no return. Whether she knew it or not, she was a goddess in his eyes. Perfect at stringing him along enough to heighten his ecstasy.

He couldn't believe she hadn't punched him in the nuts yet when he considered how he was telling her about getting mauled by a bunch of women instead of some romantic interlude with her alone. Was he screwing this up?

"You know I want you, right? More than anyone else. Not just right now, in real life, but in my dream too." He tried to gather enough brain cells to muster some coherent logic. It was tough in this state.

"It doesn't bother me. Not the way you're saying it. I know you don't care so much about them as you do about demonstrating to Ben and me how lucky we are to have you."

"Oh fuck, yes," he hissed. "Exactly."

"So what happens next?"

He might have balked or toned down his definitely X-rated mental movie if she hadn't chosen right then to cup his balls in her palm before squeezing them gently, just like he loved best.

"I try to keep my hands down and stay still but I can't, so Ben asks one of the guys for their handcuffs. He puts them on me. Tight, not gently. The pressure at my wrists only makes me harder. Then he uses another pair to pin them to the table and the same with my ankles. I can't move an inch. Can't get away as the ladies get more aggressive with me, trying to make me come but only pleasuring themselves instead. They come all over me, slathering my face and cock with their releases."

"But you don't shoot, do you?" Shari murmured before she took him into her mouth, sucking gently. The occasional scrape of her teeth seemed deliberate.

He loved it.

Fucking loved every second of it.

"Hell, no," he growled.

"And the guys?" Shari pulled off him only long enough to ask, already in tune with his lust. "Don't they get horny or jealous watching their wives? Seems like they'd want some of the action too."

"They do. They get so horny they have to fuck, but the women are sated and happy and sleepy. They don't want any part of it." He shivered with anticipation. "So Ben tells them they should try me for themselves. That they won't believe how good it feels to really fuck and not worry about hurting their partners. I'm strong. I can handle them, all of what they have to give me. And I want to. So bad."

"So who's going to fuck your ass first?" Shari wondered. As she did, she let go and he panicked, hoping she wasn't upset or grossed out. Until the glide of a drawer opening had his heart rate tripling. What did she have in there?

It didn't take long to find out.

The familiar snick of a cap opening came a few moments before a cool, slick dildo nudged between his cheeks, seeking his hole.

Son of a bitch.

He planted his feet on the bed, then lifted for her, hoping he was making himself an easy target.

"Who is this?" she asked as she prodded his ass with the toy.

"Mason." He didn't even have to think about it. "Tyler has told me how good he is in bed. He's never been with another guy. Did you know that? But he'd fuck me. Just like Ben, he'd go gay for me. Plus I've seen him at the gym. His cock is fat and long and it would feel so good as he pumped into me. I might be the one lying there helpless, but when I can hear the guys jacking off around me, hoping they can last long enough for a turn in my ass, and see their women touching themselves as they observe me get teased and tormented, I'm powerful. I may not be the one in control, but I have every bit of their attention, hoarding it for myself. I didn't have to suck a single person, or finger them, or thrust my cock in them, nothing, and yet I'm enough to fire them up just by lying there and taking it." He grunted when she pressed the dildo harder against his clenched ass. "Shari. Fuck."

Shari matched his phantom desires with the advance of her tool within him. He cried out when it breached him. It had been so long. He'd missed this so much.

Except she froze.

"Don't stop. Please, Shari."

"Mason, you mean?" The warmth in her tone relieved him. She was right there with him.

"Fuck. Yes." He grunted when she inserted her modest dildo as far as it would reach then began to fuck him slowly as she returned her mouth to his cock. The woman was an excellent multi-tasker.

"Watching them trade off and fill me up would make Ben so hard he couldn't stop himself. He'd bend you over the couch and fuck you while you were both still watching them use me and seeing how amazing I could make them feel, knowing I could do the same for you two. That I *would* later." That part almost got him. Ryan shuddered and gripped the sheets in his fists, praying for stamina.

About there was where his fantasy grew fuzzy. Usually he'd come long before he got this far down this dirty road in his imagination.

Again, Shari rose to the occasion. She let his cock slip from her mouth and her fist took over pumping him while her other hand worked the dildo in his ass. His balls were so tight he swore they had probably gone innie on him.

"Finally, we'd be so crazy in lust with you, we couldn't stand not to have you for ourselves," she murmured. "Ben would sit on the couch with his legs spread wide and order you to get in his lap. You'd take him easily, slick with everyone else's come. He'd hold you up in some crunch that showed off your flexibility and his strength while driving into you from below. Then he would stare straight at me and ask what I'm waiting for."

They both moaned then.

Shari shifted and began to rub herself on his quad, just above his knee, using him to get herself off exactly like the women in his fantasy had.

"Fuck!" Ryan shouted, his ass clenching on her dildo.

"Yes, I would." She bit his abdomen then, making a pulse of pre-come leak from his cock. "I'd straddle you, order you to help me fuck you. You'd put your hands on my waist and lift and lower me faster and faster."

She matched the movements of her hips to her words.

He swore he was there. He could feel it. Feel them.

Both of them.

Filled and filling at the same time.

Heaven.

"When Ben snarled your name and started to come, blasting his seed into your ass, I'd shatter, milking your cock. Just like now." Shari stroked him harder as passion ran wild through her. Inspired by him. It was the most alluring thing he'd ever participated in.

"Fuck!" he roared. "I'm close. So close."

"Don't you dare come yet!" she barked, surprising him. He slipped from the edge just enough to obey. "Watch what you do to me. Your body, your perfect cock, and your sexy-as-fuck mind."

His eyelids flew open. He stared in awe as Shari climbed his body then knelt beside him, towering over him.

From here, he had a perfect view of her pussy. The puffy folds were coated in her fluids, arousal he'd drawn from her, just as he had dreamed of so many times before. "Yes!"

"This is for you, Ryan," she moaned, flicking her own nipple with one hand and let her head fall back as her legs began to tremble.

Shari cried out and quaked, her fingers flying over her clit then dipping inside herself to give her clenching muscles something to hold on to. He wished it was his tongue instead. Or his cock.

He hoped she wouldn't mind when he reached out and guided her to his face seemingly just in time. She practically collapsed into his hold, letting him position her so that she sat on his face, looking toward his feet. Another climax racked her as he buried his nose, lips, tongue, and chin in her luscious pussy.

It still shocked him, though, when she had enough awareness left to shout, "God, yes! Ryan. See what your cock does to me?"

With that, she leaned forward and took him into her mouth. Her lips slid entirely to the base of his shaft and her palm cupped his balls, squeezing ever so slightly. When she swallowed around him, her intent couldn't be any clearer.

Still, she didn't leave him to wonder if he'd pleased her. She drew off and said breathlessly, "Okay, Ryan. Close your eyes again. Show me, now. Show me how hard you'd come with us."

Permission was the only thing he'd needed.

He roared and let the rapture he felt flood his system.

His fists pounded the mattress as jets of seed splattered across his chest. Ryan hoped she understood he was trying to show her with every drop that propelled from his balls how much he loved what she'd done for him. He hoped his release pleased her.

By the rocking of her hips, which ground her pussy on his face, he figured it did. He hoped her final climax was as powerful as his.

Because he was pretty sure he was never going to be the same again.

"Ryan! Oh, fuck. Ryan." She screamed out something that might have been intended as a warning. He didn't need the words. Her body prepared him for her impending explosion. He lifted her enough to wriggle two fingers inside her when the epic orgasm hit.

The clench and pulse of her muscles impressed him, and made him sure that not only did his body thrill her, so did his desires.

Thank fucking God.

He couldn't have been happier. Unless Ben were with them. Fuck.

He refused to let rogue thoughts destroy the moment.

For a while he floated, until the dildo slipped from his ass and he felt the need to clean up. "Shari, can I open my eyes?"

"Oh shit!" She laughed. "Sorry, sorry. I suck. Yes."

He blinked at the dazzling light that had more to do with her brilliant smile than the bedside lamp. "You did suck. So damn good. Never apologize for that."

Shari melted off him into an adorable pile of well-fucked woman. Hair everywhere, skin flushed, breathing like she'd sprinted across the entire ranch.

So he gathered her up and settled her next to his body, holding her close. If she also acted like the world's most amazing security blanket, protecting him from everything outside their little bubble of ecstasy, that worked for him too.

Carefully, he stole a kiss that wasn't a fraction as long or involved as he wished. He wanted to show her how deeply she'd touched him...as soon as he'd fully finished his duties.

"I gotta take care of this." He waved toward the mess he'd made of himself.

"Go ahead, you know where the bathroom is." She flopped onto her back, one hand over her mound and the other cupping a breast idly. "I'll just be here, completely dead, for a while. Ryan, it's all true. You are *spectacular* and you brought me so much pleasure I'm not sure how I survived."

"Thank you." The gruff scratch of his voice surprised him. It was more than physical, this connection they had. He kept his head bowed in reverence as he gathered their supplies then headed down the hall.

She would never know how precious the gift she'd given him was.

But he would never forget it.

And every day for the rest of his life, he vowed to honor it.

Her.

∽ TEN ∾

A rattling from the hardwood floor beside the bed jolted Shari from her semi-slumber. The daze induced by the record-breaking levels of endorphins rushing through her veins had a strong hold on her. What the heck was that noise?

She hoped it wasn't another lonely raccoon invading the cabin. The last one had nearly scarred her for life when it had popped its head through the ceiling before spotting her, hissing, then scurrying off to God knows where. For weeks after that, she'd carried a broom around in case she had to fend off a sneak attack. Living out in the middle of nowhere by yourself definitely had some disadvantages.

Except tonight she wasn't alone.

Cautiously, she drew the quilt to her chest and leaned over the edge of the bed, prepared to scream her fool head off for Ryan...and not the way she had earlier, either. She peeked in the general direction of the racket. It wasn't a rabid rodent causing the fuss. Nope, it was Ryan's pants. Buzzing like mad against the planks.

Someone was texting him.

Repeatedly.

Before she could decide if she should fish his phone from his pocket and see what the hell was so urgent, her own cell started *bing*ing and lighting up like the slot machine that had dished out Ellie's doomed jackpot that night they'd had wonderful, or awful—depending on how you looked at it—luck at the casino.

Shari lunged for the device and unlocked her screen.

She had twenty-seven messages waiting. Her mouth gaped open.

Uh oh.

Apparently they were fortunate there hadn't been a psycho raccoon about to pounce on them and bite them in their very bare asses, because they wouldn't have heard an entire family of the little bastards over the racket they'd caused.

Oopsy daisy.

Some of the texts were from her friends.

Lacey: Hey, we heard what happened today. You okay?

Ellie: If you and my brother want to crash here instead of driving all the way back to the ranch, you know you're always welcome.

Lily: Call me if you want to talk. About anything. ;)

Izzy: Yo! Where are youuuuuu? The mother hens are starting to freak.

Jambrea: I wasn't going to bug you tonight, but could you give a quick thumbs up before everyone loses their minds? We're worried.

Mason (she imagined him texting her in his best unit leader voice): *Check in. Please.*

With that last part a nod at civility having been added at Lacey's insistence.

As if that wasn't bad enough, the majority of her messages were actually in one long thread from Ben. A few hours ago, they'd started out rational enough.

"I get it if he's pissed. If you are too."

"Please just let me know you're somewhere safe."

An hour later: *"None of the Men in Blue or their girls have heard from you. Even if you drove all the way home, you should have made it there a while ago. Everything good?"*

Of course, Ben didn't realize they'd made a pretty lengthy pit stop to stock up on supplies before heading up here. Ryan shopped for ingredients like some women shopped for shoes. It had been interesting to push the cart and observe him inspecting things, smelling them, picking them up to examine them from every angle. Hell, he must have prodded each mango in the place before he found an acceptable specimen.

Then sometime after they'd finished eating and moved on to the after-dinner entertainment: *"Fuck. I'm so sorry. Please be all right."*

And finally the ones she'd just received: *"It was stupid to let you drive when everyone was upset and shit was happening so fast."*

"I shouldn't have let you leave."

"Biggest mistake of my life."

Buzz.

Another: *"I'll never forgive myself if something happened to you. Either of you. Both of you."*

Shit! Shari punched the reply button and started to type furiously.

Right then, Ryan came back in the room. His smile died when he caught sight of her frantic expression. "What the—?"

"Your phone. Check it." While glancing up, she lost her grip. Her sweaty, shaking palms caused her to fumble her cell. In the process, she sent Ben some gobbledygook instead of a well-crafted response including a sincere apology.

It was cruel to have ignored him—intentionally or not—given the losses he'd suffered. His sister's death had rocked him and bred a justified paranoia for the safety of his loved ones.

"Oh, fuck." Ryan must have a screen full of notifications similar to the ones she'd been tardy reading. He grimaced. Before he could cancel the hunt, his phone started ringing. "I've got to answer this or he's likely to haul Julie out of bed, pile her into the car, and drive up here, stopping to check every ditch along the way."

"I know. Go ahead." She flashed what she hoped was a reassuring smile. "If you want some privacy…"

"No." He plopped onto the bed, oblivious to his nudity. Then he took her hand and used it to drag her closer. "I don't want any secrets between us."

With that, he connected the call.

"Sorry," he said without so much as a hello. "Call off the search party. We're fine."

"Ryan? Fuck!" Exasperation, yep. Relief was evident in Ben's curse as well, even from what residual shouting trickled through the speaker, past Ryan's skull, and to Shari's ears.

"How much of that stuff you wrote did you really mean, now that you know we weren't hurt and were too busy getting it on to read your texts?"

"Ryan!" Shari slapped his shoulder. Why antagonize the man after they'd already tormented him? Gloating wasn't necessary, even if it had been the best not-quite-but-sort-of-sex of her life.

"You're such a fucking dickhead." To Shari's surprise, Ben didn't rage. He burst out laughing. She would never understand how guys operated. "I hope the fact that it apparently took five hours for you to blow your wad doesn't mean you had too much trouble getting it up without me."

"You wish." Ryan scrunched his eyes closed and swallowed hard enough to make his Adam's apple bob. He gripped Shari's fingers tight.

Their sparring might be effortless, but the conversation wasn't easy for him. Had he been acting this well since they'd regained their freedom? If she hadn't witnessed his pain, she wouldn't have been able to detect it in his voice. Ben surely couldn't either.

Ryan was entirely too good at hiding his hurt, taking a beating—physical or otherwise—for her liking. He would gladly sacrifice himself for the happiness of those he cared about. And had, repeatedly. Damn it.

She'd have to be more careful to make sure he wasn't ever doing that around her. That was not what she wanted for him.

He deserved better.

"So…uh…" Ben seemed reluctant to hang up now that he'd gotten relief from the fears that had been stalking him.

Ryan didn't cut him any slack or fill the awkwardly growing gap.

Neither did he end the call.

This was why they'd been locked in a stalemate for months, she figured. So much left unsaid between them. Bullshit. Too bad tonight wasn't the time to solve that problem. She was tired and, honestly, feeling a little self-centered. It was her turn. She didn't plan to waste it like Ben had.

After listening to each other breathe for a solid twenty seconds, Ben said, "It was a chaotic day…"

Shari expected him to say something like "…so I should let you go."

Instead, he said, "After you left, we found out that the roller-skating rink is double booked for next weekend. They bumped us and don't have another opening for two months."

"Oh damn." Ryan shook his head.

Even Shari knew how badly Julie had been looking forward to the outing. She'd talked about it every time they'd seen each other for the past couple of months.

"Yeah. Julie had a major meltdown. On top of everything else today, she couldn't handle it." Ben sighed, and she could picture him scrubbing his broad hands over his stubbled face. "I'm not telling you this to make you feel bad. It's just that… Look, she's had her heart set on the pony cake you were going to make for her."

"I'll still do it," he promised before Ben had even finished.

"But we had to move the party up to tomorrow. At ten."

"In the morning?" Shari's eyes went wide. It was damn near midnight now. Factor in the drive and…

They were in trouble.

No one wanted to disappoint that little girl again.

"Well, that's one hell of an effective cock-block there, Ben." Ryan huffed out a chuckle while Shari wondered if he was being serious. Could he have gone another round? Damn. "I guess I better get my ass in gear. Is the plan still to go back to the house to open presents and stuff after skating? It would buy us some time if we could meet you there."

"You'll come? We can buy a cake somewhere and you can do some quick decorations. Maybe the kind you've made before when you print the edible ink on that flat white stuff or something..."

"Shut your fucking face." Ryan seemed really insulted now. "I have the materials and equipment I need. I already ordered it all and I packed it. I spent way too much time designing this thing to crap out now. It'll be close, but I'll be there. With the cake. Done the right way."

He looked over at Shari then with a questioning glance.

"I'd be happy to drive you. It's no problem. And I'd like to at least drop off my gift for Julie, if that's okay with Ben."

"Did I hear her fucking right?" Ben growled.

"Now you did it." One corner of Ryan's mouth kicked up.

"You tell Shari that her pretty little ass is welcome here any time. Even if she did spend the whole evening too busy to answer her goddamn phone while making you a very happy man. Which I hope she did. I mean, I hope you had a good time. Both of you." He seemed genuine, if a little wistful. "I have to say this, okay? I about lost my mind there for a while. I couldn't stand it if the last things I ever said to you were shitty and angry. Even though rooming together, or whatever, didn't pan out and today was a disaster, I'm so glad you're okay. And together."

"Not to mention about to save your ass with a gigantic, glittery pony cake made with enough sugar to kill a real horse."

"Yeah, that too," he grunted. "Julie's all I've got left. If I can't even make *her* happy—"

Shari's heart ached. She wished she could give Ben a hug right then. Except she didn't know if he'd accept it. You know, if she'd been within a hundred miles of him to offer.

"Don't worry. We'll be there. Dessert, gifts, and all."

"Thank you," Ben said softly enough that Shari almost couldn't hear it despite the nearness of her head—which now rested on Ryan's shoulder—to the phone.

"You're welcome. And Ben?" Ryan looked down at her and grinned. Something about him had changed tonight. He was…determined. Less cautious. More confident.

"Yes?"

"I love you too." Instead of waiting for a response, Ryan hung up.

Tears stung Shari's eyes. She knelt on the bed and smothered Ryan in a hug. He laid his head on her boobs for a few seconds before reaching up to guide her face to his for a searing yet tender kiss.

Before they could get too carried away, he sighed and rolled gracefully from the bed to his feet. Tall and lithe, he awed her. No question, his body was as fine as he wished it to be. She could ogle him longer than she had the statues in the city's museum, which she'd visited with Lacey, Izzy, Ellie, Jambrea, and Lily on one of their recent girls' nights.

His classic good looks surpassed the famous pieces in her estimation.

"Hold that thought, Shari." He winced as he tucked his half-hard cock into his jeans and zipped them up. "We've got a spectacular confetti-filled, rainbow-sparkly pony cake to bake. I'm going to need an assistant. Unless you'd rather sleep. It *has* been a long one."

"I'm not going to bed without you. That doesn't seem very appealing anymore." With a last longing gaze at the rumpled covers and her soft pillows, she accepted the hand he held out to her. Without straining, he helped her up, then handed her his T-shirt. Shari dove into the soft cotton that smelled like vanilla and spice. Like him. Given his height, it covered the essentials. Plus, it kept his chest bare. Win-win.

"Let's go." She offered her hand, and he took it.

If she worried about what tomorrow would bring, or if Ryan would be able to leave Ben again so soon, she tried not to let those doubts spoil their fun as they mixed, baked, constructed, decorated, and had a sprinkle war in the early hours of the morning.

Even though he'd only been there for a single night, she couldn't imagine how empty her cabin would be if she came home tomorrow without him. She rubbed her chest at the thought.

"Everything okay?" he asked as he wrapped his arms around her waist from behind then licked a dab of purple icing from her cheek.

"Couldn't be better." Or could it? She sighed as she settled against him, her exhausted mind wandering again to Ben. Together they stood there for a minute, admiring the watercolor sky as dawn painted it an array of colors.

"It's a new day, Shari. Anything is possible." He dropped a kiss on the top of her head. "I've got a hunch that with you by my side, it's only up from here."

"Technically, I'm in front of you." She squealed when he tickled her. Out of breath, she held her hands up, palms out. "But I know what you meant."

If only she could shake the sense of dread she had about returning him to the city so soon. Up here, things seemed easier. Simple. Down there, he was right—anything could happen. That's exactly what she was afraid of. Ben had said it himself—he'd fucked up. Letting Ryan go had been a mistake. Maybe he was smart enough to try and fix it before it really was too late.

She wouldn't blame him.

"How about we sneak in a nap before we have to pack this up and head out?" He rubbed her shoulders, lulling her. "I don't want you to drive sleepy. I'll clean up this disaster when we get back."

When, not *if*. At least that's what he said now.

"Promise?" Did he realize she didn't give a damn about the kitchen? Really, she only prayed he would be with her when she returned.

"Yes."

↜ ELEVEN ↝

By the time Shari carefully approached the glob of vehicles choking Ben's street and found a spot long enough to parallel park her truck in, she had chewed off a solid portion of her nail polish. A cigarette sounded so good right now. If she hadn't kicked the habit a couple months ago and tossed out her stash, she'd have been lighting up no matter how much shit Ryan gave her for it. Her fingers drummed on the steering wheel as she checked her reflection in the rearview mirror, mostly to delay the inevitable.

"Hey Shar, you look great. It's going to be fine." Ryan smiled at her. "I promise no one's going to deck anybody in front of the children. Or in the presence of a half dozen cops. They don't appreciate extra paperwork on their day off."

Though that hadn't been a contributing factor to her anxiety, she added it to the list, which grew longer by the second.

What if Ben manned up and went after Ryan?

What if Ryan changed his mind and stayed with Ben?

What if being around their friends—family, really—made Ryan realize he wasn't alone even without his ex-roomie and didn't need her after all?

What if seeing or talking with Lily reminded Ryan that Shari had no experience with his kinks and he needed more than she could give?

What if they reverted to platonic interactions but never completely doused the embers smoldering between them?

Finally, Shari understood what a special hell it must have been for Jambrea and John all those years. Wanting something you knew could never happen yet unable to give up on it anyway. Being doomed to that kind of unrealized potential could break her.

"We don't have to do this. I can run the cake inside, see Julie quick, and keep my promise. Then you and I can drive away back to your place, where it's just us." He sighed, then stared straight into her eyes with that striking gaze of his. "I know things are new, still forming, I won't risk—"

That was all she needed to hear. Selfish she wasn't.

Besides, Julie was more important. The innocent girl didn't deserve another disappointment.

"It's fine. I'm being ridiculous." She shook her head and opened her door, sliding to the curb before Ryan could round the hood to lower her to the ground like he had when they'd stopped for gas.

He might have argued, or tried to reassure her again, if a shout hadn't cut through the cool noontime air followed by the bang of the screen door on the front entrance. "Uncle Ryan! Aunt Shari! You're here!"

Julie bolted down the sidewalk and plowed into Ryan's legs so hard he stumbled backward a step before crouching down to smother her in an embrace warm enough to counteract Julie's lack of a jacket. Shari could say that from experience now.

"You really came." Julie sniffled, threatening Shari's composure.

"I promised, didn't I?" Ryan finger combed the girl's hair.

"You pinky swore. I was going to be really mad if you broke it, too." She hugged him again before squirming free and bounding over to Shari to repeat the enthusiastic greeting.

"Why don't you two ladies head inside? I'll be right in. I don't want to ruin the surprise." Ryan winked at Julie when he spied Ben lingering in the doorway.

"Yeah, let's go upstairs, Aunt Shari. Everyone came to my party. At first I was sad, but it's better than I thought because it happened early. Like when you wish it was Christmas tomorrow but it takes forever to really be the right day. Except then it was here faster. My friend Hannah and some other kids from my class went roller-skating with me, only one girl fell and had to get a Band-Aid, and now all my aunts and uncles are here. Baby Ezra too…"

She kept rambling as she skipped across the porch, past Ben and up the stairs.

"Hi," Shari murmured as she turned sideways to pass him without brushing up against him.

"Hi." He shocked her when he snagged her upper arm in a single fist as she passed, swinging her around. "Thanks again for yesterday."

If she had been surprised by his voluntary contact, it made her feel like she'd stumbled into the Twilight Zone when he leaned in and kissed her, soft and quick, on the cheek before releasing her and heading outside as if nothing extraordinary had occurred.

Shari stood there, frozen, long enough to see Ben approach Ryan. No kisses there. Stiff posture, hands jammed in his jeans pockets, Ben kept his distance. Ryan, too, seemed formal and cold compared to his usual self. It should have reassured her.

Instead she felt her lower lip wobble.

It wasn't supposed to be like this between them.

"Aunt Shariiiiiiiiiiiiii! Come see my new teddy bear."

She jumped nearly as high as a startled barn cat. "Sorry. I'm coming."

Shari jogged up the stairs and into the apartment that had been so full of bitterness and frustration the day before.

Laughter and joking conversations replaced the shouting from her memories. She hoped Julie could say the same.

"Well, look who it is." Mason folded his massive arms, his eyes narrowed.

His foul mood didn't last when she strode to him and put her arms around his waist. "Thank you for your concern. I'm sorry I freaked you out. All of you."

"Our women—and some of the guys around here, too—have a habit of attracting trouble. After the shit we've seen, we tend to rush to worst-case scenarios." He ruffled her hair as if she was also eight years old. Nine, she corrected herself.

She didn't mind. Since her brother had died, and for years before, she'd missed that protective presence in her life. Sure, it could be overbearing at times, but mostly it felt nice that someone gave a damn.

"Whatever." Lacey rolled her eyes at her big, handsome husband from the lap of her other equally handsome husband, Tyler. "You've always been like this to some degree. Our…mishaps…have only made you worse."

"She has a point." Ty earned a smooch as a reward for taking Lacey's side, though every member of their group could attest that he was as hyper-vigilant as Mason when it came to guarding their own. They'd lost enough to know they didn't want to go through that agony again. Rob, Lacey's brother, had been killed in the line of duty. Razor had barely escaped the same fate. Ben's sister, destroyed in the Sex Offender scandal. JRad and Lily had lost lovers before finding each other. Izzy, a husband and her father to the same drug. Shari's own brother, John. The list went on…

Each of them was committed to keeping their group whole, safe, and happy.

The exchange might have deteriorated into some sort of testosterone display if a much smaller version of the guys hadn't interrupted. Men in Blue 2.0, Baby Ezra, who already looked so much like his daddy, Razor, he was sure to break hearts by the time he reached preschool.

He toddled into the living room and across the floor to Shari with uneven yet determined stomps of his adorable, socked baby feet. When he reached her, he put his arms up and she obliged, lifting him high in the air until he giggled. "Hey, little guy. I swear you've grown since I saw you last."

Izzy, his mom, followed close behind, zooming in for a hug of her own.

It sometimes seemed impossible that someone as petite and youthful as her could have a baby of her own. Shari tried not to let that make her feel like she'd passed her prime, isolated and lonely out in the boonies. Secretly, it kind of did, though.

Thank God her friends were kind enough, and wise enough, not to ask too many questions when she didn't have answers herself. Not yet. It was too soon to know what exactly was happening between her and Ryan. She didn't intend to jinx it by getting ahead of herself.

Jambrea provided the perfect distraction when she waddled into the living room, with an almost identical gait to Ezra's. Clint had his arm slung deceptively casually around her waist while Matt followed a step behind, surely prepared to catch her should she stumble.

"Are you sure there are only two kids in there, Jambs?" Razor asked when he saw her. "Even when Izzy was about to pop she didn't seem so...*huge*."

JRad smacked the rookie—although he'd long outgrown the official title, they still referred to him that way when he acted like one—upside the head.

"Not in a bad way!" He tried to extract his foot from his mouth. "I mean, the more the merrier, right? And look at the size of Matt. His kid will probably start out as big as a kindergartener."

"Quit while you're ahead. Well, less behind," Lily ordered, shaking her head.

Jambrea, however, only laughed. The earthy sound had always been one of her best traits. Then she went textbook nurse on his ass. "Yes. I'm having fraternal twins. The stuff I had to have done last week included some DNA testing. Guess what? I'm a freak of nature thanks to these two fine men!"

Her gleaming grin erased any negative connotations the term carried.

"What did we miss?" Ryan asked as he came through the door, carrying the amazing cake he'd baked as if it were as precious as a newborn itself. The containers he'd boxed it in kept it hidden, for the moment. Ben followed close behind, lugging the rest of the stuff Ryan needed to assemble and serve his masterpiece.

Ellie, with concern etched into her features, got up and went to help her brother. No doubt to poke and pry a little about what was going on and how he was handling the changes since yesterday.

"I was about to teach Razor about heteropaternal superfecundation."

"That's my favorite song in Mary Poppins!" Julie bounced and clapped, making everyone burst out laughing.

Shari lowered Ezra to the ground when he realized his bestie had arrived. He sped off toward Julie, who abandoned the grownups in favor of showing Ezra her new toys. Mostly he banged things together or tried to eat them.

Yep, definitely Razor's son.

"So what is that thing you said?" Ellie wondered as she returned to the living room, satisfied for now with whatever reassurance Ryan must have given her. She snuggled against Lucas, who had his feet—both the traditional fleshy variety and the super-spy tattoo-style decorated artificial model—propped up on the coffee table.

"The simple version? Two eggs. Two swimmers. Two different dads. Fraternal twins." Jambrea rubbed her belly, which truly was enormous, as pride and joy radiated from her as well as her pair of men. "I'm having one of each of their children. At the same time."

Holy shit.

Was that actually possible?

She would know. After all, she *was* a medical professional.

For a moment, Shari's overactive imagination substituted herself for Jambrea. Her gaze winged to Ryan's, then to Ben's. Both guys were staring at her in return. If looks could impregnate, she was pretty sure she would have just been hetero-fecund-whatevered right there in the middle of the living room floor.

Which only reminded her of Ryan's fantasy from the night before. It seemed like a lifetime ago because she'd hardly slept in the past thirty-six hours. It had been one hell of a day and a half.

What the hell had the guys said to each other out there?

Why were they both still looking at her like that?

Their laser beam stares were broken when the rest of their friends swarmed Jambrea, Matt, and Clint to offer them congratulations and share their excitement. While Ryan went off to the kitchen to do his thing, she settled on a stool at the bar where she could watch him without being *too* obvious, she hoped.

After ten minutes or so of listening to the chatter surrounding her, sliding into the contentment she usually experienced around her friends, a huge yawn snuck past her guard.

Ryan's head whipped around. "You're not driving home tonight."

"You didn't get any sleep either," she fired back.

"Boys and girls, there are children present," Razor faux-chided with a smirk.

"Ha ha, very funny." She blushed despite her brush off. If Ben hadn't called with his update, they probably would have done exactly what Razor implied.

"Maybe you two *should* stay in town tonight," Mason suggested. "We don't need another false alarm, or worse, a real one."

"Your room is still yours if you want it." Ben spoke a line straight out of her nightmares.

She shook her head and said, "No!"

Maybe a little too loud, or a little too emphatically, because everyone swiveled to look at her.

"Guys, she's got a business to run." JRad tried to rescue her. "If you need to get back to your guests, Shari, I don't mind giving you a ride home tonight. If you have a vacant cabin, maybe Lily and I could make an overnight out of it."

"Oh." The stain on Shari's cheeks darkened. She pressed her fingers to the flaming sections of her face. "Actually, there's no one booked right now."

"Isn't this peak season with the fall foliage and the holidays coming up?" Ben asked, frowning.

"Should be." She wilted.

"Huh?" Ryan tilted his head. "I should have realized…"

"You were too busy, pal. We got that by now." This time it was Clint who ribbed him.

"No, seriously. What's up with that, Shari?" Ben again. His brow wrinkled.

She wished she didn't have to admit how fucked up things had gotten, but she wasn't about to lie to him. Or any of their friends. "Uh, you know that new manager I hired a few months ago?"

Everyone nodded.

"I fired him." She slouched so much her spine hit the edge of the countertop. "But not before he wiped out the registration system, which sent a jacked up form letter—an automatic cancellation notice, the system default—to everyone who'd put down a deposit. He didn't mention it either. Until it became obvious no one had checked in for about a week. I lost all my bookings. I don't blame people for being pissed when I reached out to them trying to figure out the situation. A screw up of that magnitude certainly wouldn't instill confidence in me as a guest. So, yeah, most of them declined to rebook. Some others had already made alternate arrangements by the time I contacted them, and so…I decided I needed a vacation."

"Wow, that sucks." Lacey reached over to hold her hand.

"Why didn't you tell us before?" Ryan asked.

If they hadn't been interrupted last night maybe she would have mentioned it. Or maybe they would have kept giving each other stellar orgasms until they passed out and she had no functioning brain cells left to stress about it.

Either worked for her.

"Probably because I feel like a moron." She shrugged. "After the last four managers who haven't worked out, I somehow brought the worst of them yet onboard. I just need to learn this stuff myself, I guess. I thought while I was getting things off the ground it would be beneficial to have someone with experience around who could train me. You know, teach me some growth strategies, make smart decisions about where to spend my marketing budget, or share insights about what they'd seen work other places. But it seems like none of the qualified candidates are interested in living on the top of a mountain for a base salary. I'm obviously doing more harm than good at this point."

"I can help," Ben offered. "I might not work in the hospitality industry, but I do a lot of similar stuff at my job."

He was some sort of management analyst, though she'd never fully understood what that meant. When she'd asked, he'd always waved it off as dull. A way to make a living by putting money in the company coffers.

"I can at least get you back up and running until you find someone permanent. I wouldn't mind interviewing the next batch of applicants for you to make sure they're not full of shit," Ben kept going, making it awfully hard to say no.

"While he's working that end of things, I'll take a look at the reservations system." For JRad, their resident computer whiz, it would be child's play. "It shouldn't be possible to do something like that accidentally. I'll make sure it never happens again and maybe tweak the software to customize the program for any other functions Ben thinks you could use."

"Thank you." She rubbed her temples, still unsure if that would be enough to rescue her from the enormous hole her latest "help" had dug. "Then maybe you guys could be my guests for the holidays and leave honest reviews on the popular travel sites. No matter what you think, they would have to be better than the one-stars floating to the top at each website."

She nibbled on her lip, trying not to get overwhelmed. What if she couldn't turn things around? Then what would she do? Where would she go?

"Shar, you shouldn't have kept this to yourself." Ryan crossed to her side and hugged her tight. "I hope that guy who fucked you over moved out of state, or I might have to pay him a visit."

"Yep. He's long gone. By *I fired him*, I mostly mean he abandoned ship when he realized it was going down." The freedom to accept Ryan's comfort, and feel like she deserved it, made everything better. She leaned on his shoulder. "I just need to get my shit together, patch up the damage, and reopen after the holidays under *new management*. Also known as me, myself, and I."

"It's too much for one person to handle, isn't it?" Lucas asked.

"You provide meals, take care of the animals, clean the cabins, handle the bookings..." Ryan grew stiff beneath her hands, and not in a good way. "That's crazy. You're one person, not a hotel staff."

They both knew that if she took on too much, she'd never have time to make the drive all the way into the city to see him, never mind leaving her guests alone while she made a not-so-quick booty call.

Maybe more than Camp David was doomed.

Fuck.

"Uncle Ryan, do I get to blow out the candles and make a wish yet?" Julie squished between them and yanked on his hand.

"Soon." He smiled down at her before looking back to Shari. "We're not done talking about this."

Shari nodded. She had to figure it out anyway. Procrastinating on developing solutions hadn't done her much good. Having a sounding board for her problems was another luxury she hadn't been able to afford in the past. "Okay. Go ahead, now. Let's dig in to your creation. I might be biased, but I think it's the best birthday cake in the history of all birthday cakes."

Julie clapped and danced in place. "My cake is awesome, my cake is awesome."

"You haven't even seen it yet." Ryan chuckled as he picked her up and carried her into the main section of the kitchen.

"It's the best because you made it for me, Uncle Ryan. Duh." She patted his cheek with her small hand.

As everyone gathered around for the big reveal, Ben and Ryan's attention temporarily diverted, Lily approached.

"We'll make sure you're solid at the ranch," she swore as she dropped her voice to a near-whisper. "But you've got some work to do with these boys."

She jerked her chin toward the duo, who were eyeing each other when they thought their crush wasn't looking.

"I don't know where to start, Lily. Maybe you could talk to them for me...?"

"Sorry, babe. No can do. I learned my lesson about meddling in relationships." Lily winced as she glanced over at Jambrea, Matt, and Clint where they snuggled on the loveseat in the other room. "It's best if you hash things out directly. But I'm here if you have any questions or need to vent."

"How about some general advice?" Shari winced. "I've never been involved in any sort of power exchange before. Hell, Lily, I've never had a steady boyfriend. Not many eligible bachelors in the boondocks."

Lily leaned in and whispered conspiratorially, "Ryan is one of the most accomplished submissives I've ever worked with. Every bit of it comes naturally to him. He will take insanely good care of you if you let him. That means you have responsibilities too. To indulge his need to pamper you, even when it feels like you're not fending for yourself. Most of all, please never assume his sexuality makes him weak. He's fierce. Protective. And stronger than most Doms I know. You really have it good with him."

It took a couple tries before Shari could clear her throat enough to ask, "And how does Ben fit in? Do you think he could? Wants to?"

A wicked smile curled Lily's dark red lips. "You dirty girl."

"It hasn't happened...yet...but I know Ryan still wishes it could."

"And you?"

"I'd be stupid not to want them both, wouldn't I?" Shari confided.

"Yes, honey. Yes, you would." Lily patted her knee. "And I know you're no fool."

Their conversation was cut short by the rest of their friends shouting a countdown. "Five... Four... Three... Two... One!"

Then the elated squeals of one newly nine-year-old girl threatened to shatter every sliver of glass in a five-block radius. "Ohmigod! Uncle Ryan, she's so pretty. Her mane is a rainbow and *so* sparkly!"

Ben used his cell to snap a ton of pictures of Julie freaking out and Ryan's enormous grin as he basked in her excitement. Every painstaking hour he'd put into the cake had been worth it.

When he looked over to her and mouthed, *Thank you*, she nearly lost it.

It wasn't until they'd sliced it apart, devoured the even better tasting indulgence, and lolled around in a sugar coma, that she wondered what the hell was going to happen next.

It didn't take long to find out.

∽ TWELVE ∽

Even if Ben hadn't spent half the night trying to reach Shari and Ryan without luck, he would have known the moment he laid eyes on them that the two of them had occupied that time by fucking. Repeatedly. Their time in the dungeons had familiarized him with what Ryan looked like when thoroughly satisfied. Besides, the bond between him and Shari sparkled almost as much as Ben's shit would for the next week after eating whatever the hell those two had put on Julie's cake.

If he noticed the dramatic difference, so must the rest of their friends. Last night hadn't been a simple hook up. Every single person in the house, including Julie—who'd asked him last night if she could be the flower girl at Aunt Shari and Uncle Ryan's wedding—must realize he'd finally blown the last of his chances with Ryan.

Shari had been there to do what he'd been far too stupid, and probably too scared, to do. She'd made Ryan hers.

He was happy for them. He swore he was. At least the parts of him that didn't roar in denial and agony.

If he'd thought it was going to be hard to fall asleep night after night without Ryan's presence down the hall, it would be twice as difficult tonight, imagining the rapture the two of them were sharing.

Without him.

Especially because it was his own damn fault. Extra because even now he didn't have the balls, or the knowhow, to claim either or both of the people who'd had him confused as hell for months.

Soon it would be too late. If it wasn't already.

Shari and Ryan were a unit and nothing would come between them, or join them.

His luck had run out.

Ben put his hands flat on the kitchen counter, hung his head, and closed his eyes while he reminded himself of the four hundred and thirty-six reasons this was a good thing. Exactly what he'd aimed for.

He couldn't be trusted with someone else's happiness.

Especially not people he loved.

"You'd better suck it up, buttercup. Or hide it better. I don't care which." Ryan bumped his shoulder hard as he passed, knocking Ben off balance. As usual. "If Shari catches you having a meltdown in here, however quiet, she's going to feel guilty. Guiltier than she already does. I know what that feels like. You're not going to do that to her if I can help it."

His ex-roommate, ex-so-many-other-odd-and-indefinable-things, piled the now-empty cake tray and his fancy serving set into the sink then began running steamy water before adding a healthy squirt of dish detergent. He never put those things in the dishwasher. He wouldn't be here after it ran to collect his stuff even if he hadn't babied them by habit.

The realization gutted Ben.

Ryan wasn't coming back. After today, he'd have no reason to stop over other than visits with Julie or to haul away the last of the belongings he hadn't been able to carry the day before. Then what?

Then nothing.

Their friendship couldn't withstand the implosion that had led to Ryan walking out.

Ben would snuff the side of him raring to chase after Ryan and Shari and let them enjoy the lifetime of serenity they'd discovered they could have with each other before he ruined that, too.

"You're right." Ben nodded slowly, preparing to retreat to his room until everyone was ready to leave. He wasn't sure he could avoid hurting Shari, or Ryan, if he was around. Hadn't that been the problem from the start?

He wasn't willing to compromise. If it had to be their happiness or his own, he'd pick them every time.

Ben shuffled toward the hallway.

With a single question, Ryan stopped him as effectively as if he'd smeared Super Glue across the floor. "Aren't you going to ask me what it was like? If it was good?"

"No."

"You should. Because it was *fucking* incredible. Better than I could have imagined when you busted me stroking my cock the other night." Ryan turned, wiping the suds from his hands on his favorite apron, which he'd brought back with him today. The kitchen wouldn't be the same without it hanging from the hook he'd installed in the pantry.

"That's...great." He swallowed the resentment and envy that could so easily have had him foaming at the mouth at that revelation.

"She's generous in bed. Giving and compassionate, willing to listen and make my fantasies come true." Ryan glanced over his shoulder, ensuring the coast was clear before he stepped up his bragging even further. "Her pussy is so sweet and tight I wouldn't believe it if I hadn't felt it for myself."

"Why are you telling me this?" Ben's fists balled at his sides. Every detail would be burned into his brain, torturing him when he took his turn jacking off and still couldn't find relief on his own. Nothing new there.

After he'd walked in on Ryan the other night, he'd tried desperately to express the lechery his roommate had inspired in him and failed miserably. He'd practically rubbed himself raw and still fallen asleep with a boner.

"Because I want you to know exactly what you're missing out on. Everything you could have had and chose not to take." A sneer marred Ryan's golden features, turning them dark and vicious. Ben hated the change. Hated that he'd done that to the man.

See, it was best that Ryan move on while he had the chance.

"When she comes, she sounds like the best kind of porn star. You know, the ones that are legitimately into it, not just faking for the cameras. I can't wait to do it again, just so I can hear her calling out my name. Not yours. Mine." He stalked closer, overwhelming Ben's senses with his presence and his scent. The one that lingered on the pillow Ben had taken to sleep on last night.

He'd been hard when he'd gone to bed *and* when he'd woken up. His body wanted what his mind understood it shouldn't have. There was no reasoning with lust.

Ben clenched his jaw and tried to think of anything other than the nearness of his obsession and how easy it would be to show him the fallacy of his misconceptions. It got harder and harder, though, as Ryan kept spurring him as effectively as their captors had when they'd twisted his fear for his family and made him do things he wasn't proud of and couldn't face in the light of day.

"She accepts me for who I am and doesn't make me hide my fucked up desires. For the first time in forever, I don't feel like my sexuality is some aberration that makes me less than normal guys." Ryan might as well have stabbed him in the heart.

"Shut up," Ben snarled. He would *never* think such ugly things about Ryan or the easy way he connected with people of both genders. Not after he'd seen that flexibility up close. Admiration for Ryan's acceptance of himself and his desires burned through him. How dare Ryan think otherwise?

"I deserve unconditional love." Ryan chose then to decide to rebel and ignore orders, of course. Right when Ben was at the edge of his sanity. "So does Shari. I plan to give it to her. Freely. And I won't take it back once it's inconvenient or because I always imagined I preferred men to women for a life partner. I'm smart enough to know that when I meet the right person, none of the rest matters worth a fuck. I won't be a complete dumbass and throw that away. I won't die alone and miserable wondering what might have been."

Ryan shoved him, hard, in the center of his chest.

"I said, *shut up!*" He didn't mean to, but he reached for Ryan and slammed him up against the refrigerator hard enough to shift it backward and bang the appliance into the wall.

"Or what?" Ryan prodded, staring right back instead of shrinking from his jealous display.

"Or I'll remind you that she's not the only person who can make you hard in an instant." He'd absolutely lost any ability to act rationally. It was like he was back in the dungeons, operating in pure survival mode. Doing what the moment dictated without regard for long-term consequences or the implications they had on what he thought he knew about himself. Fear reignited. Last night's panic returned in a flash, adding to his adrenaline rush, stealing his ability to be calm or rational. "I'll prove that I have never thought less of you and the bond we share. Ever. Don't you see? *I* don't deserve it."

"Yeah, right." The utter disbelief in Ryan's tone, which had lost every degree of its heat and fury in the face of Ben's raw declaration, finally pushed him over the edge.

He snapped.

Ben fisted that sexy-as-fuck apron and the T-shirt beneath it in his fists. Then he used the handholds for leverage to pin Ryan. Something crashed from the top of the refrigerator onto the floor, drawing the attention of every person in the apartment.

Let them watch, he didn't give a fuck.

Ryan's jaw hung slack in shock, which made for a perfect opportunity.

Ben seized it.

His lips covered that mouth, which was capable of downright sinful things. Like sucking cock to perfection, or providing reassurance that had seen Ben through the deepest of his despair during their imprisonment. When all he'd wanted was to give up, these lips—the ones he was devouring with bruising force—had talked him through it so they could fight for their families' freedom again the next day.

It was wrong to take advantage of Ryan like this, to steal pleasure from him when he didn't know if he was capable of returning it, or how Shari would feel about it. But he was weak, and he couldn't stand by and let Ryan talk shit about himself when it simply wasn't true.

Ben was going to hell for letting Ryan think such bullshit for this long.

Twice because he should have let him think it for just a little while longer so that he could start down the road to something better with Shari.

Like a starving man, he couldn't stop at a single taste, though. It was better than he remembered, the way Ryan met him swipe for swipe, the heat and firmness of his body as it wrapped around Ben and reciprocated the angry kiss that was the oral equivalent of a hate fuck.

Hair got pulled, muscles strained, teeth scraped soft tissue. They grappled with each other, trying to climb inside one another instead of pushing each other away.

He loved every damn second of the intense exchange.

Ryan's *oomph* was the only warning Ben had that their interlude would be short-lived.

The guy in his arms thrashed, and not to get closer this time.

Ben tried to rein in his primitive response, but didn't manage to get it under control before he heard Shari say, "Happy Birthday, Julie. I've got to go."

"Are you taking Uncle Ryan away with you?" the little girl asked.

Worst of all was her tearful response. "No, sweetie. He belongs here, with your Uncle Ben, don't you think?"

"Yep. They're best friends. Aunt Jambrea told me that just because grownups fight, that doesn't mean they hate each other. Sometimes they have to fix what's broken between them and they don't know how. Maybe they learned how?"

"I think so," Shari said, and damn if she didn't sound kind of pleased despite her pain.

Ben couldn't turn around. The massive hard-on he was sporting would be obvious to Julie and he didn't plan to have *that* discussion today, too. He'd scarred her enough for one week. What the hell had he been thinking?

That was the problem. He hadn't been thinking at all.

Ryan had baited him.

It worked.

Now Shari was the one who would pay for his indiscretion. Fuck!

"See, Aunt Jambrea is pretty smart. I love you, but I have to go. Happy birthday, Julie." With that, Shari made a dash for the door.

"Don't let her leave!" Ben roared. "Someone take her keys."

Ryan, his hair standing on end, shoved past, shouting, "Shari, wait! Let me explain."

Neither of them made it very far. Mason leaned against the front door, his shoulders blocking the entire entryway.

Shari went wild. "Get out of my way."

"Nope." He refused to budge when she tried to reach around him for the doorknob.

Ben couldn't even blink when she began to swing at the police officer, her fists bouncing ineffectually off his mammoth chest. "Move, you big, dumb man. You're just like the rest of them. Why are you doing this to me? Don't let them rub it in my face."

Ryan risked having his balls smashed when he sandwiched Shari between himself and Mason, banding his arms around her and trying to shush her with soothing nonsense spoken low enough that Ben couldn't make it out over the women rushing to Shari's defense and their guys trying to keep them out of the fray.

By the time Ryan had subdued Shari and started walking backward toward his old room, hauling her with him, the gathering had erupted into anarchy. The tears streaming down Shari's face made him wish she had kneed him in the nuts. It would hurt less.

What the fuck had just happened?

What had he done?

And how could he make it right?

After months of trying to avoid hurting Ryan and Shari, he'd done exactly that.

"Uncle Ben? What's happening? Why is Aunt Shari crying? Don't let them hurt her. She should be allowed to go if she wants." Julie had run to Ellie and climbed into Ryan's sister's open arms. Her face scrunched and she looked like she was about to join in the waterworks. Figured she'd be on Team Female already. Then again, she had experience with being held against her will.

Great, he'd even blown her big day.

What a total failure he was at life.

"Hey, it's going to be okay," he lied as convincingly as he could manage. "There's nothing for you to worry about."

"She looks so sad." Julie didn't take her eyes off Shari, who had stopped struggling and let Ryan guide her deeper into the apartment. "Go cheer her up, like you do for me when I have my nightmares. Maybe she needs you to read a book and do all the fun voices."

Why couldn't it be so simple?

Torn, he couldn't leave Julie and he didn't want to let go of Ben and Shari.

"What do you say you, me, and Uncle Lucas have a sleepover at my house?" Ellie asked Julie. "You can bring your new art supplies and we can try them out. I'll help you paint like you asked."

"If I go, will Uncle Ben be able to fix things with Aunt Shari and Uncle Ryan like Aunt Jambrea said people could?" Julie clung to Ryan's sister as if she were a lifeline. How Ellie had survived far worse than he'd experienced in that hellhole and still gone on to find love with Lucas, never mind having the strength to make herself vulnerable enough to accept it...well, it awed him.

Why couldn't he seem to get past it?

"I hope so, honey." She smiled. "Why don't we let them have some time alone so they can give it a shot?"

"Okay." Julie nodded, still glancing anxiously at the place where the pair had disappeared.

"Thank you." Ben looked at Julie as he said it, observing her for signs of distress, which seemed to have disappeared with Ellie's careful handling of the situation.

"Do a good job, Uncle Ben." Julie wagged her finger at him. "I love them. And I don't want them to be sad anymore."

"Be the fixer, not the breaker," Ellie added with a glare reserved especially for him.

He didn't blame her.

"Got it." He grimaced, then leaned in to kiss Julie's cheek and smooth her hair. "I'm not sure it will matter, but I'll do my best."

"Good. Because—tough love time, Ben—I don't think that's what you've been doing lately," Lily added as she approached.

"I get that. I don't know how to do this." He held his arms out, hands extended, palms up. Helpless.

At least that was how he felt.

"Lucky for you, you don't have to figure it out on your own." She hugged him. "Be honest. Tell them what the problem is and let them help you find a solution instead of bashing your head against the wall. I'm already worried you might have dented that big brain of yours if you don't jump all over those two amazing human beings who want to be yours."

Well, when she said it like that.

"I'm going to pack a bag for Julie. I'll be right back." He didn't waste another moment before putting their plan in action.

∽ THIRTEEN ∾

Ryan kept moving, dragging Shari deeper into the apartment he'd called home for too long to change its label overnight. He steered her into his room and kicked the door closed behind them.

The limpness of her form sucked the life right out of him. Her ragdoll arms hung over his, which belted around her torso beneath her breasts. The uneven hitching of her breath concussed his wrist. "I'm sorry."

"You don't have to apologize for wanting him. It wasn't a secret that you do." Her voice seemed dull and monotone despite her encouragement.

"I know, I just...I didn't expect him to do anything about it." Ryan settled her on his bed, then knelt between her feet. Looking up at her tear-streaked face, his stomach burned like it had the time he'd taken a dare from one of his culinary schoolmates to eat a giant chunk of wasabi. Shit. "I antagonized him, though. I guess I wanted to see some acknowledgement there before I walked away for good."

"Why?" Shari flopped her hands out in a shrug. "Are you still hoping for a relationship with him? Instead of me, I mean? I thought you were ready to move on. I wouldn't have... Last night..."

"Nothing like that, I swear." It made him a shitty person to admit it, but he did anyway. "Part of me was glad to see him jealous and hungry like he's made us so that I knew, really knew for sure, that he cared. Probably it was an ego thing, too. I like when people lust after me, remember? It pisses me off when he acts like he doesn't. I saw a crack in his armor and I lashed out. It was childish. I'll never do that again, I swear. When I saw your face… Jesus, Shari. I'm sorry. Nothing could be worse than that. I didn't mean to hurt you."

Shari reached down then and drew him onto the bed beside her so they were even, eye-to-eye. "Hey, wait. After what you told me last night, I get it. It's more than pride. He's insulting a fundamental part of you. Mashing your buttons exactly right to get at the heart of you, even if he doesn't realize it."

"But you do? After a single night." He rested his forehead against hers for a moment. "Please, don't hate me for that. It was stupid and rash. Petty."

Shari threw herself into his arms and squeezed him, making the spots where Ben had roughly handled him more apparent. His back throbbed with a sweet ache and his chest probably would be bruised where Ben had lodged his fists between their torsos. Fuck, it was bad that he was getting turned on thinking about it, right?

As if she could sense his discomfort, Shari withdrew.

For a moment, they simply sat there, holding each other's hands and grounding themselves in each other's company. She eyed the slate roof beyond the window wistfully. "Do you think we could sneak out? I bet I could climb down that tree to avoid everyone and their questions. Escape without having to confront Ben again. Let's run away. Together. And this time we won't come back."

"Not an option. I'm not taking a chance that you'll slip and break something. I've done enough damage today." Ryan lifted her hand and kissed her knuckles. "If you want, I'll go out there and clear the way so we can make a quick exit. Unless you don't trust me to be alone with him. I understand if you don't."

"That's not the problem, Ryan." Shari blushed. "It's more that the underlying attraction you share is still alive. Even if you never act on it again, it's always going to be there, making me doubt that I'm really what you prefer. How can I really be good enough, when you could have *that*? I saw you making out. Holy shit. Who wouldn't want that?"

Son of a bitch!

He'd done exactly what she was afraid of and in the process obliterated any progress he'd made the night before. Reassuring Shari that she could easily be his everything would be harder now. In time, maybe he could earn her trust again.

"Egging him on like that, being so crass and blunt, was my way of saying good-fucking-bye. Breaking things off solidly. You know, shutting the door forever." Except his filthy talk hadn't worked exactly as he'd anticipated. Huh.

Shari's arched brows and the disbelieving glare she shot him clearly proclaimed him a moron.

"I didn't say it was a genius idea. Or a successful one, either." He shook his head as she laughed softly.

Thank God.

"I really am sorry, Shari. Let me make it up to you." Ryan angled toward her and cupped her jaw in his palm. When she leaned into his touch the slightest bit, his insides quit vibrating for the first time since he'd seen her horrified stare.

He sipped from her lips until she stiffened and shoved him back a bit. "Wait. I saw your kiss, Ryan. It was nothing like what we shared last night. Or this. It was rough and intense and..."

"What?"

"It made me horny as hell," she admitted with a pouty grumble.

"Did it?" He tried desperately not to let male smugness take over. Too late. A smirk snuck out anyway.

"Ryan!" She slapped his abs with the back of her hand. "Behave."

"What will you do to me if I don't?" He couldn't help taunting her. "I might like it, you know."

Before she could respond, a knock interrupted their flow. Probably for the best, to avoid strutting out of this place packing a steel rod. It wasn't like he was going to fuck her here, on his old bed. Or maybe he should. If words alone had driven Ben to that stunning kiss, what would hearing them moaning and crying out in ecstasy do to the man?

Hopefully it would leave him with a perpetual hard-on he could never slake on his own. He deserved that kind of eternal torture for being so damn dense.

No. No. No.

Ryan had meant what he'd promised. No more games that could end with Shari on the losing end of them. Besides, he'd pushed his luck too far with Julie around. The last thing he wanted to do was trigger her memories.

Shari saved him from making another giant blunder. "Come in."

He shifted so that he stood between her and whoever was about to join them. He refused to allow her to be wounded because of him ever again. She put her palm on his shoulder and pressed until he slid aside. Maybe she didn't need him to shield her in that way. He had a lot of learning to do when it came to her.

He prayed he got the opportunity.

"Can I talk to you guys for a minute?" Ben asked, uncharacteristically meek as he waited outside the door for permission to enter. Another first. Damn.

"Of course," Shari replied. She'd fluffed her hair and scrubbed away the remnants of her tears as if they'd never been there at all. Stoic, she pretended that they hadn't just played out one of her worst fears about being in a relationship with Ryan.

Ben stepped inside. Shadows beneath his eyes and the deep grooves around his mouth threatened to put Ryan back in the dungeons. The man hadn't looked this miserable since then. He didn't shut the door behind him.

"Do you mind?" Ryan pointed.

"Everyone's gone. Your sister and Lucas took Julie. They're going to keep her overnight. So we have a chance to sort things out. If you'd be willing to try that." Ben cleared his throat.

Ryan swung his gaze to Shari only to find her wearing a soft, inviting smile. She said, "Of course," before consulting him.

Fine by him.

"Are you sure? I was a total asshole out there. If you'd rather leave, that's fine. I'm not trying to come between you two." He wrung his hands, his stare shifting between Ryan and Shari.

"I hope you're trying to come *with* us." Shari wiggled her brows and lightened the mood though her declaration did absolutely nothing to calm Ryan's rapidly rejuvenating erection. Being in his bed, with these two within arm's reach, was almost enough to trigger a spontaneous orgasm. Especially after Ben had ramped him up. The impression the handle of the refrigerator door had left in his spine might never flatten out. A subtle twinge there reminded him that it had actually happened.

After so much wasted hope, it was hard to believe.

Open and honest communication with his two crushes, on top of their physical presence, was more than even his most optimistic expectations, given their propensity for dodging this exact situation. Things were changing. He only hoped it would be for the better.

Ryan didn't overthink it. He maneuvered around Shari so that his shoulders rested on his headboard, like they had on the countless nights he'd sat here and feigned watching TV while spying on Ben working out across the hall in his peripheral vision. Then he spread his legs and patted the space between them.

Without hesitation, Shari held out her arms. He wrapped his hands around her wrists and tugged her to him. Then she situated herself so that he could cradle her back against his chest, using him like he was a living, breathing throne. She fit nicely against him.

Surrounding her with his arms and legs, he hoped he could give her shelter if things went off the rails.

Ben followed suit, climbing onto the foot of the mattress. Nearby, yet not touching them.

Facing opposite directions, Ryan wondered if they could ever get all three of them going the same way. Desiring the same things. Willing and able to accept the unique qualities each of them contributed to their threesome.

His ultimate pipe dream.

Fascinated by the novelty of having his two favorite people—aside from his sister and Julie, who were family—nearby and focused on him, he didn't register the silence that lingered too long, edging into awkwardness.

Fidgeting, Ben tried to arrange his impressive frame comfortably on the bed. His walnut hair should have had a trim a few weeks ago. It feathered into his eyes. He scratched his jaw through a layer of thicker-than-usual scruff. Though it'd only been a single day since Ryan had ridden off into the sunset with Shari, Ben looked like he hadn't slept in a week. Beat down. How had Ryan not noticed earlier?

After clearing his throat, Ben lifted his gaze to theirs. "So…"

"Before you say anything," Shari interrupted, pouring on the sass Ryan had sensed lurking beneath her quiet façade. About damn time. "I'm going ask some questions. If you're not honest, I'll know. And I'm not going to stick around for some half-assed effort or more outright lies. So think hard about what you say before you open your mouth."

"Fair enough." Ben nodded, licking his lips.

Was it Ryan's imagination or were they sort of swollen from their fierce clash? Hmm, he tried not to mirror the gesture, though the heated tingle in his own mouth had him craving more. To say nothing of the rash he probably had from Ben's light beard.

"I saw you shoving your tongue down Ryan's throat. If you're so desperate for him, what the hell have you been doing with your thumb up your ass since he moved in?"

If Ryan hadn't already adored Shari, he would have after that. She cut straight to the core.

He couldn't wait to hear the answer to that himself.

"How much do you know about what happened to us during the Sex Offender scandal?" Ben prefaced his response with a question that helped bank Ryan's lingering arousal.

∽ FOURTEEN ∾

"**H**igh level, the general idea." Shari shrugged. Though compassionate, she didn't sugarcoat things when she replied, "Those immoral assholes created a highly addictive drug called Sex Offender. Your sister, April, got sucked into its hold somehow. Without her knowledge, Ellie was part of the laboratory staff working on perfecting the compound. She also got tangled in the whole mess. They were both imprisoned and used as human guinea pigs to test the formula on. They were raped, often and brutally, by elite black market buyers using Sex Offender recreationally. In addition, they were assaulted by being given the drug against their wills then set loose on clients who paid for the experience so the evil bastards running the operation could afford to continue their research. You and Ryan were brave boneheads and got yourself locked up to try to save them. Except your sister wasn't as lucky as Ellie and she didn't make it out despite your very best efforts, which is absolutely *not* a reflection on you or how hard you tried to save her."

Ben bowed his head, his fingers trembling on his knees. He'd come to rest sitting cross-legged. "Yeah, that's all true. Sort of. There were probably other things I could have tried inside..."

"Bullshit," Ryan objected. "I was there. I should know. You did *everything* you could have without needlessly sacrificing your own life. You would have done that too, more than once, if I hadn't stopped you."

Shari gasped.

"Because you never lost hope that we would survive. That we'd come through it okay." Ben spoke with such quiet regret that Ryan realized he hadn't healed, not even a fraction as much as Ryan had, from their abuse. "I got lost. Gave up. Remember when we first met Mistress Lily? I did horrible things to her. I bound her as Morselli ordered. Made her a captive like us. If it wasn't for JRad...."

"Back up, I'm sorry. I'm not following and I have to understand." Shari leaned forward, reaching for Ben's hand. Surprisingly, he let her take it and even seemed to squeeze her fingers in return as she brushed her thumb up and down his.

"It's hard to talk about this," Ben admitted. "I would rather forget it. Pretend it was like one of Julie's nightmares. Except the bad thing is, those are pretty much real, too. It happened. All of it. No matter how hard I try, I can't forget. I can't walk down the street even on the sunniest of days anymore without seeing the shadows I cast. I'm different. Forever changed."

"How does that impact how you've been treating Ryan? And me?" Shari asked quietly.

"I don't like who they turned me into." Ben looked away, staring at the area rug as if it were the most fascinating oriental instead of something they'd picked up cheap at a yard sale. "It pisses me off when I think about it. Makes me feel like shit. About myself. About how I've treated the most important people in my life. About how I've become more like them and less like me every day since they made me violate my own values."

Shari tried to give him a pass. "If this is too hard... If you can't—"

"Then I'll lose you both." He shook his head. "I refuse to let them steal anything else from me. I can't allow them to win again, can I? I won't!"

His roar deafened Ryan.

Both because of its intensity, and because he'd had no idea Ben harbored this much depression and bitterness within him. Why hadn't he confided in Ryan?

So much for their best friend status, he supposed.

Now he was ticked off, too. Violated and deceived. Had everything he'd thought he'd shared with Ben been a sham? Were they strangers after all? Who the hell was this guy across from him and Shari?

He wasn't sure he knew anymore.

For a few minutes, they sat in silent solidarity, waiting for their emotions to settle before diving in again. Eventually, Ben took a breath deep enough to expand his sculpted chest fully. If the situation hadn't been so critical, Ryan might have teased Shari about the drool practically forming on the corners of her mouth at the sight.

He could relate.

Those thoughts scattered like the marbles Julie had spilled across their hardwood floors, which they were still finding from time to time though the accident had happened in early spring. He had a feeling they'd unearth one every time they moved a piece of furniture for the rest of their lives.

Well, Ben would. Since he still lived here.

Ryan shook his head when Ben dropped another bomb. "At first, I couldn't figure out how April got trapped. She disappeared one night along with Julie. No texts, no notes, nothing. I was frantic, looking for some sign of them. It wasn't until I got the call from the OSPD that they'd impounded her car for extended parking in front of a BDSM club that I even had the tiniest clue about where to find them. By that point, I hadn't seen her or Julie in almost three weeks. I never knew why she went there in the first place, though. At least, not before I got myself locked in the dungeons."

"Wait, now you do?" Ryan eased his grip on Shari when she squeaked. "What the fuck? How? Why didn't you tell me?"

It was one of the mysteries they'd tried to solve without luck. Endless dark hours had been passed brainstorming possibilities while they recovered from a beating or a rough session in the dungeons. Betrayal unfurled in Ryan's chest, sickening him everywhere it touched. What else had Ben withheld from him?

"When we came home, after we got confirmation that she was...*gone*...I cleaned out her car to sell it. I didn't want it around. Julie was scared of it. She remembers them taking her, waking her up as they hauled her off. April screaming—"

"Yeah, I know. It was like a week after the Men in Blue cracked the case." Ryan cocked his head. What the fuck had Ben been hiding since then? Why? That fucker! He hadn't given Ryan the chance to help him through whatever had obviously been eating him alive.

"That's when I found her diary wedged under the seat." He slapped the comforter near his feet hard enough to jolt Shari against Ryan's chest. "It turns out my sister was selling herself to get by. I didn't know. I swear I didn't. I would have taken a third job, sold a kidney. Anything to keep her from resorting to that. In one of her entries, she wrote about how she heard rumors some guys from a BDSM club were paying extra for women willing to take a sex drug before appointments, and she did it. While Julie was out in the motherfucking car, sleeping.

"The shit was so powerful, it only took one hit for some people to become irreversibly addicted, and she was one of them. She never came home again. Neither did Julie. April was one of the first women to be enslaved and used as a glorified lab rat. Lily remembers seeing her early on in the process. She tried to rescue my sister, too. The drug had her enslaved. She rejected Lily's assistance for herself and Julie, whom she didn't want out of her sight, even while April was fucked up on Sex Offender. April stayed when she could have escaped. Even her own daughter's safety couldn't convince her to flee. Probably for the sake of a couple hundred bucks I would have loaned her—hell, given her—in a heartbeat. If she'd asked."

"Oh God, Ben." Shari wept openly now, not hiding the fat tears that rolled down her face and splashed onto Ryan's forearm. He found himself numb. Unable to cry after so much heartbreak. The dampness on his skin from Shari's crying made him feel semi-human again. "I'm so sorry. You know she was already doomed. Nothing you tried could have saved her. I've seen what the aftereffects of Sex Offender do to Ellie, even now... That was some evil stuff."

Ryan didn't dare speak. Rage boiled his blood. Ben had put himself in danger for that woman, risked his life. It had been in vain. He had to remind himself April had also been a victim, not a willing participant in that initial drugging. Nothing she did after that had truly been a choice.

Like they explained to Julie, it had been a sickness. The terminal variety.

Still, Ben had earned himself a set of scars—both physical and emotional—on her behalf.

No. In the end, their suffering had been for Julie. And Ellie. Both of whom deserved a normal life after so much torment.

But what about Ben? And him?

Fuck.

No wonder Ben's overprotective streak had only seemed to deepen when they moved to this place. He'd learned how one tiny mistake could ricochet through lives, tearing them apart.

Ryan shook himself from his thoughts when Ben responded to Shari.

"I guess I know that. Maybe. But I'll never be sure." He explained, "After several people identified her, bragging about having used her *services* in the underground ring, I pretended to be interested in the drug myself. It was only being sold outright in tiny quantities to ultra-rich douchebags like Izzy's ex-husband and her father, who was in tight with the scientist Ellie worked for. There was only one way to get in on it for a guy like me. They needed more subjects to test Sex Offender on as they had a tendency to OD or go insane pretty damn quick. I agreed to be a sex slave in exchange for a taste of the drug, though they never did give me one. Thank God. I was used to make money. Which is how I met Ryan. In the holding pens. After he'd been as desperate to find Ellie as I was to find April and her co-workers had pointed him in the same direction."

Ryan's breathing hitched as he remembered the horrors they'd endured. No way would either of them share explicit details with Shari. She didn't need to know how atrocious things had been to understand how their time locked up had shaped them. Besides, she was smart. She'd connect the dots on her own anyway.

"Can I ask you something?" Ryan asked, surprised at the tremble in his voice. He hadn't realized he was shaking until Shari put her palm on his thigh and rubbed it without letting go of Ben with her other hand. Linked, they seemed stronger.

Ben nodded, warily.

"Is that why you pulled away from me?" Ryan's throat threatened to close, cutting off his windpipe as he nearly choked on the rest of his question. "Because Ellie made it out and April didn't? It was after they ID'd her body that everything seemed...different."

"*What?*" Ben rocked forward onto his knees. "How can you even say something so disgusting to me? I should knock your perfect teeth out. Fuck, no. I love Ellie. It kills me that she spent a single minute in that hellacious place. Did you *really* believe that?"

"I couldn't think of any other reason that makes sense." He deflated.

Impossible to separate his own feelings from their mess and be objective, he appreciated Shari's input on the situation.

"Ry, it's not that," she interjected when Ben didn't seem able to explain. "He feels guilty. About April. I bet he distanced himself from you right around the time he found her diary, not when he found out she'd passed away in the dungeons. They just happened close together, so you assumed as well as you could with what you knew."

Ben struggled to speak. He started and stopped a dozen times, his face nearly purple with the strain. When Shari tried to pull him closer, he resisted. Ashamed or angry, maybe both, he couldn't go on.

Neither Shari nor Ryan pressured him.

They sat there with him, giving him a chance to work through his feelings with their unwavering support. Okay, fine, with *Shari's* unwavering support. Ryan wavered all over the fucking place. If he'd been driving, the Men in Blue would have pulled his ass over for suspected DUI given how he vacillated between outrage, shock, anger, misery, offense, and a baker's dozen other emotions, which zipped through him too quickly to name.

Finally, Ben croaked, "It's not just April I feel guilty about. It's Ryan, too. I let him down. Took advantage."

This time Shari seemed confused.

Ryan wasn't.

Not in the least.

That didn't mean he agreed with Ben's assessment. They'd had this argument plenty of times before. And it looked like they were about to have it again.

Today he'd make sure Ben fully understood how wrong he was.

Once and for all.

FIFTEEN

Ben's chest could easily have contained one of the exaggerated cartoon disasters depicted on those posters for heart attack warning signs, which they plastered around the cardiac center where he'd settled for a decent paying gig as a management analyst. Except he felt anything but numbness.

It was more like he experienced that horrible zinging pain that took over your body when blood rushed back into body parts. Maybe that was what this was. Him finally returning to the same plane as other people, who were fully alive.

Emerging from emotional hibernation.

Since he'd discovered his sister's diary, he'd been cut off from so much—the world, his full feelings, Ryan. Especially Ryan.

He looked at his roommate, the guy who had beat astronomical odds with him. The person he'd shut out of his life lately because he couldn't bear it otherwise. Admitting how unbalanced their exchanges had been wrecked him. Especially since he craved more of some of the acts they'd committed...in there.

The other thing he could do to prove both to himself and to Ryan that he could rise above his base nature, the one that had been enhanced by their stay in Morselli's lair, had been to deny the dark urges. He stared at Ryan, hoping the other man could understand.

With Ryan's single nod, he knew the guy had, though he didn't appear to agree.

Great, another argument. Exactly what he *didn't* want.

Ryan pinched the bridge of his nose between two fingers like he did when he had a tension headache. More often lately.

"What the hell is he talking about?" Shari asked in a near whisper.

Ben didn't bother to stop Ryan from spilling his deepest, darkest secrets to her. Maybe this time she would realize he'd been right to shove them both away. He didn't deserve them.

"It was easier for me, Shar." Ryan nuzzled her hair, as if drawing strength from her nearness. He used to do that with Ben, too—recover faster, fight harder—when they spent time together in their cell. Had Ben snatched coping mechanisms from Ryan too? Fuck, he was worthless. "I came into the dungeons later than Ben. Plus, I'm bi and I've been cool with that forever, so it didn't matter who they put me with. Man or woman, it wasn't any better or worse for me. And, you know, I'm kind of a slut who's into being bossed around anyway, so—"

"Don't do that!" Ben commanded. "Don't put yourself down. I won't let you ever again. Enough. We both did what we had to in order to survive. Except you stepped up and took some of my share of that shit when I'd reached my limit. You protected me when my attitude and my deranged stunts looking for April and Julie wrote checks my ass couldn't cash."

Shari caught on. "You feel like you used Ryan to avoid something."

"So many awful things. A couple times, they beat him so bad I don't know how he didn't die. They used him like savages. They gave him to a roomful of people who'd taken Sex Offender while he, on the other hand, was lucid and his sex drive was unenhanced. They fucked him raw. Once…the worst...they kept me in the room while they did the drug and the mist and fumes were enough to give me a contact high. Not a full dose, but bad enough that I can't imagine what Ellie—or my sister, or Lily, or any of them—went through. Then they sat around and laughed while they watched me tear into him. I couldn't stop myself." Ben covered his eyes with his hands. His shoulders shook. "After, *he* comforted *me*. Told me it was okay, that he'd enjoyed it even though that can't be possible. I was so rough. Greedy. Still, he kept me safe from poachers or even myself while I went through the downside of the high. I never would have made it without him. Not even another day past when we met, never mind the weeks we were down there after that. Then I went and did that. I could have broken him. I was out of my mind with lust like I've never felt before."

Shari tried to cut him some slack. "I'm sure the fact that you're naturally attracted to him magnified the effects of Sex Offender."

Except he couldn't be sure she was right. "But I've never even thought about fucking a guy before Ryan. How can you be sure that how I feel isn't...manufactured? A side effect of what we went through, or that day? Sex Offender."

Ryan flinched as if Ben had sucker punched him.

Another reason he'd never had the balls to have this conversation fully before.

Bile scorched his throat. He had to come clean. "It can have permanent effects on your system. Look at Ellie. Sometimes I still feel it. Ravaging me. Making me want to tear into him like I did that day."

"Did you hear me complaining?" Ryan practically purred. What the hell was wrong with that guy? He could not possibly have enjoyed such savagery. A glutton for pain, he kept setting himself up over and over for Ben to accidentally knock down.

Maybe it was best they put distance between them. He shouldn't have called Ryan last night, shouldn't have invited him to come today. Except Julie would have been crushed. She thought of Ryan as a second dad. And she'd already lost so much, he hadn't had the heart to rip that from her, too.

Still, he couldn't let Ryan brush off his concerns. They were too important to ignore.

Dangerous.

"That's exactly what I'm trying to say. You *should* have. But you never did. Maybe you never would, because you're strong enough to put other people first. Above yourself. It's not right! I won't take advantage of you ever again."

Shari tried to intervene. "Hang on, Ben. I think you're confused."

He didn't relent. Clarity had come to him a while ago on this point. It was just another thing those monsters had robbed from them both. The chance to definitively separate the unusual magnetism they had from the taint of those events.

"No, I'm clear on this. Certain. I could never turn around and treat him like they did. *That's* why I've been keeping my goddamned hands to myself since then. If I was a true friend—half as decent as he is—I would have kicked him out months ago, so that he could thrive on his own instead of binding him to me tighter to help myself get through the nights when I know there's no future for us."

"Why? Why can't there be?" Ryan blurted. "I love being bound for you. To you. Are you saying it's because you only fucked women before? I get it if you did things with me down there that you aren't into in regular life. Desperate times and all that…"

Ben loved the guy, but he had to be joking. Had he really been thinking all this shit?

So wrong.

Add gay-shaming to the list of injuries he'd inflicted due to his negligence.

"Ry, I don't think that's the problem." Shari smiled softly as she patted him on the knee. "He may never have been involved with a man before you, but he's completely into you. I wish you could have seen what I did when he jumped you in the kitchen before." Then she turned to Ben again. "He wants you. You definitely want him…"

"Aren't you two listening to me?" he shouted. When they only blinked in response, he tried to school his features into a blank mask and concentrated on lowering his voice so they couldn't mistake what he said next. "How can I ask him to serve me when I'm the one who owes him my life? How can I take you from him, make him share your affection, when all he ever did for me was be generous? How could I possibly let go of my control long enough to fuck him, when I'm not positive that I wouldn't hurt him again?"

If Ryan's reflection of his agony was any indication, he already failed on that point.

Undiluted sorrow shredded his insides.

"You idiot!" Ryan howled. "You've been beating yourself up for nothing."

"Oh, Ben." Shari sighed his name, like it was carried on a gentle summer breeze. Everything he prized in the world these days, yet was afraid he would stomp all over given his nature and the un-improvements his time in hell had wrought.

So he tried one final time to warn them off, before his restraint cracked and he took what he so desperately needed. Them. "It's not right to accept his affection when I'm not one-hundred percent certain that what I feel comes from my soul, like I believe, or a side effect of what they did to us. Same for him. Maybe he would never have fallen for me if it hadn't been for those monsters and what they did. If that's true, then I'm only prolonging their theft of his freewill. It's not right."

"We're telling you, you're mixed up. We're here for you. Willing to take a risk to show you that you're not the horrible person they've conditioned you to think you are." Shari's conviction began to persuade him. She was impartial. Had never been exposed to Sex Offender or the evil people who had wielded it. Her perspective wasn't warped by circumstance. "When we look at you, we see something totally different than the distorted impression they've planted in your brain. Remember, it was one enormous experiment. Don't let them keep stealing your choices because you're afraid."

"Even if that's true, I don't deserve you. Either of you. You're good and kind and so damn sexy. I can't be trusted to keep you safe. Like April..."

"Shut the fuck up." The iron in Ryan's snarl surprised him, snapping him out of his line of reasoning. "The world sucks sometimes, Ben. We both know that without a doubt. Even if something horrible happened to one of us, unless you did it, you're *not responsible*. Right now, you are harming me. You're hurting Shari too by keeping yourself away from us when that's not what we would choose for ourselves. Can't you see? You're doing exactly what you're so damn scared of to begin with."

Ben shook his head, trying to keep Ryan from starting to make sense.

"You have the power to fix this. You are in control of your fate," Shari crooned to him. "Don't let those brutes take another thing from you by twisting you around until you make bad decisions. Be with us. Let us heal you. Or at least try to make you feel better until the wounds can scab over. In the process, you can do the same for us."

"You're lost, Ben. A fucking mess." A slight smile crossed Ryan's face when Ben snorted at his honest assessment.

"Now *that* I believe." He might even have grinned some in return.

"Let us help you. Shari is everything good and light in the world. Untouched by the shit we went through. She'll find a path out of the darkness and keep the shadows away. And I'm still here for you, every step of the way. Like I was in that shithole. I'll always have your back. I thought you would know that by now." Ryan's hands balled into fists before he purposefully unfurled them, finger by finger.

"What if I do this?" Ben asked softly, lured into having faith by their unwavering determination and his underlying desires. "What if something happens and I lose you two? I can't do it again. I can't. I'm fucked up and I'll never recover. I have to hold it together for Julie, but I'm not doing a great job of that, and you're slipping away. I want to rip things apart with my bare hands. Then last night I couldn't find you. I thought..."

"Oh fuck." Realization dawned in Ryan's eyes.

He'd said too much. It hadn't been his intent to overwhelm them with remorse.

Only to explain, honestly and completely for once, what he was feeling so they might understand and pardon his errors in judgment.

Shari too must have realized what their disappearing act had led him to believe. She lunged from Ryan's hold and practically tackled Ben. They tumbled until she blanketed him, smothering him in warmth and softness.

Ryan didn't object as she covered Ben's face with butterfly kisses, comforting him in a way his instincts could process despite the depth of his despair. His hands shifted as if he was possessed, coming to rest ever so gently on her back. For once, he didn't brush her aside. He stayed stock still, as if any motion would scare her off, then accepted the comfort she rained on him.

The truth was clear to him in that moment. No words would ever convince him like this simple show of her sincerity and yearning. One Ryan seemed to approve.

When she hesitated, staring straight into his eyes before sinking lower so that she could take her first taste of his lips, Ben glanced at Ryan out of the corners of his eyes. The other guy looked like he might break out into one of his patented happy dances, complete with expert-level twerking.

"Mind if I kiss the shit out of him, Ryan?" Shari verified, though Ben could read the answer plainly in his best friend's eyes.

"Don't ask, Shar. If it feels right, go for it. That's what I want for you. For each of us." Maturity didn't always suit Ryan. Right then was the exception. He seemed genius to Ben, who'd struggled for so long with trying to simplify things between them. It didn't last long, though. "Besides, if I wasn't afraid of shattering this Hallmark moment, I'd probably already have my hands in my pants and be playing with my cock while you two make out. Go ahead, put on a sexy show for me."

Laughter buffeted Ben's lips.

Then he was doomed. No way could he help but taste elation that pure and freely given.

He craned his neck upward, closing the gap between himself and Shari. The moist heat of her lips soothed the bruised flesh he'd won as a consolation prize from his tongue twister with Ryan earlier. Her petite hands petted his shoulders, helping him relax and enjoy instead of pillaging her mouth. Despite his fears, she calmed him.

Her passion burned away some of the pain. For them both, he supposed.

As their tongues touched, swirled, and licked, his hands roamed lower, to her waist. He held her hips securely on top of him, keeping her from slipping to the floor when she lost track of their surroundings. Instead, he rolled, putting her beneath him.

Something inside him unfurled, coming back to life. And he wasn't just talking about his dick, which grew stiffer by the heartbeat. Levered up on his elbows, peering into her pretty coffee eyes, he felt more like himself than he had in ages.

Not only because she was so utterly feminine compared to Ryan's cut form.

Also because she lent him some of her strength. Damn, did she have a lot of it.

Shari squirmed beneath him. He thought he might be crushing her until he realized her instincts had her attempting to align their bodies so their pleasure points connected. If they'd been naked, he could easily have pressed his cock to her and begun to ease inside.

Fuck, he wanted that.

To feel her pussy sheathing him as she looked at him like this, like he wasn't the horrible deadbeat he'd convinced himself he must be. Or at least started chipping away at the roadblocks that had been keeping him from her.

From them.

Ben reached out, searching for Ryan. The other man didn't leave him hanging.

Their hands locked together in an unbreakable grasp that caused him to redouble the attention he was paying to Shari's kisses and the curvaceous body trapped between him and the mattress. He didn't stop sipping from her lips until it was that or black out from the lack of oxygen.

When she'd caught her breath, far sooner than he could manage, she smiled up at him while caressing his back.

"It's not going to go away overnight, this shit they did to you both or the lingering trauma." Shari kissed him so softly, he wondered if he'd imagined it. "But if we keep working on it and stay honest with each other, we'll get past it. I can feel it."

Terrifying hope bloomed within Ben like a tiny crocus trying to be the first to break through the late-spring snow. He hoped he wasn't peeking out just in time to be slammed with an unseasonable frost. Frozen solid, he'd never manage to thaw again.

Shari refused to let him duck back underground now that he'd sprouted. "We're here for you. I believe that having you will be good for Ryan, too. You're worried about taking advantage, but Ben...can't you see? He needs you. Do what's truly best for him, since it's what you also want. Love him. In every way your heart craves."

"Fuck, yes," Ryan hissed. "Please. Do that."

"I shouldn't. But I have to." Ben couldn't resist them both allied against him. "I'm going to go to hell for this—"

"Shhh." Another kiss from Shari swallowed his negativity.

"Do it." Ryan stared at them with that endless blue gaze that had reminded him of the sky every time he thought there'd be nothing but midnight surrounding them again. It was no different now. Refreshing and rousing.

"I need you both." Ben closed his eyes as he breathed hard, waffling between what his brain told him was right and what the whole rest of his being felt was perfection. So close. Attainable. All he had to do was man up and grab it. "Forgive me."

"Of course," Shari whispered at the same time Ryan said, "Done."

So Ben pounced, dragging Ryan down beside Shari so that he could study them both, laid out on the bed before him like his most incredible—and lewd—dreams were about to come true.

Because they were.

∽ SIXTEEN ∽

Shari clasped Ryan's hand as they reclined side-by-side, looking up adoringly at the man who'd bruised their hearts because his own had been mangled. They'd almost left him to the phantoms of his past, which haunted him. Blame had no place here anymore. It had already caused enough harm.

Of the three of them, she was clearly the one who needed the most guidance now.

She had no idea where the heck to start when presented with two gorgeous men like these—experienced maestros of seduction, even the one with the submissive streak. *Especially* that one.

"Last one naked gets a spanking," Ryan joked, breaking the tension while tossing her a hint.

She didn't need any additional instruction. With a shimmy and a couple of yanks, she had her eyelet dress peeled over her head and fluttering into a heap on the floor.

Ben paused with his shirt a few inches above the waistband of his jeans, baring his six-pack as he admired her in her underwear. "Damn."

"Guess I was in a hurry." She shrugged one shoulder.

"Or you don't like spankings very much," Ryan teased.

"Don't worry. He likes them enough for you both." Ben shook his head slightly. "I know your tricks, boy."

Ryan, who hadn't removed a single stitch yet, only smiled.

"Would you mind if we didn't get around to that today?" Ben seemed genuinely curious. "I'm in the mood for something less...denigrating."

"I'm a fan of anything that means I wind up in bed with the two of you." This time there wasn't a hint of sarcasm or playfulness about Ryan's confession.

Shari sort of regretted her hastiness as her gaze ping-ponged between the two still-clothed men, though she supposed she'd bared her body while they bared their souls. Certainly a harder task.

"Besides, I kind of liked the vanilla topping Shari gave me last night." Ryan winked at her.

"You already went for food in bed?" Ben grunted. "I know you're a chef but—"

"He's not talking about Cool Whip," she interrupted before he could put more mouthwatering ideas in her mind. Too late, now she wanted to try that too. Later.

"Although now that I'm horny and thinking about that, it sounds kind of kinky, huh?" Ryan tapped his index finger on his chin. "Possibilities."

Shari laughed at how alike their thought processes were.

"Tell me what you mean." The directness of Ben's request didn't allow her to consider objecting, not that she would have anyway. Still, he was much better at this domineering thing than she had been.

So good that Ryan answered immediately, beating her to it. "She totally mind-fucked me. Subtly yet really effectively, by getting me to share a fantasy, while sort of acting it out."

"Was that kind of thing enough of a power exchange to get you off?" Ben asked as he continued where he'd left off, deliberately walking his T-shirt up his torso. As distractions went, it was pretty phenomenal. Shari forgot to be nervous about Ryan's response, too busy staring at the impressive display of well-muscled man Ben revealed bit by bit.

"Why don't you ask her?" Ryan laughed. "She watched me shoot about a gallon of come across my chest."

"True story." She pinched his upper arm, so much more relaxed around him after that adventure. "You did seem pretty pleased with yourself and that long cock of yours. But seriously, is it good enough, Ryan? Or do you need more? I kind of liked finding out what I have to give. I just worry I'm not everything you need."

"Right now, I'm happier than I've ever been. That's all I know." He turned his head and kissed her knuckles, then took her finger in his mouth and sucked lightly. "I think we might be about to shatter that record, though."

"What can I do to make today better?" she wondered.

Before Ryan could answer, Ben said, "Let me guess, his naughty little daydream included being tied up."

As he spoke, he shucked his jeans and underwear simultaneously. When he stood fully upright again, he wasn't the only straight and tall thing in the room. His cock jutted from his body, erect and...massive. Thick and dark, his erection had her licking her lips.

"Eyes up here, Shari," he mocked her. "I asked you a question."

She shivered. Was this what it would be like to give someone else control?

"Okay, I can see why this turns you on," she muttered in Ryan's direction without taking her eyes off Ben.

Who knew she might like to sample each of their flavors? Huh.

"You'd better answer him, Shar." Ryan, still fully dressed, rolled toward her. "Or he might put you over his knee yet."

She imagined what that might feel like. His heavy hand on her lower back, pinning her to those massive thighs. The heat of his palm caressing her cheeks before a stinging impact caused her to wriggle on his lap. It might be worth it to feel his cock at her hip, knowing she had the power to turn him on.

Damn, she could be in trouble.

"Shari." Ben crawled to her on the bed, his knees on either side of her and that imposing shaft searing her belly as gravity pulled it toward her.

"Oh. Yes. He mentioned handcuffs."

"I'll have to ask Mason to lend me some." Ben smiled, then kissed her lightly. "Good girl."

Ryan groaned. Though she could see the erection clearly stretching along his groin beneath his denim, he didn't cup himself. Expectantly, he stared up at Ben.

"You were the one who didn't strip. Not my fault." He shrugged. "Help me finish Shari, then I'll see about having you join us. Next time maybe you shouldn't screw around when we're about to get serious with each other."

"Yes, sir." The title rolled off Ryan's tongue, clearly more than a simple sign of respect, and certainly not a smarmy mockery. He paid Ben respect, and meant it.

Shari pressed her thighs together, trying to curb the ache between her legs.

These two might kill her. But she would die happy.

"Go ahead." Ben lifted his chin toward Shari.

She squeaked when Ryan swooped over her, lifted her shoulders, and unwrapped her for Ben. The scrap of lace panties she'd worn just for him followed shortly after.

It was the first time Ben had seen her nude, and she found herself reluctant to meet his stare. What if he didn't like what he saw?

"No wonder you didn't answer the phone, you lucky fucker." His envy turned his tone warm as he rubbed the nape of Ryan's neck.

"She's gorgeous," Ryan affirmed.

"Better than I pictured the million times I imagined her naked, even," Ben agreed. "Her body is compact and strong. You can tell she works on the ranch. But still curvy. Stacked."

"So soft," Ryan murmured before leaning in to pillow his head on her breasts. While he was there, he put his lips around her nipple and suckled.

Shari sighed. Could it be this easy?

For months she'd wondered about how she would be able to handle the pair of them when she'd barely slept with one man in the past. She wasn't a temptress like Lacey, or a Mistress like Lily, or as no-nonsense as Jambrea. Whatever she was, they seemed to like it, though.

When things went right they were every bit as effortless as they had been tense before. Why the hell hadn't she confronted them sooner?

Because they hadn't been ready.

Ben might never have been if he hadn't believed he'd lost everything the night before. Sometimes people had to hit rock bottom before they were ready to tackle their fears and make tough changes.

She didn't know if she was supposed to be still, but she didn't feel like it, so she went with her gut. Shari buried her fingers in Ryan's hair and held him to her chest. With the other, she reached out. Ben entwined their fingers.

"I should look at you two all day. Just like this." With his free hand, Ben wrapped his fist around his cock and began to stroke. Leisurely.

"Don't. Please," Ryan begged.

"Only because I can't," Ben said. "I've waited long enough already."

"Amen," Shari muttered under her breath.

Ryan's soft laughter jiggled her breasts.

"Fine." A wicked grin curved up one side of Ben's mouth. "I might not have any cuffs, but I've got something even better. Want to see what happens when Ryan loses his mind?"

"Mmmhmm." She did. She *definitely* did.

"You might be a sadist yet." Though he ragged on her, Ryan didn't seem to mind.

Ben reached across them both to yank open the nightstand drawer. He took from within a short length of rope and a bottle of clear liquid she pegged for lube. On the way back, he trailed the rough hemp over Ryan's hip. The slightest contact—even through his clothes—made him gasp.

"Didn't think I knew this was in there, did you?" Ben snapped it so it whipped Ryan's thigh. It couldn't have stung much, since he was still dressed, but it had an impact. "I hope you weren't doing anything that could get you in trouble."

Ryan moaned. He shook his head then said, "I can't pull it tight enough by myself, and I only did it when you were home. Never anywhere crazy like my neck. Only my ankles or sometimes my wrists as best I could."

"Let me guess, you used the slack in the rope loop so that you could fuck between your wrists and the rope? Did it get you off faster to chafe your dick with this scratchy thing?"

"Yes." Ryan didn't bother to deny it.

Shari pictured him going to those lengths to find some relief. To secure a clearly half-assed release. If she had suspected, she would have come to his aid.

"I might have been humiliated, but I could have called you for help if I had to. How did you find it?"

"It was sticking out of the drawer one day when I passed by. You must have been drunk on the pleasure of using it and not noticed before you passed out one night. I tucked it back in so Julie wouldn't notice and ask a thousand questions I can't answer for at least another twenty years." Ben dangled the rope in front of Ryan, who tracked its arc back and forth as if it hypnotized him.

She couldn't pinpoint what prompted her to say it. The words flew from her lips before she could stop them. "I think you should let me strip him and bind him for you. If working on a ranch is good for something, it's learning how to tie solid knots. There won't be any getting out of my handiwork if you don't let him out."

"Fuck, Shari." Ryan literally twitched beneath her, his entire body jolting as if she'd shocked him with one of the cattle prods she kept out in her barn. For that matter, he might have liked that too.

Ben hummed his approval. "I admit, I didn't expect you to be quite so…"

"Enthusiastic?" she supplied.

"Perfect," Ben finished instead.

"I'll assume that's a yes from you, then." She grinned, feeling significant and sexy in a way she never had before. To be sure, she asked Ryan also, "Would you let me do that to you? Right now?"

"Yeah," he groaned. "But if you do, you'd better be ready for the fuck of a lifetime."

She raised her brows at him, imagining her thighs spread around his trim hips getting a workout. Being on top wasn't her favorite, but she could manage. "You mean the *ride* of a lifetime?"

"Hell, no. Well, unless that's what you want. I like that too. But it's been so long, I won't be able to keep myself calm or still. So either tie all of me really well, or go for my wrists. I love having them bound. Then let me fuck the shit out of you like that."

"Endurance is one of his finer qualities." Ben smiled down at them both, his eyes slumberous as arousal began to take hold.

Shari beamed as she faced Ryan and unbuttoned his shirt. She did it deliberately. Slow and with intention, so that he could savor the anticipation. After last night, she knew how that factored in to building his arousal. And she wanted this experience to shake his foundation. Life could be crazy sometimes, each of them knew that. If she only ever got one chance to share this with these two men, she wanted to do it right. "I noticed last night."

She laid a string of kisses down his sternum as she revealed his smooth chest. Did he wax?

He must, and she liked it.

Shari kneaded his pecs while Ben started at the other end, taking off Ryan's socks before working on his belt. The sight of those long, olive-skinned fingers threading the leather through Ryan's buckle hit her hard. She shuddered and moaned.

Ryan matched her as Ben moved on to the button. Then the zipper.

"You could use that on me," Ryan offered just before the wad of leather, metal, and denim hit the floorboards.

"Not today. I've got other plans for your ass," Ben declined as he appraised Ryan, who didn't attempt to hide a single speck of himself from either Shari or Ben.

Naked and unafraid, Ryan left himself open to their scrutiny.

Shari couldn't have found a single thing wrong with his lithe body or his new attitude. Both were marvelous to her.

"Do those plans involve my favorite position?" he asked on a half-groan, half-whimper.

"Maybe." Ben shrugged, though his hungry stare made it clear he was into it too, whatever *it* might be.

"Which is what?" she couldn't help but wonder aloud.

Ryan looked to Ben, pleading for him to respond since he seemed incapable of coherent speech while the majority of his blood rushed straight to his exposed cock.

"He loves to fuck while being fucked."

"Uh huh." Ryan nodded vehemently, then cupped his shaft and balls, giving them a squeeze, as if to relieve some of the pressure that had to be building there.

"Did I tell you you were allowed to do that?" Ben asked with precisely the right amount of steel in his tone to jolt Shari.

Ryan's hands fell to his sides, limp, palms up, though his fingers twitched as if it took much more effort than he let on to keep from touching himself in their presence.

She could relate.

"Shari, you'd better tie him so he doesn't get carried away again. I don't want to have to punish anyone today." Ben held the rope out to her and she clasped it, surprised at how prickly the texture of the raw material was compared to the nylon or cotton varieties she used back home.

This was really what he preferred?

A single glance at his wide eyes, shallow breathing, and slack jaw confirmed it.

"Give me your hands."

He did immediately.

So she wrapped his wrists then fastened the hemp in a knot that would allow her to release him quickly if necessary, but wouldn't loosen on its own.

"Tighter," Ben instructed when she cinched the final strand.

"Are you sure?" she asked them both at once.

"Yes," they responded in unison.

So she gave them what they asked for, only making sure she could slip a finger beneath the cord to ensure Ryan's circulation wouldn't be impacted.

"Fuck yes," he hissed, his eyes falling closed as he savored his bondage.

Shari took a deep breath, trying to force some oxygen into her lungs, which burned as if she powered through the steepest uphill section of her favorite hiking path in the woods.

"I think our girl needs some of your attention," Ben told Ryan.

"Where?" he asked.

"Get her ready to take you. I want you on your knees."

When Ryan climbed to them on the mattress, his cock swaying below him, Ben slapped his ass.

"Thank you." Ryan's response came even before the crack of Ben's palm had finished echoing through the room.

"You're welcome. But not like that. Get on the floor. I know how much you like kneeling on hard surfaces. Let's see if we can leave some marks on those legs, shall we?"

"Fuck, yes." Ryan obeyed faster than Shari could process what Ben had said. He slithered to the ground without the use of his hands, landing with a *thunk* on the hardwood planks that made it clearer to her.

He liked...

Ah.

Well, then. She supposed she'd blown that one by letting him sprawl on the bed between her legs while he'd pleasured her the night before. More than willing to make up for her mistakes, Shari giggled when Ben hooked his hands beneath her thighs then yanked her until her ass balanced precariously on the edge of the mattress.

No way would they let her fall.

Ryan glanced up at Ben, who smiled and ruffled his hair. "Go ahead. Make her come. As many times as you can in the next ten minutes. Then, if I'm happy with the job you've done, I'll let you fuck her."

"And you'll fuck me too?" Ryan asked. "I want that. The three of us. Linked together. Finally."

"It's going to happen. Don't worry." Ben tapped Ryan's cheek.

"Why do I feel like he's leaving out some important information?" Shari squinted at the two of them, not entirely sure what game they were playing yet. Not that she minded, especially the part about being Ryan's all-you-can-eat buffet again for a while.

He could do a lot with that time—she knew from experience.

"Because I did. Are you sure you've never played like this before?" Ben chuckled.

Who knew he could be so devious? Maybe Ryan brought out this side of him.

Together, the three of them transformed each other into the perfect partners for each other.

Shari couldn't wait to see what it would be like when they became more familiar.

Then again, her heart might not be able to handle it.

She was pretty sure it was a lost cause already.

"Get to work." Ben fisted Ryan's hair and directed him where he wanted him—with his face buried in Shari's pussy.

From zero to warp speed.

Shari closed her eyes against the disorienting onslaught of pleasure. Holy shit. Could she really survive six hundred seconds of ecstasy that intense?

They were about to find out.

"That's right," Ben murmured in her ear. She hadn't realized it, but he'd circled the bed so he could lean down and whisper. "Hang on. Let him treat you. The better he does, the less I'll torture him. So help the boy out."

Shari didn't think that would be a problem. Already her muscles spasmed as his tongue flicked over her clit in the pattern he'd discovered most effective the night before.

"Oh God," she moaned.

Ben's naughty instruction definitely acted as a bonus, magnifying her arousal. He nibbled her earlobe before continuing in a whisper only she could hear. "After these ten minutes are up, he's going to have to fuck you for twenty, minus a minute for every time you come on his face right now. I won't let him shoot, no matter how much you strangle his cock with that pretty pussy. And I know you will. He fucks like he was born for it."

Shari's eyes rolled back and her body gathered, preparing to knock sixty seconds off Ryan's sentence already.

"Yes, come for him. Because holding back tortures me too. Only after he's finished his *penalty* will I put my cock in his ass. You'll need that time to loosen up. Wait until you see how wild it makes him to take a man inside him like that. The sight alone will have you shattering around him again."

It would have been impossible to resist the lascivious picture Ben was painting.

Shari's pussy clenched, hard, then released. Contractions racked her body as she cried out Ryan's name, then Ben's. Both men were there, Ben squeezing her hand and Ryan her knee, where his bound hands rested, while they went about their business, delighting her.

Bent over her, his chin to her forehead, Ben wrapped his other hand around her neck, pressing slightly. Enough to trigger a second orgasm. Score for Ryan.

"You like that?" He didn't miss her elevated excitement.

Shari moaned, "Yes."

"And this?" Ben surprised her then, hunching even lower to capture her lips tenderly. He might have been upside down, and turning her inside out, but their first kiss would be one she never forgot.

He tasted different than Ryan, like exotic spices from his ancestors' homeland.

No wonder he appealed to Ryan's sensibilities.

From between her legs, Ryan moaned, vibrating her clit perfectly to trigger another climax when coupled with the sweet liplock Ben had engaged her in. She was glad he enjoyed seeing them swap affection as much as he had forecasted he would.

Ben lifted up, causing her to whimper in regret. He smiled and rubbed his nose along hers before murmuring, "More of that later, I promise."

Then he cupped her breast, squeezing. He flicked a thumb over her nipple. The gesture triggered another wave of rapture. Only then did he return to the other side of the bed to monitor Ryan's feast. "Enough cheating. I've given you a head start. You'd better try harder. Only seven minutes to go."

Shari slapped her hands on the sheets and curled her toes where they rested on Ryan's shoulders. Sweet torment. She let him take her up and over too many times for her to count considering the haze of lust that fogged her mind.

All she knew was that by the time Ben looked at the bedside clock and said, "Enough," she thought she might never move again. The barrage of pleasure had liquefied her bones yet left her starving for something more...substantial.

Ben hauled Ryan to his feet with one hand on each of his roommate's upper arms.

"I've always thought he looked hotter than usual with a woman's come on his face." Ben showered Ryan with approval, leaning down to lick a sample from his cheek. "Fuck, you *are* delicious. Both of you mixed together like that."

Though Shari thought she might get a replay of their kitchen make-out, instead Ben approached her. He inserted his index and middle fingers inside her without much fanfare. He hummed as he verified Ryan had thoroughly soaked her pussy. Then he withdrew, making her moan at the loss.

"Clean them," he ordered Ryan, who opened his mouth and let Ben stick his fingers into his mouth. The scrape of his teeth along the digits had to be intentional.

Ryan's cock jumped, dislodging the bead of precome at its tip.

"Are you ready to fuck her?" Ben asked innocently.

SEVENTEEN

Shari knew what their future held. And she couldn't wait.
Ryan didn't, but he trusted Ben—and her—enough to keep playing along anyway. "Hell, yes. I have to get inside her. Please. Where are your condoms?"

"I—" Ben blinked. "Shit!"

"No. No shit allowed. What's wrong?" Shari surfaced from her daze at his harsh exclamation.

"I think they're expired. It's been...forever. I didn't even think about it. Fuck. I could've put you at risk."

Huh? The guys had been tested. She distinctly remembered what a relief it had been to them, and their friends, to find out that they'd gotten a clean bill of health. Ellie too, despite the dozens of people who'd used her without regard to her safety. It was kind of a miracle, really.

"I'll go to the store." Ryan dove for his discarded jeans, bending awkwardly to one side to snatch them with his bound hands. "Just don't change your minds while I'm gone."

"Guys, hang on. I'm clean, too. And on the pill." Shari blushed at that despite what they'd shared. She was still new to these sorts of intimate personal discussions.

"You are?" Ben swung around, his cock still rock hard.

"Seriously, you wouldn't mind?" Ryan winced. "You know, after everything they did and how many partners I've had. I won't be offended—"

"There are only two people you fuck who matter to me, Ry. Ben and me. So shut up and get to it already, would you? I'm dying over here." She held her arms wide open on the bed, inviting him into her embrace.

Ben slapped Ryan's ass when he hesitated a moment longer than he deemed appropriate. "You heard the lady. Put that cock in her."

Shari sighed.

"Tell him what the deal was," Ben directed.

"You have to fuck me for twenty minutes minus one for every orgasm you gave me." Math was beyond her by then, so she figured she let them figure that part out on their own. "You can't come or he won't... You have to last. Only when you've passed the mark will he take you, too. He wants us to come together. The three of us."

"I love your fucking devious mind." Ryan spun around, went onto his tiptoes, and crushed his mouth against Ben's. The other man didn't object or even try to direct the moment. It didn't need his influence to be flawless.

When they separated with a groan, Ben muttered, "You better hurry up. I can't wait to have my cock buried in your tight ass. The sooner you start, the sooner you're mine."

"I've been yours for a while." Ryan ducked his head as he proclaimed it softly. "You just didn't notice."

The assertion rang through the room despite its low volume.

Shari's heart did a double thump in her chest.

Then Ryan was there. He planted his bound wrists above her head, tugging against the rope as if he enjoyed the burn from the coarse cable. Carefully, he knelt between her legs then draped his body over hers, bringing his face close enough for her to revere. She showed him with every swipe of her lips and tongue and teeth over his mouth how much she adored him. Consumed by the moment, she didn't have a chance to tense or worry when his bare cock nudged her opening.

"Need a hand?" Ben asked.

"Yeah. Shit. Help me. Ben, put my cock in her," Ryan panted between devouring her mouth.

"You meant please, didn't you?" Ben swatted Ryan's bare ass, wedging the blunt head of his erection more tightly against her opening.

"Yes. Please. Ben. Come on. Please." Ryan's desperation moved her. She hugged him tight as he pled with Ben. "I gotta fuck. Help me."

Shari lifted her head long enough to watch Ben take hold of Ryan's cock and steady it, guiding it into her pussy as Ryan worked to penetrate her. He rocked into her with short jabs that advanced him through her clamping rings of muscle. With each bit he spread her, stretched her, and delighted her.

She cried out.

Finally!

"Fuck, yes," Ben egged him on. "She loves that. Give her more. Let her have all of you. I want you balls-deep. *Now.*"

Ryan's hips hitched backward then plunged forward, embedding his shaft completely.

Shari arched off the bed, overwhelmed with sensations—mostly phenomenal, with a sprinkle of discomfort. After appraising Ryan's long hard-on the night before, it thrilled her that it didn't hurt more, as she'd expected it might.

By the time he'd withdrawn then returned with a few gliding strokes, she'd forgotten about the soreness in favor of the sparkling pleasure that bubbled up from her center. When her body responded automatically, hugging him within her, he groaned.

"How long?" he asked Ben over his shoulder.

"Thirteen minutes," he replied, then slapped Ryan's ass. "Go!"

Ryan bit his lip, hard. She could see his mouth moving, as if he was repeating some sort of mantra, or maybe something to distract himself from the wonderful sensations he was creating between her legs.

"I'll try not to come," she whispered to him, unsure of exactly how she'd pull that off when the firm length of his cock felt utterly fantastic inside her.

"Don't do that." He kissed her, sucking gently on her lower lip before releasing it. "Never do that. I want to bring you as much bliss as I can. Until you're delirious with it. I can handle it. Feel me in you."

Shari moaned.

Because she could. So clearly.

Not only where his cock prodded her most sensitive places, either.

She felt him taking up permanent residence in her heart. Entwining with her soul. Two people—no, *three* people—couldn't possibly be this in sync with each other without forming some sort of permanent bond. At least she hoped not.

Now that she had them, she didn't plan to let go.

Not in twelve more minutes.

Not in a lifetime.

"You know how I'm a pretty good cook?" Ryan asked with a wry grin that didn't do much to disguise how spectacular it felt from his end of things or how hard he had to focus to keep from spilling his come inside her.

"Yeah." She would have gushed about the meal he'd made for her the night before if she could have uttered more than a single syllable right then.

"I'm *way* better at this."

"That's true." Ben paced beside them, his fingers trailing along the exposed length of Ryan's spine then down his flank. "If there were sex Olympics, you'd need a warehouse to store your gold medals. So quit slacking and make her come already."

Shari threw her head back when Ryan added a well-placed swivel of his hips to his thrusting. The first time it electrified her. The second, it shattered her.

Despite her lingering resolution to make things easier for him, she couldn't. She came so hard she was afraid she'd leave a permanent dent in his cock. The orgasms he'd given her with his mouth had been fantastic. Compared to this, she realized they had only been an appetizer.

He uncovered the main course.

Ravenous, she met him pound for pound.

"Jesus, you two are spectacular." Ben observed their mating with awe in his golden eyes. He stroked himself in the same rhythm Ryan used while pumping into her. "What the hell do you need me for?"

"Join us and find out," Ryan taunted, trying to get Ben to break his self-imposed time out.

"Soon," Ben promised.

He sidled closer, putting his groin at face level. She was so busy gawking at his enormous cock that she didn't realize what he intended until Ryan dipped down and caught the fat head in his mouth without ever faltering as he shuttled within her.

Ben gripped Ryan's hair, then speared the other into hers. She gladly followed his direction when he pressed her closer to his shaft. Shari licked him, sampled his unique musk, and breathed deep of his scent. Only when she'd taken her fill did she open her mouth wider and duck her chin to take his heavy balls into her mouth and bathe them with the flat of her tongue.

"Fuck. Yes!" Ben thrust deeper into Ryan's mouth to give her room to work his sac.

So she did.

Knowing that she could inspire even a fraction of the extreme sensations they sparked in her tipped her over the edge again. If it was possible to overdose on endorphins from orgasms, she was in serious danger.

Time warped, slowing to a crawl, which made her hyperaware of every moment while also flying by. She reached a place she'd never imagined where her rapture became constant. Not a peak-and-valley landscape where she was coming or not coming, but one where an incessant tide of pleasure kept her floating on ecstasy.

Eventually, Ben withdrew, mumbling something about facials and temptation.

It wasn't long after that Ryan faltered for the first time. Of course, the variety in his movement only added to her rising satisfaction levels. Everything they did to her increased her enjoyment.

Especially when she realized what had happened. Ben tossed the bottle of lube to the bed, having slicked his fingers and presumably Ryan's ass with the substance. He stood behind Ryan, gripping his hip with one hand while the other disappeared between his cheeks.

Shari realized right away how controlled her lover had been when he bucked frantically, slamming into her and filling her slightly beyond the limits of her body. The intensity of the sensation sparked another explosion within her.

Oh God. She couldn't take much more.

"Ben," she cried.

"Yes?" He whipped his stare to her, assessing even as he lit up with affection and...respect?

"Hurry, please."

He nodded. "It's time."

Ben withdrew his fingers, wiping them on one of the T-shirts that littered the floor. He climbed onto the bed behind them, making it dip. "You ready for me?"

"So ready," Ryan assured him, although Shari suspected Ben had cut his preparations short for her sake.

"Have you been playing with that plug in your drawer? That thing is huge."

"Yeah. Like you." Ryan might have earned himself another spank for that if both men weren't so close to the edge. "I wanted to be prepared, just in case."

His eyes seemed brighter then, as Shari watched so closely.

It was like he'd been given another chance at something he assumed he'd never have.

To share this with him—with them—was a humbling experience.

"Kiss me," she whispered, and he did.

"I'm glad you stayed primed," Ben growled as he bit Ryan's shoulder. "Because this isn't going to be some drawn out affair. Watching the two of you has me crazy. Living with you without touching you has been like months of foreplay. I need relief. And I'm going to use you to get it."

"Yes!" Ryan pushed his ass back, slipping slightly from her pussy. "Let me give you that."

Then there was no more talking, only action. Ben and Ryan gasped in unison.

Ryan clenched his jaw until she distracted him with another lingering kiss at odds with the relentless slap of his pelvis against hers. He groaned into her mouth, trying to speak. Instead he only managed a few incoherent pleas that had her hoping she was giving him everything he needed.

They moved as one then, sometimes in harmony and sometimes in counterpoint, but always in the style that maximized each of their pleasure. Over and over, Ryan chanted their names and Ben swore, "I'm here. I've got you. And I'm never letting go again."

"Have to come!" Ryan shouted. "So close."

Shari looked up into the faces of two men she could easily fall for. Both of them wore the same expression. One of utter shock, relief, and euphoria.

Come to think of it, hers probably matched exactly.

She was right there with them.

"Yes. Do it. Now." Ben granted Ryan release, and in doing so, gave himself the same permission.

Shari too.

Together, they came.

Ryan flooded her pussy with hot blasts of fluid that quickly overflowed her. She could only imagine that Ben did the same to Ryan's ass by the groans and curses the men shouted as they jerked above her. Their combined weight and the pressure of their hips bumping into hers added to her enjoyment.

Even as she continued to spasm, she laughed. And laughed.

Until she cried.

∽ EIGHTEEN ∾

"Um, Shar. You...okay?" Ryan asked between great huffs of air.

Way to act the psycho chick, Shari.

"Relieved." The more she tried to hold in her sobs, the faster they erupted from her.

"Hey, it's okay. We're here. We've got you." Ryan kissed the tears from her cheeks. When he groaned, she figured Ben had withdrawn.

That only made her more upset, that she might have cut his pleasure short. Forced them to separate after only just coming together again.

Softening rapidly, Ryan's cock slipped from her pussy and a warm rush of his semen followed behind, leaving her afraid to move and stain the blankets more than she probably already had.

Overwhelmed, she clung to him.

Ben rounded the bed and crouched near her head. He swiped her hair, damp with perspiration, from her face and tucked it behind her ears. When she tried to duck her head, neither of the guys would permit her to hide.

"It's fine to get this out," Ben murmured in her ear as they peppered her with kisses. "However you feel, that's okay."

"Almost gave up." A hiccup cut her explanation in half. "What if I never got to share that with you two? What if I'd lived my whole life and never knew what I was missing?"

"It would have been my fault." He brushed the corners of her eyes with the backs of his knuckles.

"That doesn't matter anymore," Ryan added. "Because it did happen. And it will again. Like seventeen times a week if I have anything to say about it."

Shari laughed at that. "Ambitious. I might have to train for a sexathon like that."

Now that her endocrine system had shifted out of overdrive, she could feel how hard she'd pushed her body. A wince must have clued in the guys too.

"Why don't I get you cleaned up?" Ryan asked as he pushed onto straight-locked arms, then glanced between them.

"Uh oh."

Ben's gaze whipped to her groin, where Ryan was staring, looking rather alarmed.

Shari struggled to get her elbows beneath her so she could see the alien baby she half expected to find there, given his wide eyes.

"Ben, why didn't you tell me to be more careful?" He scrubbed his hand through his hair. "I lost track of everything except burying myself in her. Shit, I made her bleed."

"What?" Ben was there, inspecting both her pussy and the traces of red streaking Ryan's dick. "Did this happen last night? Or were you gentle with her when you made love?"

Ryan cleared his throat then peeked down at her. Oh, hell no. She wasn't fielding that one.

"Uh…"

"I won't freak out. Though I wish I could have seen that, since I'm apparently never going to be able to keep myself under wraps long enough for that kind of sweet sex myself." Ben looked between them, clearly trying to decode their glances.

"I'm not worried about that. We'll try it, someday." Ryan met Ben's stare. "Last night, though, we sort of didn't get that far. You know, before we answered your calls. And then there was cake-making, which took all night..."

"Are you kidding me? You obviously spent the entire evening in bed together. Are you telling me you *didn't* fuck each other's brains out?" Ben's skepticism twisted his features. "I could tell everything had changed between you when you showed up today. What happened?"

Shari felt her cheeks heat as he carefully examined her tender flesh while Ryan looked on.

"I might have been preoccupied with eating her instead. Her pussy is sweet. And she sounds so beautiful when she comes. It's like a siren song making me want to hear her scream my name again and again." He rubbed his rejuvenating hard-on. "Shit. I'm going to get another boner thinking about it. Maybe we should do some more of that."

"Damn, we should probably have worked up to that wild ride then. Do you feel okay?" Ben asked her before reassuring his partner. "I don't think it's as scary as it looks, Ry. There's a tiny tear at the bottom, right here. I'm gonna guess it's still bleeding a little because she's so wet. Or maybe it's like when you nick your neck shaving and it just won't quit. I can call Lacey or Jambrea if you think we should, though."

"No!" Shari shot to a sitting position then. "Hey docs, I'm right here, and I'm fine. The best I've ever felt, actually. Do *not* call them. They'll freak out and overreact and next thing we know there will be half of the OSPD crowded around this freaking bed taking an incident report that's really a play-by-play of how well you fucked my brains out. Absolutely not. No one else is poking around down there tonight."

Ryan grinned at that. "You're right. She's fine."

"Has this ever happened to you before?" Ben asked. "Next time I hope you'll tell us if you're uncomfortable. It's like I was afraid of, you know, that we might be too rough—too much for you—since..."

"Hey. Quit that." She went to him, rising with assistance from Ryan's palm under her elbow. Then she snuggled against Ben's chest. "I loved every minute. I swear. I didn't feel real pain. A twinge of discomfort while Ry was first getting settled in, maybe, but that's it. Everything you two did was incredible. I promise."

Ryan stroked her hair while Ben rocked her gently. She could fall asleep right there between them so easily.

"Answer his question, though, Shar," Ryan insisted. "Is this normal for you? Otherwise, maybe we *should* have one of the nurses take a look."

"Oh. Well, I don't exactly have a lot of experience," she mumbled, figuring the odds that they'd let this topic drop were probably about as bad as the probability of winning the Mega Millions, considering she'd never bothered to make the trek into the city to buy a ticket.

"What does that mean?" Ben's spine stiffened beneath her wandering hands.

"Please tell me you were not a virgin an hour ago," Ryan begged.

"I wasn't, but let's say that if we count both of you, I've now been with three guys. And the first time was a couple years ago. One of John's soldier friends did the honors up against a barn wall. When he realized he'd popped my cherry, he pulled out, zipped up, then bolted before he even came. Probably worried my brother would have sliced him to bits in his sleep, which he was very capable of doing. Other than that, there wasn't really anyone around to hook up with. I wasn't lying before. I've spent most of my life alone."

The guys eyeing each other over her head pissed her off.

"I didn't tell you that so you'd pity me. Just know my history was nothing special, and definitely not enough data for me to know what's *normal*. I've never managed to do that to myself and I have a pretty extensive vibrator collection—thank you, online shopping. None of my battery-operated boyfriends are as well-endowed as you guys, though."

"Oh shit, now *that* I have to see. Why didn't you mention that last night?" Ryan leaned in, nuzzling her neck. "I assumed the friend of yours I met was the only one in that drawer or I would have gladly returned the favor."

"I was hoping you were going to be my real live boy toy." She turned and grinned at him. "Until we got interrupted."

"Damn, man," Ryan faux-glared at Ben. "You owe me one."

"Here I thought I just gave you one." Ben's smile illuminated his face. It elevated him from smoldering to cover-worthy hotness.

Shari hadn't known Ben before the Sex Offender scandal had reforged him into the man he was today, but she imagined that was how he'd been most of the time. Her heart ached to see how different he was, even as a shred of hope made her determined to put this look on his face as often as possible from here on out.

Ryan gazed over at her and nodded as if he gave her mental plan a thumbs-up.

"Well, if she's okay, then I suggest we move on. Next time, we'll be more mindful of our differences." Ben rubbed Ryan's back, as if trying to convince him he was absolved of any perceived wrongdoing.

"Can I take care of her, please?" Ryan asked Ben.

"Why don't you ask her what she wants?"

"Please, Shar." His expressive eyes were impossible to resist. Not that she could function properly on her own at the moment in any case.

Ben mistook her delayed response as a result of her addled mind for hesitation.

"Let him," Ben suggested. "This is part of what he needs."

When she nodded, Ryan picked her up and cradled her in his arms. So she rested her head on his strong shoulder.

"Thank you for trusting me. For letting me serve you." Ryan's hoarseness caught her attention. When she glanced up, his eyes shone.

What was that about?

"Since you've got her, I'm going to my room to grab a quick shower. I'll meet you back here when you're finished," Ben said.

"Sounds good," Ryan agreed.

Ben put his arms around Ryan, and her by default. He hugged them both then dropped a kiss on each of their lips before strutting down the hall.

Both she and Ryan stared until his bare ass and broad shoulders were out of sight.

Hell, even his calves were sexy.

Shari patted Ryan's chest. "We're awfully blessed, you know that?"

"I sure do." He flashed her that full-on smile that brightened her world a few shades every time she earned it from him.

Then he walked a few doors down to the bathroom usually reserved for Julie, if the purple sparkly accessories were any indication.

Pipes clanked in the wall when a shower switched on in the bathroom she knew the guys shared next door. Ryan perched on the closed toilet lid and cradled her on his lap, leaning over to turn the antique brass fixture marked with an H.

"Am I squashing you? I can get in now." She shifted restlessly.

His arms banded tighter around her waist. "That tub is no joke. It's cast iron and cold as a well digger's ass if you don't let the water heat it up first. We spent enough nights freezing our balls off on a concrete floor that I don't ever want to feel that uncomfortable again. You either."

"All right. I don't want to take advantage of your nature, though. Tell me when you're tired of lugging me around, huh?" She laughed, but he didn't.

"I *like* doing things for you. Let me spoil you," he implored. "I've spent most of my life taking care of Ellie since our parents died. Now she's got Lucas, and with things between me and Ben the way they were, I've felt kind of...useless...for a while. I need to be needed. Hell, last week Julie started climbing on the counters to get stuff off the top shelf. She's so independent for her age that was pretty much the only thing I was good for anymore."

"I highly doubt that's true, but I'm more than willing to sacrifice if it means I get to stay here in your arms."

For a while he tended to her in silence, dumping some of Julie's bubble bath into the steamy water then lighting a candle on the surround. Their mutual calm temporarily dissipated when Ben's off-key singing cut through their moment, making them both chuckle.

"No matter how much I do for you, it'll never be as much as you've done for him already." Ryan tipped his chin toward his chest so that he could kiss her with slow, sensual glides of his lips as Ben's impromptu serenade faded. Then he simply held her and let her do the same for him in return.

The blank space gave her mind room to wander. He'd done such an amazing job essentially raising Ellie, and now Julie. Eventually, she asked, "Do you want kids of your own someday? You're so good with them."

He smiled warmly then. "It wasn't something I thought was in the cards for me, except for maybe adopting. To be honest, I always kind of suspected I'd end up with a trans woman. You know, rocking body, nice tits, and a huge cock. But...everything else aside, yeah. I'd like that. A lot."

"Me too." She imagined what it would be like to have a huge family. Plenty of people to fill up the long dining room table at the ranch. They'd never be alone again.

It sounded perfect to her.

When Ryan was satisfied with the level in the tub, he placed her carefully in the citrus-scented water. Right then, the shower cut off in the adjoining bathroom. She daydreamed about what Ben's body would look like as droplets of water sluiced off it.

"Hey, Ben," Ryan hollered, startling her.

"Yeah?" he boomed from the room next door.

"You up for a half-dozen rug rats?"

"As long as you're on diaper duty."

"Deal." Ryan grinned down at her. "That was easy."

She splashed him. "I was being serious."

"Me too." He dunked a clean cloth in the water before soaping it and spreading the suds across her upper body. Every pass of his fabric-covered hand relaxed her further. "You've seen Ben with Julie. She's his whole world. He loves having her in his life. We may not always know the right way to handle things, but we're learning. I think we make pretty great parents, actually."

"Judging by how happy you made that little girl today, I'd say you're right." Shari lost another piece of her heart to them just thinking about it.

"She does love cake. I think she gets that from me." Ryan grinned.

"Probably so," she agreed. "But I was referring to the look on her face when she flung herself at you on the sidewalk. It was *you* she wanted more than anything."

"Don't know why. I kind of ruined her party, didn't I?" He rubbed his temples.

"Next time you come up to the ranch, I'll let her ride my horse. I'm pretty sure that'll make up for it."

"I'll be uncle of the century." He smiled softly as he shook his head. "You know, it's unbelievable the prospects that can emerge from the darkest days of your life. If you hang in there long enough to get past the shit, you never know what could be waiting on the other side."

"I'm so proud you never gave up. For all of our sakes."

"Me too." He finished attending to her with meticulous care. She had about as much resistance left in her as a wet noodle by the time he'd washed her hair, scrubbed her back, then gently cleaned between her legs. Aware he also removed the last traces of his own semen from her skin, she would have been bummed except she planned to have him paint her with his lust again soon.

And often.

By the time he dried her off, thoroughly and gently, she swayed on her feet.

"Whoa." He dropped the towel, steadying her before swinging her into his arms once more.

"Sorry." She struggled to keep her eyes open without much success.

"Go ahead. Sleep." He kissed her forehead. "I'll tuck you in."

"You're not going to leave me by myself, right?" she asked without caring that the question made her sound clingy and sort of desperate. He wanted her to need him. She did. So much.

"Hell, no," he swore. "I'm going to give you to Ben while I clean up and then I'll join the two of you. It'll be a tight squeeze, but hey, I'm always up for a snugglefest. Tomorrow, while Ben's at work and Julie's at school, maybe you and I can go bed shopping for something that the three of us will fit more comfortably in."

She smiled, her eyes already drifting shut as he carried her into his room.

They were still open enough to spot Ben there, waiting for them, exactly as he'd promised. He'd changed the sheets and borrowed some pillows from another room, probably his own, which meant they'd smell extraordinary. Pajamas he hadn't bothered with. Naked, he looked like a sultan lounging in his harem—exotic, compelling, and in command.

He held his arms up and Ryan settled her into them. Curling into his side, she absorbed his heat and the security of his biceps, which immediately coiled around her. Ryan drew the covers over them before giving her a chaste kiss.

Then he did the same to Ben.

Shari sighed, nodding off.

The last thing she heard was Ben murmuring, "You're good for him, Shari. I always knew you would be."

"*We're* good for him."

"I'm starting to believe you might be right." He hugged her, though not so tight that she couldn't feel the tremble in his hands or hear the racing of his heart.

Sometime in the middle of the night, one of her lovers resettled himself and she roused. Not enough for full consciousness to take hold, but enough that she detected Ryan's presence behind her, spooning her. He wrapped around her body, his arm reaching over her to rest across Ben's abdomen.

From where her cheek was pillowed on Ben's lightly furred chest, she glimpsed a piece of his smile in the starlight, which beamed through the window. Contentment. It was a look she'd never seen him wear before. Hopefully he would more often from then on.

With that memory permanently etched into her heart, she sank back into a deep and dreamless slumber.

∽ NINETEEN ∾

Shari felt downright lazy, still lounging around early the next afternoon. Ben had left for work long before she'd gotten up to pee then stumbled back to bed, crashing for another few glorious hours of rest. Did that mean she'd slept twelve hours straight? Or nine hours followed by a three-hour nap? Either way, it had been glorious.

Then Ryan had made and served her brunch in bed. Stuffed with the fluffiest omelet she'd ever had along with a healthy serving of cinnamon crepes and fresh fruit, she hadn't been able to bring herself to move even after he'd cleared away the tray. Now she read a book while watching him work out in the guys' home gym across the hall. "I can see why you used to spy on Ben while he was lifting weights."

"I know, right?" Ryan flexed, letting her admire the results of his hard work.

She'd made a half-assed comment about joining him, planning to use the treadmill. With very little effort, he'd convinced her that she shouldn't feel peer pressured.

Sold.

Tomorrow she'd be less of a slug, she promised herself.

If she was being honest, she was kind of sore and feeling raw emotionally from their interlude. Not to mention so damn sated, she wasn't sure she'd ever find a shred of motivation again. Except maybe for buying that bed Ryan had mentioned last night. Sleeping with both him and Ben had been one of the best experiences of her life, but probably they could use a few more inches of mattress for her men to spread out on.

She liked the way that sounded in her mind.

"What are you smiling about over there?" Ryan asked.

"Mind if I pick out a bed online and have it delivered? I think I can manage that, at least."

"Great idea. Go for it. Make sure it's huge, okay?" He grinned now, too. "We need lots of room for all the positions I want to try."

"Check. I'll also find one that has a canopy or maybe ironwork. Something we can tie you to well enough that you can thrash all you want without ever getting away from Ben and me as we take turns devouring you." She winked at him.

"Shar..." he growled, then dropped his weights, making a deafening clatter. "Do you know how uncomfortable it is to work out with a boner? Besides, I promised Ben I'd let you recover today. Don't make me a liar."

"Who, me?" She smiled. "Besides, you don't have time for a quickie if you plan on taking a shower before we need to leave for Julie's bus stop. You said two-thirty, right?"

"Yeah." He wandered to her then knelt in front of the bed so that he could take her lips in a seductive kiss. "Damn, that's good. Mmm. I'll never get tired of tasting you."

Shari took another sample. He was pretty damn delicious himself.

With a sigh, he rolled to his feet then headed for the shower. From the hall, he called, "Hey, would you mind picking up Julie from the bus stop by yourself? I'm thinking about braising some short ribs for dinner. They're Ben's favorite. Figures, they take fucking forever to cook. If I wait until after she's out of school, there won't be enough time for them to get nice and tender."

"I'll do anything for your meat," she joked, just so she could hear his rich laughter some more.

In reality, she couldn't wait to see the girl again. Hopefully Julie hadn't minded staying with her honorary aunt and uncle after her birthday party.

As far as Shari was concerned, more time spent with her was a huge benefit to a relationship with her uncles.

―――

Shari leaned against a tall oak tree and pretended to scroll through her social media profile so she didn't look as out of place as she felt. A few parents milled about, though no one spoke to her. Hadn't since she explained who she was there for and watched the raised brows and sly looks the rest of the group exchanged. She wondered if they ostracized the guys, too. Either because they were two unrelated dudes living together while raising a little girl, or because they'd heard rumors of the Sex Offender trials.

Well, fuck that. She was willing to admit she might be defensive, overprotective even. But heaven help them if they so much as turned their noses up at Julie. Those cows, even the dad cows, didn't know what awesome people they were missing out on having as part of their lives.

Shari definitely did.

Not a moment too soon, the yellow bus waddled around the corner and stopped with a hiss. Kids with backpacks half the size of their entire body, cartoon lunchboxes, and colorful layers of clothing bounced down the bus stairs one by one. They skipped or ran ahead of their various parents as they headed for home and the freedom of afterschool playtime.

Soon, Shari was the final person waiting.

The bus driver peered down at her from her ugly green plastic throne. "Who're you supposed to get?"

"Julie Weber."

"She didn't get on the bus today, ma'am. Let me radio the school and see what's going on."

Shari bit her lip as she strained to catch the bus driver's conversation over the scratchy radio. Her gaze flew down the row of windows as if Julie might have simply forgotten this was her stop.

"Okay, thanks, I'll let her know," the bus driver said as she hung up the mouthpiece.

"Is she still there?"

"Nope."

Blackness encroached on Shari's field of view. Stars flickered on the very edges.

"Calm down, honey." The bus driver smiled when Shari felt like doing anything but that. "They said one of her uncles—a Brian, maybe—picked her up."

"He did *what*?" Shari felt her panic drain, replaced by relief. Then confusion. Then fury.

To be sure there hadn't been some mix up, she whipped her phone from her pocket and checked her messages for a change of plans.

None.

How could Ryan do that to her?

"Thanks," she said curtly with a halfhearted wave to the bus driver before beginning her march to their apartment. As soon as she hugged the shit out of Julie, she was going to talk to Ryan. Or at least she'd try. Yelling at him might be more like it. Sure, they were just getting started, but he couldn't change his mind like that and not inform her. Jesus.

Her hands shook, making the breeze chill her skin, which was covered with an icy terror sweat.

Screw marching. Shari began to jog.

She took the stairs two at a time, bursting through the cracked-open door. Ryan had barely stepped into the kitchen, his arms piled with grocery bags. He spun around and gaped, as if she looked half as bonkers as she felt right then.

"Shar? What's up?"

"Where is she?" Shari shoved past him, needing to set her eyes on Julie to finally silence the alarm bells ringing in her brain.

"Who?" he asked.

"Julie!"

"What? I thought you were going to get her from the bus stop?" He dropped his load on the counter, without seeming to give a single fuck that they'd spilled all over.

"I did! I mean, I went to the bus stop." The sickness spread through her gut now. "She didn't get off the bus. They said one of her uncles had picked her up at school. Brian, they told me. I just assumed..."

"It wasn't me." He rushed to her, grabbing her shoulders. "I wouldn't do that to you. Are you sure?"

"Yes." She nodded furiously as her throat began closing off. "They said Brian. I thought they must have misspoke."

"What the fuck?" He was already snagging his phone to verify with the school.

Shari didn't waste any time either. She dialed Lucas.

While Ryan roared in the background, ripping the administrators for allowing Julie to leave the premises with someone other than an actual approved family member, Shari plugged the ear not pressed to her own phone.

"Hey, Shari," Lucas answered.

"Oh my God." She could hardly force words out of her chest, which seemed to get tighter by the second.

"What's up?" He may have sounded calm, but she knew him well enough to know he'd flipped into soldier mode. Instinctively.

So she didn't bother with pleasantries. "Did you pick Julie up from school?"

"No. We dropped her off this morning. Walked her to her classroom, then came home."

"Shit!"

"Calm down." He tried to coach her. "Tell me what's happening. Facts only. Quick."

"She didn't get off the bus. The school says one of her uncles picked her up. It's not Ryan, he's here. Ben's at work. I have a horrible feeling." She tried not to burst into tears. Double when she glanced up and saw Ryan smack his palm against the refrigerator.

"Has anyone checked with Ben, in case he got off early?" Lucas asked, making her feel stupid.

"Ben?" Ryan took deep breaths. The deceptive calm of his voice was at complete odds with his tortured expression and his posture now that he folded in half, propping one hand on his knee. "Hey, checking to see what time you're going to be home. Want dinner to be ready when you get here."

A pause.

"Not until six? No, that's fine. I'll let you get back to work since it's a busy day. See you then." He hung up before he could drop any hints. The last thing they needed was to stomp on every one of Ben's triggers after they'd convinced him to be more vulnerable.

"Shari?" Lucas called, a little louder this time.

"No. He doesn't have her. Ryan checked."

"Oh, fuck. Okay. One of you stay put in case she wanders home. The other can drive around and look for her. I hear your panic. Take deeper breaths. Hold one in. You can't hyperventilate now or you'll only slow us down, having to take care of you."

She didn't bother to respond before doing as he instructed.

"Now let it out slow."

Shari obeyed.

"Keep doing that."

When the world stopped tilting, he continued, "Okay, here's the plan. I'm going to call Mason and we'll put the Men in Blue on it. You hang tight. Want Ellie to call you and stay on the line while we're waiting for next steps?"

"No. I'll be okay. Do your thing. Fast."

"Will do. Later." He disconnected without wasting a single second more.

"Shari, where is she?" Ryan had never looked so pale.

"I don't know. I'm sorry. The first time I'm responsible for her and look what happens."

"Not your fault. I have to go look for her." He jogged into the kitchen and snatched his keys from where he'd dropped them on the counter. "This can't be happening."

"I'll stay here. Lucas is calling Mason. Every cop in the city will be searching for her within five minutes." She rushed to Ryan and flung her arms around his waist. "Be careful, please. Drive safe. I know you're upset…"

"I won't do anything crazy. Promise." He kissed her forehead then bolted from the apartment, leaving her reeling in the quiet.

Absolutely alone.

Just like every other time in her life, she was left behind to wait and see how things turned out while other people, men she loved, did the grunt work.

Never again, she decided right then and there. Next time she would be on the front lines while someone else held down the fort and chewed their nails to the quick.

It didn't take long for her phone to start lighting up like one of those Christmas light displays timed to rock music. Lacey, Lily, Jambrea, Izzy, and Ellie called nearly simultaneously.

Bad news traveled fast in their circle.

Izzy, who lived closest, also texted. *I'm on my way over.*

Thank God. Shari grabbed a tissue.

By the time she answered the phone and patched everyone into a group conversation, she had officially started bawling. "Where can she be?"

Their chorus of "we'll find her", "don't worry", and "things like this happen all the time" were drowned out by another thought.

"How will I tell Ben that she's gone? He sent her away because of me. This never would have happened if it had been a normal day. The school probably got confused because she has so many uncles and they'd met another new one this morning." Now she sobbed.

"You are not responsible for this, Shari." Lily used her most intimidating Mistress tone to try to hammer that fact into her brain.

It only sort of worked.

The next two hours passed in a blur of commotion, officers calling in reports, and their ladies filling the apartment with support as they came over one by one. Finally, Ryan dragged himself through door, utterly dejected.

"I can't find her anywhere." He crossed to her and held her so tight she could hardly breathe. "I checked her friends' houses, the skating rink, every park and playground we've ever taken her to around here, the candy store, the pet shop… She's not there. We have to call Ben. We have to tell him."

"Tell me what?" The man himself asked from the doorway. His rapidly darkening gaze hopped from person to person in the room. "Is someone going to fill me in on what the fuck is happening? There are enough cop cars outside to thwart a bank robbery. Is someone hurt? Worse? I was afraid something happened to one of you. Julie?"

The dread in his expression socked Shari straight in the heart.

Shari ran to him then. She leapt from a few feet away, wrapping her arms around his shoulders and her legs around his hips as he caught her with a single huge hand, which spanned her ass. "I'm so sorry, Ben. We didn't want to worry you in case it was a simple misunderstanding."

She couldn't see him, but she felt Ryan at her back. He said the words she couldn't. "Julie's missing. Someone we can't identify picked her up from school today and we haven't been able to find her *yet*."

Ben stumbled backward as if he'd been shot point blank.

Ryan shouted and reached for him, keeping him—and Shari too—from crashing to the floor. She unwound herself from him, then helped Ryan as they supported him, leading him to the couch. He sank onto the cushions as if his skeleton had turned to jelly.

His slack features, devoid of any emotion, terrified her more than if he'd smashed furniture or wailed in anguish or…anything else, really.

"The Men in Blue are on the case, Ben," Lacey informed him when neither Shari nor Ryan could drum up the right words.

"We're going to get her back," Mason promised as he came inside.

"Keep faith in that," Ryan instructed. "Remember the stuff we talked about last night. It's just like that. She's fine. She's out there. And we're going to bring her home soon. Really soon."

"Okay." Ben nodded stiffly, then repeated it to himself about a hundred times.

Only problem was…they didn't.

↶ TWENTY ↷

Ben paced the halls, still wearing his work clothes from the day before. Minus his tie. Plus a whole lot of wrinkles. His socks probably had holes worn in them by now, and the last time he'd caught sight of his hair in the bathroom mirror he'd wondered how it had stuck up that straight.

His thoughts jumbled. Though he tried to keep telling himself that they were going to find Julie, each iteration became harder to believe. Or say. He felt like a lunatic mumbling the same things over and over beneath his breath.

He'd been awake for something like thirty-six hours straight. No way could he shut his eyes when his niece was missing. Again.

Pain he wished was unimaginable—yet was very familiar to him—came rushing back.

He'd thought the agony had stalked him in his nightmares. No, feeling it again while fully conscious, he remembered how much worse it was to live through it than to dream about it.

How had he been stupid enough to think he could take the risk of experiencing this again by letting Shari and Ryan into his heart? Julie was like his own daughter, and they could easily be his soul mates. Each one of them precious to him.

He could never handle something happening to them. And clearly he sucked at protecting those he loved.

The hallway seemed to narrow and lengthen. Claustrophobia attacked him.

Ben wasn't proud of it, but he ducked into Julie's room, then shoved open the window. Instead of the fresh air he desperately needed, he got a lungful of cigarette smoke. "Shari, what the fuck are you doing out there?"

She didn't say anything. He still got answers.

The redness of her eyes screamed *crying*. The gray tendrils floating behind her clearly said *smoking*. The balance check she did, grabbing the gutter to steady herself, indicated *almost falling off the damn roof and breaking my fool neck*.

"Put that thing out and get your ass in here." He leaned out of the casing far enough that he fisted her shirt in his hand, just in case she stumbled.

Her glare combined with her lack of argument made it seem like she might be torn between outrage and remorse for being busted. She stabbed the butt of her cigarette against the slate roof.

As soon as it was extinguished, he hauled her inside, confiscated the partial pack of cigarettes in her back pocket along with her lighter, then flung them both out the window, into the yard.

From below someone—it sounded like Razor—yelled, "Hey, it's raining smokes. Cool!"

"Don't treat me like a child." Shari shoved his chest. The gesture didn't even threaten to sway him.

"Don't act like one," he snarled. "What if you slipped? Ryan's already crushed. That would be too much for him."

He wasn't tough enough right then to admit he was really worried about himself and how he'd reached his quota for disasters. Even thinking about her crumpled on the sidewalk outside for a moment made him want to puke. So he kept raging, because that he could handle. "And smoking? You quit for a reason. Given your family history on top of the usual, it's not a good idea. Don't slip back into bad habits. Destructive ones. Julie wouldn't want that."

She crossed her arms and harrumphed. "Look who's talking! Mr. I-Don't-Need-Anyone-Not-Even-The-Two-People-I-Fucked-Like-A-Maniac-And-Acted-Like-I-Wanted-A-Relationship-With-Until-I-Got-Scared-Shitless!"

"Oops!" The door opened a bit then shut again as Jambrea said, "I guess *that's* what that racket was."

Then she called out, louder, "Ryan! Your boyfriend and girlfriend are having their first fight. You want in on it?"

Ben didn't wait for a referee to intervene. He kept digging himself deeper. "Bad shit can happen in the blink of an eye. I let myself get distracted for one damn day, and look what happened!"

He punched the wall, leaving a hole the landlord would not approve of—considering the hell Ben had gotten for the one the guy had patched a couple days ago—along with some of the skin from his knuckles. No more pounding the sheetrock, he promised his security deposit. Fuck, that stung.

Not nearly as bad as the lance that pierced his chest when he saw Shari's expression.

He might as well have smacked her.

"Fine, I'll leave if I'm such a horrible reminder of your mistakes." She wobbled as she reached for the doorknob. Though everything in him yearned to correct her invalid conclusion and beg her to stay, he figured it was better to let her go.

Except that would have required walking through Ryan, who burst through the door just then.

"What's going on here?"

"I'm leaving."

"The hell you are!" He snagged Shari's wrist and pulled her deeper into the room, slamming the door behind him.

Shaking off his grip, she sank to the window seat, tucked her feet beneath her, and plucked Julie's new teddy bear from the open toy chest, hugging it to her chest as she wept. Now was probably not the right time for Ben to mention that he thought the thing was sinister with those black eyes that seemed a little too...real. Like they followed him around the room.

He wouldn't mind chucking it out the window, too.

Then again, she might have bought the stuffed animal for Julie. He couldn't remember where it had come from. At that moment, he didn't have the brainpower for much of anything non-critical.

"Enough. Both of you." Ryan rubbed Shari's shoulder even as he held his hand out to Ben.

Instead of accepting it, he clasped his fingers behind his back.

"None of us has any clarity at the moment," Ryan said. "We're exhausted, terrified, angry, and confused. This is not the time to make decisions or say things we might regret later. It's definitely not a good idea to hurt each other because we're limping along already. Besides, it didn't work worth shit when I tried leaving the other day. It's still not the solution."

"You know how you always say you like to be needed?" Shari asked Ryan.

"Yeah."

"I need you so bad right now. Hold me, please?" She awed and baffled Ben by simply and directly asking for what she required instead of trying to protect herself from further injury by admitting her vulnerabilities.

As he watched, Ryan sat beside her and opened his arms. She flew into them, burrowing against his chest as he wrapped her in the strength she couldn't provide for herself right then.

Ben wished it could be that easy for him.

"There's room for you, too," Ryan offered.

Ben held his head in his hands, squeezing his skull as he tried to sort out right from wrong. In the end, he went with what his heart demanded instead of what his brain tried to reason. He'd almost made the same mistake twice.

Shit!

Shari peeked up at him from where she huddled against Ryan. If this was a test, he knew he couldn't afford to fail again. Nor did he plan to.

"I'm sorry, Shari." Ben staggered to the bench as if he'd downed the entire bottle of cognac Ryan had tucked in the cabinet for pan sauces. He crashed onto it, then rested his forehead next to hers on Ryan's collarbone. A strange sensation stung his eyes, one that he hadn't permitted in decades. Not even at his sister's funeral had he shed a tear.

Because he'd feared he might never stop.

Now it was impossible to hold back.

With them, he didn't have to. They'd shelter him while he was exposed. Ben let Ryan and Shari surround him with their forgiving and liberal embraces. They drew his grief and horror from him like a doctor siphoning poison from a wound. He didn't give a fuck if the entire apartment full of their friends heard him sobbing like a baby. Because the only two people whose opinion on the matter he gave a shit about were there, reassuring him it was okay. That they didn't think less of him for breaking.

Some time later, when his wails turned to blubbering then died down to moans, they were there to rebuild him piece by jagged piece. Ryan handed him a handkerchief to mop his face and blow his nose. Shari crooned to him as she caressed his back.

Though his throat was raw, his nose was stopped up, and his eyes might never focus again, oddly, he did feel better. Not because he'd lost control but maybe because he'd finally grieved.

For April.

For himself.

But not for Julie. Because Ryan's murmuring had sunk in.

"We're going to bring her home. Just wait. The Men in Blue are tracking down leads. It won't be long now before we have a breakthrough. I know it. We will *not* give up on her. None of us or any of our friends will either."

"Okay." Ben nodded. "I'm sorry I doubted. I forgot for a second..."

"That's over now." Shari kissed him softly, raking his hair into some semblance of order. "We only move forward, not back. Which is why I'm never going to smoke again, all right?"

The thought of her sick and dying like her mother...that was why he'd freaked out on her. He didn't have the tact to explain that now, in a way that would sound supportive instead of accusatory, but later he owed her an explanation.

She gave him a reason to grow, to get better at the hard stuff in life, so that he could be the man she deserved. Ryan too.

About to tell them, he didn't get the chance.

A tap came at the door. Lily spoke loud enough to be heard through the solid wood. "Sorry to interrupt. Jeremy's got an update and he brought a couple people with him that he'd like you to meet. Do you need a few minutes more?"

"No." Ben found it was true. More quietly, only for his lovers, he said, "As long as you two will be by my sides."

"We will be," Shari confirmed.

"Always," Ryan added.

"We're coming," he shouted to Lily then pushed to his feet, giving each of his partners a hand up, like they had done for him.

↷ TWENTY-ONE ↶

Julie squished her face to the sliver of the window that wasn't covered by cardboard and duct tape. Through it she could see her house. She wasn't sure if it made her feel better or worse to know her Uncle Ben was right there and he still couldn't hear her screaming even at her very loudest.

She should know—she'd spent the entire day trying. Now her voice was scratchy and she could hardly swallow. It was like the time she'd had strep throat and Uncle Ryan had made her magic rainbow popsicles to take away the hurt. She wished she had one of those now.

Uncle Ryan and Aunt Shari were close by too. At least Aunt Shari's truck hadn't moved from where she'd parked when she'd come to Julie's birthday party two days ago.

How had things gone from so happy to so crappy that fast?

Were they as scared as she was? Were they trying to find her?

Did they know someone had taken her or did they think she ran away like her mommy?

Her breath started to go in and out really fast, making it hard to think.

They would look for her, right?

Uncle Ben had told her how hard he'd searched for her when the bad men had taken her. That must be why all her other uncles were there too. She'd never seen as many police cars in her whole life as lined the street just then.

Knowing they were out there helped her calm down and force more air into her lungs.

She remembered what Uncle Ryan had said about when he went through the bad stuff. He told himself over and over that somehow, someway, he would get out and never let himself stop believing that was true.

So she tried that. "I'm going home. They're going to find me. They won't ever stop looking. I'm right here! They'll notice me soon."

When her voice stopped working, she curled into a ball in the corner and tried not to snivel. She couldn't remember why that was so important until a flash of memory from the bad stuff played like a movie on her scrunched eyelids.

It was her mommy, crying.

"Quit that or we'll give you something to be upset about. You want us to hurt that little girl of yours? We've kept our word so far, but that can change if you don't cooperate."

"NO!" Her mommy's howl snapped her back to the present.

Julie wanted to scream. She couldn't. She wanted to cry. She shouldn't.

She had to be strong so her uncles could find her.

They would, if she never gave up.

How could she do that when she wasn't anywhere near as brave as Uncle Ryan or as strong as Uncle Ben?

Her eyes went wide as she remembered Aunt Shari marching up the stairs to their apartment the other day, flashing her tattoo. Visions of Aunt Ellie's artwork came to her mind too. Aunt Lily had lots of ink. And so did some of her uncles. Uncle Lucas had gotten lots after his accident.

They were the most awesome people she could imagine.

Julie stomped over to the bucket of markers and paper the new bad man had put by the door "to keep yourself occupied" before he'd locked her in this room then left for work this morning. She decided it felt better to be angry than sad so she kicked it hard enough that if she were playing in the schoolyard at recess, she probably would have scored a home run.

She sent everything flying before crumpling the paper into balls and throwing them too.

Only when she'd burned off some of her *nervous energy* did she plop onto the floor with her legs crossed. Reaching beside her, she plucked a blue marker from the carpet then ripped off the cap. She squinted at her hand, imaging what it might look like if she had the kind of tattoos that would give her superpowers, like her aunts and uncles.

Sticking her tongue out like she always did when she concentrated really hard, she put the tip of the marker against her wrist and began to draw. With every swirl, design, and color she added, she felt less like the Cowardly Lion and more like Dorothy.

How much better would it be if she had all of her family with her?

Aunt Shari must have thought the same thing, since she put her brother's name on her side.

Julie imagined each of them and what their favorite color was, writing their names on her arm. Uncle Ben in red, Uncle Ryan next to him in blue, and Aunt Shari too, in green. Really big, taking up one whole leg, she put A-P-R-I-L in pink. That was her mommy's name. Around them she drew flowers and hearts and stars and doodles.

Maybe the too-small tank top and skirt the new bad man had forced her to wear weren't so terrible after all. The clothes gave her lots of spaces to tattoo. Her handwriting wasn't as pretty as Aunt Ellie's, but she smiled for the first time since the new bad man had trapped her in here when she saw them.

And when the new bad man came home, flinging open her door hard enough that it crashed into the wall, she didn't scurry away or try to hide. Because that was not what any of these people she carried with her on her skin would do. Instead, she got to her feet and stared straight at him.

"What the hell did you do to yourself?" he shouted.

"Gave myself tattoos. Do you like them?" She twisted her arms back and forth so he could read the names of the people she loved. The ones who loved her back and wouldn't ever give up on finding her.

"I liked you better without them." He stared at her until she felt kind of sick. "After dinner, we're going to have to wash them off."

"No!" She would bite him, and kick him, and scratch him before she let him get rid of them.

"Oh yes. I brought you some more princess dresses for you to model like you did last night when we played dress up with your teddy bear."

That was before she'd realized her new friend was actually a bad man and didn't plan to let her go home. He'd seemed so nice when he'd picked her up from school, telling her that Uncle Ryan had gone home with Aunt Shari so Uncle Ben had sent him to get her. Then he'd talked about how he would take her to play with all her new birthday presents or the puppy, which he didn't even have in this house. He'd tricked her.

So she didn't believe him when he said, "Princesses don't have tattoos."

"The cool ones do." She put her hands on her hips. "They're probably just under their dresses where you can't see them in the movies."

"Oh, we'll see these. Though I don't think that's what people will pay for. Besides, it's too much information."

She had no idea what he meant about that, but something he said had caught her attention. Her stomach rumbled. "Did you say we can have dinner now?"

He nodded.

"Pizza again?" It was what they'd had for supper last night.

"If any other place delivered in this shitty town..."

"That's a curse word." She knew he was a bad man.

He rolled his eyes. "Okay, fine. Pizza, coming right up. Let me order it for you, your highness. Who knew a kid could be such a pain in the ass?"

"That's another curse," she pointed out.

He smacked his forehead with his palm.

"Besides, I know how to order my own pizza. Uncle Ben lets me do it." She wasn't allowed to use grownup cell phones very much, but sometimes they let her play games on them when they were waiting in a really long line or do things like order the pizza when they were supervising.

Even better, Uncle Ben had forced her to memorize his phone number in case of emergency.

This definitely counted.

If she could use the new bad man's phone, maybe he wouldn't notice what buttons she pushed.

"Great, make yourself useful." The new bad man crushed her hopes when he took his phone from the pocket and pulled up the pizza shop's phone number from his contacts before hitting the green go button and handing it to her. "Get a large pepperoni pie."

He waved her down the stairs as they were waiting for the pizza place to answer.

Julie wished he'd go to the bathroom, or turn on the TV, anything to give her a chance to call for help instead. But he didn't. He sat on the couch and stared that weird stare again, never even hardly blinking as he watched her.

Poop!

She remembered what he'd said last night, when she threw a fit about not sleeping in her own bed. If she tried to run away, he'd hurt her. He'd stop being her friend. Would a real friend make her stay when she wanted to go home?

"Peppy Pizza. I've got 324 Ridgeway for this number, that correct?"

"Yes."

"Want the same thing as last night? Large pepperoni?"

"Yes." Julie felt her chance slipping away. She had to try something. "With a large *help*ing of pepperoni, please."

New bad man snatched his phone back. "Don't do anything stupid."

From where she stood she heard the pizza man say, "You got it. It'll be there in thirty minutes or it's free."

Without even saying thank you, Rudeface mashed the red hang-up button.

He glared at her, but she pretended like she didn't know why. Twirling her hair, in the stupid pigtails he'd put it in that morning, seemed to work.

Like before, he acted nice again. Not scary at all.

He showed her the toys he had in the living room, including more bears like the one he'd given her the day Uncles Ben and Ryan were fighting. She didn't want to play with them anymore.

Except he got grumpy if she didn't.

She was so bored by the time the pizza man rang the doorbell, she stayed in the living room, away from the windows, like the new bad man had told her to the night before. Before she could come up with a plan, he'd opened the door, snatched their dinner, then slammed it shut without any talking at all. Uncle Ben never acted like that. The new bad man carried their food to the kitchen. He'd gotten halfway there when a knock came at the door followed by a muffled shout.

"What the hell is he saying?" new bad man asked.

"He needs you to sign the receipt."

"Son of a bitch," he grumbled. That was *definitely* a curse. "You do it. Fast. Then get away from the door. And don't you dare try to run or I'll come get you back. You won't know when or how I'll take you, but you'll never be safe. Next time I'll catch your family too. They'll hate you for getting them in trouble. You hear me?"

No. He couldn't, could he? Why not? Someone had done exactly that to her mom.

And she'd never come home. She'd gone to heaven instead.

Julie didn't want any more of her aunts and uncles to leave forever.

"Okay, I won't. I promise. Leave them alone. But what's your name?" she asked.

"Don't worry about that. Scribble something. Anything. It doesn't matter what."

Another lie. It mattered an awful lot to Julie.

She yanked open the door, nearly crying again when she smelled the fresh air and thought about how quickly she could sprint home. Except she would never put her family in danger like that.

No way.

"Oh, hey." The pizza man smiled. "Wow. You got some tattoos, huh? Those are pretty great."

"Yes!" She could have hugged him for noticing. "I did them myself."

"I guess that's why your dad is so cranky, huh?" he teased in a nice way.

"What did I tell you? Hurry the hell up, kid," the new bad man shouted. "That's enough chitchat."

Julie flinched.

"Didn't mean to get you in more trouble," the pizza man said with a frown. "Is everything okay here?"

"Yes," she said, but she tried to shake her head no, a teeny tiny bit, as she did.

"Now! Sign it and let's eat," the bad man yelled again.

So she did as he ordered.

As much as she dared.

Then stared at the delivery guy as she handed him the receipt and his pen, and shut the door in his face. The whole time she thought really hard.

Help me, help me, HELP ME!

Would it be enough?

"Get over here and have some pizza," new bad man snarled. "It's almost bath time. We're going to take your teddy bear with us and make it a long one, so we can get all that shit off you. Good thing I think your fans won't mind too much."

Huh?

She didn't understand, but she did what he said.

Hopefully, if she kept him as unmean as possible, she could stand him better until Uncle Ben could find her. They had to.

Hurry, please.

⌒ TWENTY-TWO ⌒

When Ryan entered the living room, shoulder to shoulder with Shari and Ben, holding hands, he couldn't have been more proud. Either of his roommate—no, *boyfriend*, because Jambrea'd had it right, he certainly had the right to call Ben that now—or of himself. To be claimed so openly by a dedicated, all-around awesome man like Ben *and* a wonderful, courageous woman like Shari gave him an ego boost bigger than the one he'd experienced when he'd received a rave review from one of the world's top food critics last month.

Ben stood between them, clutching each of their hands, finally allowing himself to draw strength from their bond instead of believing it made him weak. Didn't he see? When they were together, they were damn near unstoppable.

The sight of Ben, broken and weeping, had ripped Ryan apart. Not even in the dungeons had he lost it like that. At least, not on the outside. Maybe he was finally being honest about his feelings so that he could process them without so much guilt eating him alive.

That was a huge improvement.

Shari had changed him, somehow opened him to the possibility when Ryan had been unable to do it on his own. He would be forever grateful for that. He'd never seen anything as intoxicatingly beautiful as the two people he loved—and after today, he was sure that he did love them, was *in* love with them—sharing their feelings openly with each other.

"You've got this," Lily said softly, patting his ass before leaving them to stand near her husband.

Otherwise, no one said anything. For a group of people who were so often boisterous and never shut the hell up, it was weird. Clint broke the tension with a slow clap and a huge grin. "So does this mean it's official? Have we successfully corrupted three more people into joining the ménage lifestyle?"

Matt punched his partner's upper arm lightly. "Leave them alone. You might have noticed today's not a good day to fuck with them."

Surprisingly, Ben laughed even if it was strained. "Yeah. I'm officially done being a dumbass. These two are mine and anyone who says otherwise will have to answer to me."

Whoa.

Ryan felt himself in danger of popping a woody right there in front of a slew of their friends, and a couple strangers as well. Inappropriate! He chastised his dick.

Out of the corner of his eye, he caught Shari doing a fist pump and chuckled.

Their reprieve from the horror of their situation was shortlived, though.

"Sorry, we tend to overshare around here," JRad apologized to the newcomers in their midst. Then he turned to the rest of the group. "I'd like you to meet Special Agent Gregory Salinas. We've been trying to lure him away from some no-name agency that our good friends Lucas, and Shari's brother John, may or may not have once been associated with. If we're really lucky and you all don't scare him away, he might accept a position on the OSPD since the Chief is interested in beefing up our technology staff."

"Hello, and no problem. You guys are great. Even during what has to be one of the worst times of your life. A definite perk when working on these types of cases. I'm sorry for what you're going through right now. We'll do everything we can to get your little girl back." Special Agent Salinas, who appeared too young to be as successful as he must have been to attract JRad's admiration, made up for his perceived lack of experience with boatloads of enthusiasm. He waved to them. "Pause a second, though. I recognize Lucas, of course, but...what's your last name?"

When he pointed at Shari, she smiled softly before saying, "David. Shari David. Very nice to meet you. We appreciate your help."

Poor Gregory's eyes nearly popped out of his head and blew up to four times their usual size, like he starred in an old-fashioned cartoon. "*John David* was your brother?"

She nodded.

"I'm so sorry for your loss. He's a hero." Special Agent Salinas earned some major brownie points with Ryan for honoring Shari's sacrifice. "An absolute legend."

Lucas too, it seemed. "Seriously, the best."

Maybe even with Jambrea, who sniffled. When most everyone glanced over to make sure she was all right, she shrugged. "Sorry. Super pregnant, remember? Hormone overload."

They all knew it was more than that. She'd loved John once. Still did, he supposed. Matt and Clint surrounded her, cloaking her from view while she composed herself.

In typical Razor fashion, he brought them back to a less tense place with his immature antics. He didn't quite sulk when he asked, "Wait. JRad, does this mean you're gonna be the boss of the geek squad?"

"When and if there's a division to be head of, they're considering me for the position. Yes." Jeremy nodded. After the work he'd done on the Sex Offender case, Ryan thought he deserved any job he damn well wanted on the state's payroll. "First we have to convince Special Agent Salinas to stick around. So try not to be an idiot."

"Might as well ask him to quit screwing Izzy." Tyler laughed.

"Hey, kid zone." Isabella shook her finger at them as Ezra buzzed around her ankles.

Mason stepped forward then. "I thought we could also use some expert advice from the Division of Crimes Against Children. So we've added Detective Raya Tran to our team. We've worked with her on other cases and I assure you, Ben, she's an all-star in her field."

"Thank you," Detective Tran nodded.

The crispness of her uniform and the extreme ponytail she'd pulled her thick, glossy black hair into were a piss-poor disguise for how striking the fine-boned Asian detective was. Her porcelain skin and delicate features along with her ultra-petite stature probably meant she could easily infiltrate schools while undercover. Invaluable, yet probably also a pain in the ass when she wanted to be taken seriously.

Her ramrod straight posture and the brusqueness of her communications made him certain that she was often underestimated. Ryan would never be that idiotic. He bet she could give Lily a run for her money when it came to issuing orders. Frankly, he'd pay good money to see that.

Hey, he was a guy. If visions of the two tough women battling it out while dressed only in chains and latex—don't forget the thigh-high boots—before making out flashed through his brain, it was only natural, right?

When he peeked over at Shari, she was giving him *the look*. Could she read his mind? Or was he that obvious?

Uh oh.

Raya cleared her throat, drawing their attention back to her. "Mason asked me to meet you here so that Agent Salinas could analyze the surveillance footage we were able to recover from the schoolyard."

Ben just about crushed Ryan's fingers at that. "You have a lead? Solid information?"

"We have the suspect on film, sir. That's all I can promise you at this time." Detective Tran softened a smidge when she addressed Ben. "I'd like you to come take a look, if it's not too difficult for you. To see if you might recognize this scumbag."

"Of course. Anything I can do to help." Ben practically yanked Ryan's arm out of the socket when he zoomed over to the kitchen table, where Jeremy had set up an impromptu computer lab.

He never once let go of Ryan or Shari, even though it was a tight fit for them around the monitor. The rest of the Men in Blue and their ladies huddled up for a glimpse too.

"So here's what we've got." Detective Tran tossed a USB drive to JRad. "Don't get your hopes up too high. It's not exactly cinematic quality."

Understatement of the century.

When Jeremy pulled up the file and pressed play, Ryan thought he might need glasses. It was blurry, kind of grainy, obviously blown up far larger than originally intended. The sound was mostly a garbled mess. As if a playground wasn't already an assault on any human being's ears, this was worse, distorted by the autumn wind, traffic on the street outside the chain-link fence, and distance.

Ryan's shoulders slumped.

"Don't get too discouraged yet," Special Agent Salinas admonished. "I'll be able to clean this up some. Isolate the different audio inputs and edit out the static. Sure, it's not going to be studio quality, but it'll be better than this."

"I can do the same for the video. We might be able to add more chances for success if we can read their lips along with the edited audio."

"With everyone putting their heads together, we'll find her. We'll get her back safe," Ben uttered beneath his breath.

Detective Tran had obviously screened this footage about a million times. She knew it second by second. "Okay, get ready, here they come."

A teacher Ryan recognized from his own pick-up or drop-off duties, parent conferences, and holiday concerts came onscreen, escorting the kidnapper. She had her trusty clipboard with the release information and checked something off on her list.

Ryan fumed. She'd half-assed her duties. Sure, Julie had a shit-ton of honorary aunts and uncles. Plus, their non-traditional work schedules meant that they relied on a variety of family friends to help out periodically. But, really, she hadn't even asked for ID.

"Ms. Edwards has been placed on leave pending a school board review of this incident," Detective Tran informed them.

What a sanitary way to describe the theft of a child, Ryan thought.

"They're going to turn in a moment and you'll have a better view."

Ryan studied the back of the bastard's head, not that he could tell much from the shot other than pettily noticing the man had a thinning spot on the crown of his head. Dark hair. Average build. Not much to go on.

Shit.

Then Ms. Edwards called, "Julie!"

That part was clear enough to make out plainly.

Ryan's pulse tripped when she trotted into the frame, her brand-new purple pony backpack bobbing behind her. Ben inhaled sharp and deep.

Shari was there in an instant, ducking under his arm to wrap her free arm around his waist and help prop him up. Ryan squeezed his fingers, reassured when Ben returned the sign. He was hanging in there as well as could be expected.

Julie's face lit up when she spotted her abductor.

"One reason Ms. Edwards didn't question the pick-up was because Julie clearly knew this man." Detective Tran broke the news. "So I hope you do, too. Wait for it. Detective Radisson, please freeze the frame...right...here."

He did.

But Ryan drew a complete blank. The guy had pasty white skin, a pointy nose, and a chin too small to be proportional to the rest of his face. He squinted and tilted his head from side to side to be sure given the distortion of the video but...no.

If he'd seen that guy before, he would have remembered.

"Fuck," Ben barked.

"You know him?" Detective Tran asked.

"No. Never seen him in my life." He let his head fall back for a moment before meeting her stare. "So how the hell does my niece? You don't understand. I never take my eyes off her. Not after what we've been through. Other than when she's at school, me—or one of the other people in this room—are always with her."

Ben looked around. Everyone was studying the image, most shaking their heads.

"No one recognizes him?" Tyler asked, for verification.

A shower of negatives confirmed it.

Shari spoke up then. "I don't know him either, but...can you go forward a little? What's that he's holding?"

Detective Tran eased her grimace at that. "Very observant, Ms. David. That's what I was going to ask next."

To Jeremy, she said, "Roll forward about fifteen frames, please."

He tapped a couple keys and the image skipped.

Ryan felt sick. "Oh shit."

"I *touched* that thing!" Shari shrieked.

Ben released Ryan's hand then so he could catch her before she hit the floor, passed out cold.

"Here, give her to me. Show them," Ryan said to Ben.

By the time he'd scooped Shari up and crossed to the couch, she was stirring. She'd hardly settled onto the cushions before Lacey and Jambrea were there, shooing him away. "Give her space to breathe."

Lacey snagged a stack of pillows and jammed them under Shari's feet while Jambrea unbuttoned the top several buttons of Shari's flannel shirt. "Hey, honey. You're fine. Just relax a minute or two before you try to stand up, okay?"

When Shari began to realize what had happened, she covered her face with her hands. "Oh my God. That bear. I was just holding it."

"Hang on, you have it? Here?" Mason risked getting his balls ripped off by one of the nurses when he approached Shari despite their glares.

"Yes." Satisfied she would recover, Ben motioned to the officer. "It's in Julie's room. I thought it was a birthday present..."

"No," Shari moaned from the couch. "She had it two days ago. When you two were fighting."

"She did?" Ryan asked, certain he'd never seen it before today.

JRad stood and crossed to Ben and Mason. "I think we should go slow. I only poked around on that footage for a few seconds, but I'm picking up some kind of interference. I think that's why the quality is so bad."

"Does that mean what I think?" Special Agent Salinas asked.

"It could." Jeremy nodded solemnly.

Ryan thought his head might start spinning around from looking back and forth between Shari, Ben, and the cops so often, so quickly.

Izzy said what they were all thinking from where she bounced Ezra on her hip compulsively. "Spell it out for the civilians among you, please."

"Sometimes a bear isn't just a bear." JRad punched his palm. "Give me a minute to grab some equipment out of my car. Don't go near it until I say so."

Ryan knew it had to be awful if they wouldn't explain without proof.

Fuck.

He returned his attention to Shari, who was slapping Lacey's hands away and struggling to sit up on her own. Ryan squatted beside her, keeping her company while holding her in place. They didn't need her cracking her skull open because she was too stubborn for her own good.

It wasn't long before Jeremy jogged back into the room, a briefcase in tow. "Okay, show me where it is. Don't say anything. Not a word, got it?"

"Yes," Mason said. Then he and JRad disappeared down the hallway.

For the ninety seconds it took for their resident techno-whiz to work his magic, no one made a peep. Hell, Ryan hardly breathed. He rocked Shari, and she hugged him back.

Then from Julie's room, Jeremy shouted, "Got it! It's disarmed."

He reappeared with Ben, who looked as white as a ghost. Lacey forced him to sit beside Shari and shoved his head between his knees so they didn't have a repeat performance.

"What? What is it?" Lily wondered.

"Give me something sharp," JRad demanded.

Detective Tran reached for Ryan's prized ceramic chef's knife and handed it over. Any other time, he would have objected to such an unsuitable usage.

Jeremy took it and, with one motion, beheaded the bear. He stuffed his fist inside and yanked out its brains. Actually, one of its eyes. Because the eye turned out to be the lens of a compact action cam.

"Fuck, no!" Ryan looked over at Shari, then Ben.

"Someone's been watching her? Us?" Ben's face turned purple then.

Ryan wasn't sure he'd every truly seen the man full of rage before.

He never wanted to witness it again.

"Oh fuck, that's disgusting." Razor even seemed kind of ill and the Men in Blue had seen it all.

Detective Tran was suspiciously silent.

"Did you suspect this?" Ryan asked her pointblank.

She nodded. "I'm sorry. I didn't want to frighten you needlessly. One of the priorities for Special Agent Salinas is to compare the voice samples from the surveillance footage to known child pornographers. It's a leading motive for abductions."

Ellie fled the room, followed closely by Lucas. "E, wait!"

Considering the horrible violations she'd endured, Ryan didn't blame her. Things were so much worse than he'd imagined. God knew he'd had plenty of horrible scenarios running through his mind. This topped them all.

When he turned to Ben, prepared to find him regressed to hopelessness or hiding behind a blank mask, he saw his lips moving instead. His hands were clasped, his elbows resting on his knees, and over and over he said to himself, "We're going to find her. They're going to bring her home safe. She's okay. We're going to find her."

Now it was Ryan's turn to choke back tears. It was either that or howl like a wounded animal. Shari leaned her head on his shoulder.

Special Agent Salinas had a fancy headset on and seemed to be hard at work already. As JRad slipped a jeweler's loupe over his head and began the painstaking process of taking the nanotech apart teeny screw by teeny screw, a knock came at the door.

Razor was closest, so he cracked it open to see who was interrupting their breakthrough discovery. He shouted over his shoulder, "Did someone order a pizza? Good thinking, I'm starving."

Then the person outside said something Ryan couldn't hear from across the room.

Razor said, "Huh? Seriously? What the fuck?"

Every cop in the room stood at attention, as if their Men in Blue senses started tingling at precisely the same moment.

"You'd better get in here." The rookie hauled a pizza guy inside and slammed the door. The blood draining from the newcomer's face made it likely he was going to pass out like Shari had, or piss his pants. Odds were even. "Tell them what you just told me."

"I was making a delivery up the street and something seemed off." He stammered as he continued, "T-there's a little girl in a house over there. I think her dad might be beating her or something. He's...not right. And when she signed for the pie, she did this—"

He reached into his pocket and withdrew a crumpled slip.

"I saw all these cop cars over here and thought maybe you could make a quick house call. Check it out or something. I hope I'm not gonna get in trouble for this."

"Definitely not. You did good, buddy." Razor reassured the guy with a clap on the shoulder that nearly sent him sprawling.

Detective Tran retrieved the paper, then glanced at it. The widening of her eyes spoke as loudly as a shout from one of the other officers. With a few brisk steps, she crossed the room and extended her hand, so they could see it for themselves.

"Is this your niece's handwriting?" she asked Ben.

Ryan and Shari leaned in for a look too.

They took a single glance at the word *HELP* scrawled there, and all three said at once, "Yes."

When Ryan's ears stopped ringing, he realized the pizza dude was rambling on in the background, being grilled by Clint and Matt.

"I think the guy is new to town. He's been ordering pizza the past week or so. And there are lots of boxes stacked in the entryway. His kid's stuff, I guess. A ton of teddy bears. She must collect them. There's a whole mountain of them."

Ryan had to hold Ben back then. He strained forward as if he was about to bolt before he even knew what direction to run in.

"Address?" Detective Tran fired the question at him.

"324 Ridgeway. H-half a block that way, across the street. The blue Victorian with the black shutters." The pizza guy cowered when faced with their collective intensity.

Matt and Mason stepped toward each other, creating an impenetrable wall in front of Ben. Matt boomed, "Stop right there."

"You've got to let us do our jobs." Tyler wasn't about to bend. None of them were. "If we don't do this by the book, he could walk when he gets his day in court."

"If you take me with you, we won't have to worry about that," Ben threatened in the coldest voice Ryan could have imagined. It chilled his soul.

Razor attempted to be the voice of reason for once. "I also don't like to arrest my friends for murder."

When that didn't cool Ben off, Clint said, "Worse, that fucker could get spooked. He could take her and run. Or…"

"Quit arguing," Ryan urged. "We're wasting time."

"Fine. I'll hang behind. As soon as it's clear, I'm going to her," Ben compromised, which was more than any of them had a right to expect of him.

"Take that deal, guys," Lucas spoke up, acting as their mediator. "It's only fair. A hell of a lot more reasonable than I would be if I were him."

"Fine." Mason nodded.

Then Ryan, Shari, and Ben tried to fade into the wallpaper so the Men in Blue could fly into action. The rest of the civilians left the room entirely, giving the cops space to do their thing.

Having never been on this end of things, it was enthralling to watch. Their teamwork had been responsible for saving his own life. And Ben's. And Julie's. And Ellie's. And Izzy's. And Lacey's. And Lily's. And Jambrea's. And each others' several times over. Countless other strangers' as well.

A whole new level of respect grew within Ryan for what they had chosen to do with their lives.

They made a difference.

A huge one.

He prayed that today would be no different.

A win for the good guys and the innocent.

Please, God, if you're listening, let this go our way.

TWENTY-THREE

Ben had déjà vu. He felt hollow and disconnected from the action around him. Exactly like he had the moment Lily and JRad had shouted for him and Ryan as they approached Lily's harem in one of the labyrinthine hallways of Morselli's dungeon, pleading for them to help get Ellie and Lucas to safety. Ryan had blasted past him, collecting his sister, who had been bombarded by a massive dose of Sex Offender. Though they didn't know it at the time, Lucas had just suffered the catastrophic impact that would lead to him losing his leg. Shocked the man could move at all as he attempted to drag himself to safety, Ben had assisted him the rest of the way, then fashioned a tourniquet around his crushed limb.

Between the drama that had buffeted them from every direction, Ben had visually searched the bloody, terrified, battered crowd of people without luck. His sister wasn't there. They hadn't found her. Or Julie, who had been released later by the Men in Blue—from the cage where she'd been locked with her mother's corpse. He still dreaded the day she recalled that particular detail of her internment.

Like then, an odd blend of hope and dismay assaulted him.

They knew where she was. So close this whole fucking time.

But they didn't have her back yet.

So much could still go wrong. He had to see her. Hug her. Show her she was safe again. Reassure her that even though bad shit happened in life, she was a survivor. Until he did, he could hardly stand to breathe.

It seemed like several hours had passed, though it had taken less than ten minutes for the Men in Blue to formulate a plan, get it approved by the chief, and assemble for action. Other than Shari, who refused to stay behind this time, and Lacey, who was their backup in case of a medical emergency, and Lucas, who would be an asset to any covert operation, the rest of the non-officers wished them luck then huddled up, waiting for news.

Mason briefed Ben, Ryan, Shari, and Lacey. "You four hang back. Street level is okay, but I want you out of sight. Stay behind that overgrown hedge in your neighbor's yard until you hear me shout the all clear. Then you can haul your asses over as fast as you can. Lacey, if we need you, we'll send an officer to escort you and provide cover if necessary. Do not run out in the open on your own under any circumstances."

She bit her lip.

Mason knew his woman too well for that to fly. "Promise, Lacey. Even if you see me take a bullet or—God forbid—Tyler, you *will not* put yourself at risk to save us."

"If I won't?"

"Your pretty ass will stay up here with the rest of the civilians."

"How did I know you were going to say that?" She rolled her eyes. "Fine. I won't move without a police escort until you give the all clear."

"That's my girl." He kissed her cheek, then marched to the door. "Anyone need more time?"

No one spoke up.

Mason took his firearm out, switched off the safety, then led the charge out the door.

Ben counted out loud to fifty as they'd agreed, then crept down the stairs and into the yard with his group. If he hadn't been one-hundred percent certain they weren't punking him, he would have thought the officers, detectives, agents, and their pet super spy were hiding behind the house.

He didn't see a single one of them, no matter where he looked.

Damn, they were good.

The four of them crept into place and peeped as best they could through the dense, thorny branches. It seemed that they were slightly less invisible to their trained friends. As soon as they were in place, hell broke loose.

Ben couldn't quite see what exactly happened, or in what order. Still, he was sure someone had jumped or fallen off the roof from one of the attic dormers. "Julie!"

"It wasn't her." Ryan gripped the waistband of his jeans to keep Ben from violating his oaths to Mason. "It was an adult. Maybe the guy."

Shouting ensued as radio silence became a thing of the past. He heard people calling out locations and finally someone—Lucas, he thought—hollered, "I can take a clean shot."

"Hold your fire!" Mason responded, negative. "This is a residential neighborhood. And Julie's somewhere inside. We're not taking any chances here."

"Damn it!" Lucas again. "I lost him. I don't have the right foot on for this terrain."

"Fall back." Mason again. "Outside team, watch our backs. We're going in."

Ben drew an enormous, shaky breath, then held it until his lungs felt as if they were engulfed in flames. Time slowed. He swore he could hear Ryan, Shari, and Lacey's hearts pounding in time to his own.

None of them budged, straining for the two words that would free them.

"All clear!"

Ben didn't care about his ripping clothes or the rending of his exposed flesh—he cannonballed through the hedge then sprinted up the street. His early morning runs had not prepared him for this sort of dash. He was fairly sure he set a world record.

Ryan, Shari, and Lacey's footfalls echoed behind him, but he wasn't about to wait.

As he was tearing clumps of the kidnapper's lawn out with his sneakers, the silhouette of a child appeared in the foyer. "Julie!"

He stumbled, knowing right away it was her.

Why wasn't she running to him as fast as he was rushing to her?

Ben slowed, wondering if he was scaring her. His face was probably a grotesque twisted mess.

He took the stairs to the porch with two humongous leaps, tripping on an uneven board. He crashed to his knees about ten feet from the front door. "Julie, are you okay?"

"Uncle Ben! Is it really you? You found me!" She trotted closer.

He held his arms out. "Yes, it's me. I'm here."

She froze on the threshold.

"Are you hurt?" he asked, and scooted closer. She stumbled back a step or two.

"No."

Something inside him began to loosen.

"She's scared, Ben," Ryan said gently from somewhere behind him, likely the yard.

"It's okay, honey." He tried again to reassure her. "We're here. Me, Uncle Ryan, Aunt Shari, all our friends. Look at how many policemen there are to protect you. You're safe. It's okay now. Come on out and we'll go home."

"I can't!" She began to sob. "If I leave, he'll find me. He told me he'll hunt me down. Next he'll come for you, and Uncle Ryan, and Aunt Shari, even. He told me he knows about you. Where you work, and where we live, and…no. Just leave me here. Go. Run away before he comes back and sees you talking to me. He's going to catch you, too."

"Julie, none of that is true. He's a bad man. He was lying to you." Ben held his hands out, feeling useless.

Knowing that words alone could be used as a weapon this powerful, to warp an impressionable young person's mind and turn it into an effective weapon of self-destruction, seemed like the most heinous crime he'd seen committed.

And he'd seen his share.

He wished they'd caught the fucker even more now. Although Razor had made a good point about murder charges.

Ben stood up and edged closer.

Julie screamed, "Stop. Stop! Uncle Ben, don't. I don't want him to get you."

Why hadn't they thought to call Julie's therapist? They could use Dr. Epstein right now. He turned then and looked to Ryan and Shari and Lacey for help.

"Hi, Julie," Shari said then, approaching but staying off the front steps. "What if we run away together? You, me, Uncle Ben, and Uncle Ryan. We'll go to my house. You know how far away it is. The bad man doesn't know how to get there. Remember how I told you about my brother?"

"Yes." Her tears slowed and she elaborated, if weakly, "He was a soldier. Like Uncle Lucas."

"Even better than me, Julie," Lucas promised. "He was the best. And he built lots of alarms and booby traps around Aunt Shari's house to keep her extra safe when he was away. I absolutely swear to you that no one will be able to get you, or your family, if they are staying there."

"Can you come too? To watch them?" Julie scrubbed her hands over her eyes, leaving streaks of…marker?…on her cheeks. What the hell?

"Of course." Lucas earned even more of Ben's respect. "I'll always take care of you."

"No, them. I don't want him to get them because of me breaking the rules and being bad."

"Honey, you're not bad. Never bad. That man was the bad one, so his rules don't count." Ben made a mental note to email Dr. Epstein as soon as they were in the truck and out on the highway. Whatever it cost, he'd try to persuade her to make a mountain call…

Ben dropped to his knees and held out his arms again. "Do you trust me?"

"Yes."

"Am I a bad man?" He hoped she knew better. If she didn't, it wouldn't be her fault. Confused, and troubled—hell, traumatized—she might not be able to tell anymore.

"No. You're the best."

"I love you very much, Julie."

"I love you too, Uncle Ben."

"So how about I make some new rules? You can come out of that house right now. If you do, we will go home, pack some clothes quick, and leave here. When we get to Aunt Shari's resort, my rules say no one bad can come inside and no one bad can hurt you. Or us. Okay?"

"Okay." This time Julie flew to him, landing against his chest with enough force to rock him back. He tried his best not to crush her as he hugged her, tucking her face against his neck. Oddly, he didn't feel the least bit like crying anymore, though relief did threaten to leave him in a boneless puddle on the floor.

He wasn't sure how long they'd stayed there like that before Lacey cleared her throat. "Maybe I should give her a quick lookover?"

She might as well have poured a bucket of ice water over his head.

The tiny tank top and too-tight pleather skirt Julie wore finally registered on him. Did they think...?

When he looked up, the concerned look on Detective Tran's usually carefully neutral face made him realize they did. He asked Julie, "Are you hurt anywhere? Did that bad man touch you?"

She shook her head. "No. We were eating and then he was going to give me a bath. He didn't like my tattoos much."

Jesus, please let that be true.

"Well, I love them." Lacey tried to act like everything was normal as she examined Julie without letting her catch on. "May I see the ones on your arms?"

"Yeah. I put Uncle Ben, and Uncle Ryan, and Aunt Shari over here. Aunt Shari said her tattoo makes her tough and she has her brother's name on her side. So I thought if I put you all on here, the new bad man wouldn't be able to hurt me ever. You found me and he ran away. It worked!"

Ben caught sight of April's name, big and bold. She would be proud of her daughter today, he thought, swallowing hard.

"It sure did." Lacey inspected every inch of Julie's arms and legs. When the nurse leaned in and whispered a question Ben was sure he didn't want to hear—couldn't hear without turning into the Hulk and smashing half the block—Julie emphatically shook her head no.

"Nothing like that, Aunt Lacey. Can we go now? I don't want to stay here. I don't even want to go inside our house. I just want to get in Aunt Shari's truck and drive far, far away so he can't come back and get any of you. Okay?"

"Okay." She smiled softly and nodded. "You're a sweet girl."

"Thanks." Julie shrugged. "Come on, Uncle Ben. Let's move it."

He smiled as she yanked until he did as she said. Most of the other Men in Blue were chuckling at how a nine-year-old could lead him around, but he knew every one of them would do the same thing if Julie was their daughter.

"You going to wait in the truck with Aunt Shari, Uncle Ryan, and Uncle Lucas?" he asked Julie, though the last thing he wanted to do was let go of her small hand.

"Yep."

"I'm going to go pack some stuff really fast. I'll be right back, okay?"

"Yes, but..."

"Hmm?" He glanced down at her as they walked across their street and toward Shari's truck.

"Don't bring that new teddy bear. I don't like it."

"I don't like it either. How about I throw it away?" he asked, thinking of its dismembered corpse currently being entered into evidence.

"Good idea."

Ben stopped and put his hands out. Julie raised her arms. He picked her up and hugged her again before handing her off to Ryan.

Then he bolted up the stairs to their apartment.

He only had time to yell, "We got her. She's okay," as he flew through the rest of their friends in the living room on his way to collect some necessities.

Honestly, he didn't feel much like he was fleeing. Rather, he felt like he was running toward a life he actually wished he could have. Disenfranchised with his fellow human beings, being surrounded by the tranquility of nature and the few people he loved and trusted most sounded perfect to him.

A quiet life, away from crowds and the hustle of the city, appealed more by the moment.

Just them and their little unit.

He smiled at the thought as he shoveled a random assortment of clothes, toiletries, and toys for Julie into a couple of soft-sided suitcases. He hadn't gotten very far when Ryan called out his name.

"Back here," he shouted. "Almost finished."

Had the kidnapper come back?

Was Julie okay?

Ryan and Shari?

"Julie decided she didn't want to be apart from you. I also thought maybe she could change her clothes quick." Shari smiled, though it was clear her nerves were as frazzled as his. "So we're going to pack together, okay?"

"Good call." Ben nodded.

They worked as a team, getting Julie ready—adding that horrible outfit to the evidence pile—while he finished gathering supplies. Ryan and Shari were each holding one of Julie's hands, flanking her. As soon as he indicated he was ready, Lucas took point in front of them and Ben brought up the rear.

The rest of the Men in Blue flooded the yard to ensure their safe passage.

At the last moment, Ben looked over his shoulder at the ruined apartment and knew that he'd never call it home again. Too many bad memories haunted the place.

Ready to make some new ones, somewhere happier, he smiled as he watched his little family pile into Shari's monster-sized truck. They were finally on the right road.

Before he took his place behind them, he spun around and gave their apartment a double one-fingered salute while taking the last few steps backwards. Unfortunately, Julie had eagle eyes.

"Hey, Aunt Shari, why is Uncle Ben making unicorn puppets? Doesn't he know we have to leave? I don't want to stay."

Ryan and Shari lost it. Cracking up, they waited for him to contort himself into the backseat of the truck next to his niece. The rest of the Men in Blue couldn't keep a straight face either when she pretended to play along, fashioning her own unicorns to trot along the edge of her window at them.

Ben didn't have the heart to tell her to stop. Not even when they pulled away with Lucas and Ellie following right behind them.

Every honk they earned from cars they passed on the way out of the city made Shari and Ryan snicker and snort. Julie giggled too, though she had no idea what was really going on.

It felt good to laugh.

To know that even after the awful things they'd endured, they were still capable of finding joy with each other.

∽ TWENTY-FOUR ∾

Two days after they'd retreated to Shari's resort while the Men in Blue searched for the kidnapper, Ryan felt like someone had trapped him in a pressure cooker. If he didn't do something to relieve the tension, he was going to explode. Just like the time they'd had one of the kitchen gadgets malfunction during his culinary institute days, it would probably cause a big enough detonation to rip a gaping hole in the roof at this point.

So he snuck into the bathroom and called Lucas. "Hey man, did you have a chance to put that stuff I asked for in the barn by the lake?"

"Yup. I even got Ellie in on it. She made it way prettier than I could have imagined. Romantic. You're definitely going to get laid if you take your guy and girl over there."

"Thanks, I owe you."

"Want us to hang out with Julie right now? Ellie has some art supplies to keep her entertained."

"Okay, seriously, I owe you two. Best future brother-in-law ever."

"Don't worry, this makes up for the times we've been late to your fancy dinner parties because I was busy banging your sister. Did you really believe we'd gotten three different flat tires this summer?"

"Willful ignorance. By the way, I owe you nothing. Get your ass over here, and don't be *late* either."

Lucas roared with laughter, something he hadn't done much before Ellie had resurrected his sense of humor. Among other things. "Yes, sir."

Ryan muttered to himself about filthy Special Forces super spies as he collected light jackets for himself, Shari, and Ben, then wandered into the living room around the same time Lucas knocked.

When he called, "Come in," Lucas opened the door for Ellie as if he were a perfect gentleman.

What a crock of shit.

His sister's cheeks blazed. Probably because she'd overheard her fiancé torturing Ryan with their sexual exploits.

"Aunt Ellie! Uncle Lucas!" Julie hopped up and skipped over to them. When she noticed the paintbrushes Ellie had in her hand, she squealed, "Are you going to teach me more art?"

"If you want me to."

"Please. Please. Please." Julie took her hand and led Ellie to the table. "I want to try flowers again. And maybe a kitty sitting in them this time. Aunt Shari told me there are a bunch of cats that live here in the barns. That's *so* cool. I wish we could have a cat, but there are no pets allowed at our apartment."

"Time for us to go, kids." Ryan nudged Ben and Shari where they were cuddled together on the sofa.

Ben hadn't left Julie's side since they'd rescued her. He looked over his shoulder then back to Shari and Ryan at least seven times before he gulped and said, "Okay. Just for a quick walk or something, though, right?"

"Something. Right." Ryan nodded.

"I've got this." Lucas stood with his arms crossed, his legs spread, and his shoulders straight. Prosthetic foot or not, he could kick pretty much anyone's ass. Add in the gun and knives they all knew the guy had hidden somewhere on his body, and Julie couldn't be much safer.

"Come with me." Ryan held a hand out to each of his lovers, thrilled when they took them and let him help them to their feet. He grabbed their jackets and eased their arms into the sleeves.

"It's so cute when he dresses you," Lucas ribbed, in rare form today.

After making sure Julie was engrossed in unpacking the supplies, Ryan shot the guy a "unicorn".

Ben wandered over to Julie and finger combed her hair. "Will you be okay if we take a break for a bit?"

"You're coming back, though, right?" she asked. "And Aunt Ellie and Uncle Lucas will be with me the whole time, right?"

"Right," Ryan promised her.

"Then yep. Go outside and do your mushy stuff. Nobody wants to see all that kissing anyway."

Ellie slapped a hand over her mouth and Lucas was already texting the rest of the Men in Blue a quote as notable as that, Ryan was sure.

"Uh. Okay then. We'll be back soon." Ben shook his head ruefully, having been summarily put in his place by a nine-year-old. Nothing new there.

"Who raised that girl?" Shari teased as they strolled down the porch steps, hand in hand.

"I think she's kind of a brainiac." Ryan shrugged. "It's not like I was bringing you out here to play hopscotch."

"Wait, you really were planning to seduce us?" Shari glanced up at him.

"Maybe. Why don't we go check out that barn you told us about?"

"The booty shack?" She laughed. "Sure. Not much to see, though. It's been empty for a while. Never really got used for what it was intended for."

"Well, I'd rather use it for this than anything else, I think." He grinned, practically dragging them to their destination when they didn't move fast enough for his liking. Then again, they'd have to have been running at the speed of light to appease him.

When Ben did the honors, lifting the bar across the heavy wooden doors before throwing them open, even Ryan was impressed.

"Wow, Ry," Shari gasped, clutching her hands to her chest.

A long whistle preceded Ben when he asked, "How the hell did you pull this off?"

"With a little help from our friends." He took in the battery-powered LED lights wrapped around the posts and beams, the space heater chugging along to keep the place toasty, and plaid fleece blankets laid out over a thick bed of hay in one corner. Buckets of mums in full bloom surrounded the area with rich hues of maroon and mustard.

Okay, fine, maybe he would owe Lucas one. But only one.

They wandered closer to the center stage, and she whispered, "It's beautiful."

"Not nearly as stunning as you." Ben stole the words out of Ryan's thoughts. He didn't mind.

Being that connected to someone, so in tune, amplified his attraction and his desire.

Ryan eased behind Shari, resting his hands on her waist. If he pulled her closer to him so that his cock nestled along her ass, well, who could blame him?

Approaching them slowly, like a predator on the hunt, Ben hummed as he took in the picture they made. He inched nearer until he stood toe to toe with Shari. Then he lifted his hands and clasped her face reverently between his palms, which swallowed her up.

"I'm going to do this right," he whispered.

"So far, so good." She shivered in Ryan's hold as Ben came nearer. His lips hovered a hairsbreadth from hers as he simply stared into her eyes, letting her see the undeniable affection there.

Ryan couldn't stand the anticipation another moment. He reached around them to slide his hand into the back pocket of Ben's jeans. Then he yanked, eliminating any gaps between the three of them.

The sound Shari made was gratifying, and arousing. A cross between a whine and a sigh.

If his cock hadn't already been straining against his zipper, it would have gone insta-hard when she lifted one arm behind her and clutched the back of his head. Her nails pressed into his scalp lightly, inflicting precisely the right amount of sensation.

He couldn't resist.

Ryan lowered his face so that he could bury his nose in her soft hair and breathe deep before nudging the layers aside for access to her neck. He blew lightly to scatter a few remaining strands and was rewarded with a moan.

Ben sealed their mouths tighter as he swallowed it, then set about eliciting several more.

While Ben was busy savoring Shari's kisses, Ryan set out to discover her most sensitive erogenous zones. As if he were conducting a search and rescue mission, he mapped each square inch of her neck with his lips and tongue.

When she shuddered and rocked her ass backward, into his groin, he figured he'd scored a direct hit. That place he suckled, applying light, fluttery motions of his tongue. He'd learned these techniques were often the most productive on women he served.

Shari was no exception.

She broke from Ben, gasping. "I could come just from this. Holy crap, you guys. Don't stop."

"I'd like to see that." Ben scanned her flushed face before trailing his fingertips along her jaw, down her neck, and over her collarbone. "Ryan, get that shirt off her."

"Yes, sir." His balls ached as he gladly followed the direct order.

He took the hem in his hands and lifted, facilitated by Ben, who nudged her arms upward so he could peel the thing off in a single motion. Beneath, she wore a pretty pink lace bra that added to the impression of softness made by her pale skin. He imagined it would smell like baby powder and freshly fallen leaves.

Natural.

Nude.

Perfect.

"I swear you get more lovely every time I see you like this," Ben muttered.

"Thank you." She smiled.

Ryan couldn't remember a time that she hadn't shaken off their compliments. Maybe they had finally started to sink in. After years, or an entire lifetime, perhaps she would understand exactly how amazing she was to him. To them both.

Same for Ben.

"We're going to fuck you so well you won't even be able to remember old what's-his-face's name when I'm finished." The Ben Ryan had always known was hiding inside his roommate's shell emerged like a badass butterfly from a pitch black cocoon. It was astounding to watch him spread his wings.

Astonishing and a complete turn-on.

Ryan groaned, wondering what the man had in store for him.

The sound drew Ben's attention. "I'd like to bury myself in you, too. You have no idea how badly. Except I'm not really prepared for that and I'd never take you dry. Not happening."

"Ah, yeah, I'd rather you hold off with that beast of a cock then." Ryan laughed, a little nervously. "I figured I'd pushed Lucas enough. I wasn't about to ask him to scrounge up some lube. I'll take a rain check. Besides, today should be about Shari and making new memories."

"Good living through better barn sex." Ben grinned. "After this you won't remember any shitty first time. This will be the only time that matters."

"It already is." She reached for them, hugging one with each of her arms. "I don't mind sharing. If you want lube, I have some in my stash. It would only take a few minutes for me to run over to the main house quick—"

"Hell, no." Ryan cut her off, and Ben backed him up.

"You're not going anywhere until I've worn this pussy out." He stripped his T-shirt over his head, dropping it on the ground.

When he put it like that, she quit resisting. So Ben guided her down to the makeshift mattress.

Ryan shucked his clothes then balled up his shirt and Ben's too, making a pretty decent pillow for Shari. From that angle she'd be able to watch as Ben fit his cock to her opening and began to spread her wide around the fat head.

Ryan had looked huge between her legs. How would she ever take all of Ben?

From the way she hooked her leg around Ben's hip and began to grind on him, it was clear she wanted to. But...damn. Even Ryan wasn't sure she could. He'd do his best to facilitate their introduction.

In a way, it *was* their first time. Hers and Ben's, anyway.

The thought made him smile.

It also added to his horniness factor.

Ryan looked to Ben, who was busy making out with Shari again, this time a little more feverishly. Ben was a pretty decent multi-tasker, removing her underwear without breaking their contact.

Besides, he couldn't wait another moment to touch himself as he watched his lovers love each other. Ryan wrapped his hand around his cock and began to stroke. He might catch hell for doing it without permission, but that would be fine with him too. Occasionally he cupped his balls and rolled them in his palm or pinched his nipples, but he had to be careful with those extra stimulations.

He was close enough to embarrassing himself already.

For a submissive with a reputation for lasting as long as his Dom required, that was unheard of as well as unacceptable. He wanted to be ready to give them any pleasure they would take from him, up to and including the use of his stiff dick.

All of him belonged to them.

"Do you see what you do to him?" Ben asked Shari in a gruff rasp. He took her jaw in his hand and turned her head so that her face was practically touching Ryan's shaft. He hadn't realized he'd crept that close.

"Mmm. Yes," she purred. "Will you let me suck that cock? Don't you see how big it is? How hard? I want to taste it. It'll make me wetter. Go crazy."

"Damn, Shari." Ben nipped her lower lip.

Ryan knew that monologue had been for his benefit. She was remembering his fantasies and bringing them to life. He loved her for it.

"So can I? Please?" she begged.

∽ TWENTY-FIVE ∽

"You're lucky, boy. I want to spoil her. And the lady wants your dick in her mouth." Ben reached out and fisted Ryan's erection. He pumped it, hard and kind of rough. Exactly how Ryan liked it.

When Ryan clenched his jaw to keep from coming, Ben backed off. He slapped Ryan's dick like he'd seen Mistress Lily do in her harem once.

Just like then, it fueled his arousal.

Then he surrounded Ryan's cock once more. Except this time, he guided the tip to Shari's eager mouth. She opened, permitting him inside. Soft suction and the rubbing of her tongue along the underside of his shaft made him buck. He might have fed her too much at once if Ben hadn't still been holding on to him, prohibiting him from going too deep.

"Easy now, boy," Ben coached. "I've got other business to attend to over here. You stay still so Shari can keep that pretty mouth full of gorgeous cock. Don't disappoint her or I'll be upset."

"I won't." Unless Ben kept tempting him like that.

He had to close his eyes for a moment to regain a modicum of composure.

The tremors that ran along his shaft when Shari squealed nearly did him in, though.

His eyes flew open in time to watch Ben plumping her breasts while he dragged his teeth across her distended nipples one at a time, over and over. While he investigated how she liked to be touched, licked, and sucked at her chest, his hand meandered from her softly rounded belly to her mound.

Ben cupped her pussy in his huge hand, massaging her clit with his thumb as he palmed her sex. Her moans grew louder and more insistent. Just when Ryan feared she might forget about him stuffing her face with his dick and bite him while she came, Ben stopped abruptly.

She stared up at Ryan with a combination of panic, disappointment, and hunger.

Oh, she was going to like playing with Ben.

Lightly, he slapped her pussy over and over, tapping the engorged tissue with his fingers.

Even that seemed like it might be too much stimulation for her right then.

"No, no, Shari," Ben mock-chastised her. "You're not coming again until you're packed with my dick. I want to feel you come apart. Hold on to that feeling. Save it for me this time. It's going to be the best orgasm of your life when I finally tell you to let go and we fall over the edge together. Can you do that for me?"

She nodded, essentially mouth-fucking Ryan's cock. They were going to destroy him.

Hell, he was already ruined for anyone else.

Fascinated, he stared at the places Shari and Ben touched. It was as if he could see the pleasure arcing between them. "Is she doing a good job on that dick?" Ben asked him.

"Yes, sir."

"Should I give her my cock? Or make her wait for it?"

Shari used what leverage she had. She let her teeth rasp over Ryan's shaft. If she thought that was a deterrent, she was sadly mistaken. He reached up and pinched his own nipples, loving the harsher edge to his rapture. "Oh shit."

"I'm going to take that as, 'Go ahead and cram her full. She's a good girl, and she deserves your fat cock, sir.'"

"Uh huh. That," was the best he could do.

Ben laughed. In the middle of the most intense sexual encounter of Ryan's life, the man was fucking laughing. They'd unleashed a beast.

And he was going to love every moment of his life if it was anything like this.

Instead of diving into Shari's pussy, Ben got to his feet. He stood with his legs spread, directly in front of Ryan. Though he knew where this was going, he waited patiently for his prize.

"Get me nice and wet. I'm going to need some help fitting in there," Ben ordered. He took Ryan's head in his hands and guided it to his crotch.

He didn't need to be told twice.

Ryan practically inhaled Ben's cock, or as much of it as he could fit in his mouth. He slobbered on it, coating it with his saliva. When he went too far and would have gagged, Ryan got yanked backward by Ben's fist in his hair.

It had been worth it, to feel that sublime pressure on his scalp.

"Behave yourself." Ben tapped Ryan's cheek with his open hand before returning to Shari. He settled between her legs then set the fat head of his now lubricated cock against her opening.

Shari tensed.

Ryan knew that would only make the bite of discomfort worse. It also slowed Ben's progress.

"Boy, get your tongue over here and help her relax. If I can't drill all the way in there, I'm going to take it out on your ass. Understand?"

"Yes, sir." He straddled Shari's head, facing her feet. The position gave her an excellent view of his taut sac. Then he leaned forward so they could sixty-nine. Though, honestly, now he wasn't sure which team he rooted for. Either sounded amazing. Watch up close as her pussy swallowed Ben's cock, or find out that she was simply too petite, please her anyway, then let Ben pretend to be annoyed by what would surely be the best sex of his life and get off hard in the process.

No way to lose.

Careful to hold himself off Shari and spread his legs wide enough that he didn't smother her, he got down to business. Gently at first, he worked his way from her outer lips toward her clit to be sure she could tolerate the direct stimulation.

When he wrapped his lips around the bundle of nerves and began to suck lightly, her legs twitched. He figured he was on the right track. Ben must have agreed because he pressed forward then, beginning to embed himself in the warm, wet paradise of her pussy.

"If I had known she would feel this good, I would have taken your place the other day, boy." Ben groaned when Ryan let his tongue go wild and slip around the head of Ben's cock.

"Play nice!" Ben leaned forward and spanked Ryan, hard enough to leave a bright red handprint he hoped.

That did not dissuade him from naughtiness in the least.

In fact, Ryan started to work his tongue in a figure eight that swiped across Shari's clit, then Ben's cock, then back. Neither of them complained.

Ben was quiet as he concentrated on fitting them together without a replay of their last encounter, when Ryan had gotten out of hand. Shari wasn't making it easy on them, though. She bucked her hips upward, trying to swallow more of both of their cocks—in her greedy mouth as well as her pussy.

"Hold her still," Ben demanded.

Ryan leaned on her a little more, surprised when her pussy clenched before his eyes. Maybe he wasn't the only one in their trio who enjoyed being bound by the others. He'd ask Ben to explore that some other time.

Despite his regulated pace and Ryan's prep, Ben couldn't quite seem to work himself inside Shari. Ryan tapped Ben's quadriceps before opening his mouth wide. Ben groaned, then accepted a quick refresh of the moisture covering him. He pulled his cock from Shari's pussy and pumped it into Ryan's mouth a couple times.

Then he tunneled a little farther into Shari when he returned.

Ben alternated fucking Shari's pussy and Ryan's mouth, sharing the taste of her arousal.

After a while, Ryan realized Ben no longer needed the help to slide completely within her, but he seemed to like their new game. He would pump into Shari a few times, then withdraw, letting Ryan lick her honey from Ben's shaft.

The inconsistent stimulation kept Shari riding the razor's edge of passion.

Each time Ben returned to her, he prodded deeper and ground harder.

The things she was doing to Ryan's cock should be illegal. It was by far the best blowjob he'd ever had. Mostly because he suspected she was using him like a pacifier, to calm herself and weather the storm of ecstasy Ben had whipped up around them like a tornado.

Ryan had his head down, lapping furiously at Shari's clit, when Ben bellowed, "Fuck, that's good. You've got me, Shari. All of me. I'm yours."

Sure enough, he'd fit every last inch of his shaft inside her. Ryan kissed Ben's abdomen where it now pressed to his face. He swiped his tongue over Shari's clit again, loving that now he could flick it against them both at the same time.

They didn't seem to mind.

Ben began to thrust then, setting them into the final phase of this incredible sexual experience. Ryan couldn't still his instinctive flexing, which allowed him to fuck Shari's mouth just a little.

She repaid him in kind, reaching around his thigh to spread his cheeks.

When Ben realized what was about to happen, he moaned, then said. "Give me your hand, Shari."

Ryan couldn't see what was going on above him. The sucking and slurping made him pretty sure Ben had leaned forward to do the same as Ryan had for Ben's cock, though. The difference in size between her tiny digit and his erection was laughable.

Besides, he was trained to take much more.

When Ben released her and she advanced her mission, Ryan realized nothing in his past mattered. Because the simple pressure of her finger on his puckered ass was enough to put him in danger of disappointing Ben. Ryan looked up, desperate.

"Don't you shoot," Ben growled. "Not yet."

Ryan redoubled his efforts, eating Shari better than he had the past two times he'd tried to inhale her. Her pussy must have tightened around Ben, who also showed signs of cracking. He fucked her faster now, harder, too. Sweat began to roll down his sleek abdomen.

"Ryan, I said not yet." Ben must have something in mind, and Ryan wanted him to have everything he desired.

How he kept from coming down Shari's throat, he had no idea. But it wasn't more than a dozen additional furious strokes before Ben put them out of their glorious misery. "She's so goddamn tight, Ryan. You should feel this. It's impossible to resist."

"Give it to her then," Ryan encouraged when Shari found his prostate and began to massage it. The woman was pure seductress. "Let her come with you. Fill her up. I want to watch."

Thankfully, Ben relented.

"Fuck, Shari!" he grunted, then his entire body heaved. Shari moaned, then bucked as if she could feel his come pumping inside her, blasting her pussy with his semen.

"May I have some too?" Ryan asked as he studied Ben's balls unloading from inches away.

Ben withdrew, triggering additional aftershocks in Shari as his veins stroked her most sensitive places. She seized beneath them in the grips of rapture so divine to behold it stole Ryan's breath. Then Ben was there. He fisted his glistening cock and managed to aim it, even as he jacked himself off. The final two or three streams of his come iced Ryan's cheek, lips, and tongue, which stuck out of his wide-open mouth.

He stayed still as Ben decorated him.

"Good boy," Ben rasped, then popped the tip of his dick into Ryan's mouth with an enormous exhalation. "Clean it off. Don't waste a drop."

Ryan sucked softly, hoping to preserve Ben's buzz as long as possible.

"Guys?" Shari called softly.

"Yes?" Ben responded. "You okay?"

"Best I've ever been. Still horny. I see a pretty cock right here. Can I have it?" She licked along Ryan's shaft, nearly making him spill his release without permission.

"Would you like that, boy?" Ben asked, knowing full well he would do damn near anything to slide through Ben's fluids while being hugged by Shari's pussy. Mingle them inseparably.

"Yes. Need to."

"Go ahead."

Shari's finger slipped from his ass as he slithered down her body. While he missed the sensation, he knew he was going to have plenty to enjoy in a moment.

Ryan peeked at her slit, making sure she wasn't bleeding this time. She wasn't.

"I'm fine. Get in there before I change my mind."

"It's a little scary how fast a learner you are," he laughed.

"I'm not joking, Ryan." She didn't even crack a smile. "I want that cock. Give it to me. Now."

Ben sat hard on the blankets then lifted Shari's shoulders so she rested against his abdomen. He hugged her tight as he observed Ryan doing their bidding.

Ryan pressed inside her, wondering if she'd even notice after taking Ben's fat cock. No worries there. She still sheathed him like a humid glove. Even better, he felt how slick and hot she was from Ben's come, which pooled within her.

Each time Ryan withdrew, he stared at the pearly fluid decorating his shaft.

Ben spoke softly to Shari the whole time. He told her how much he'd enjoyed fucking her. How desperate she was making Ryan. How badly he wanted to see her shatter around Ryan's cock so that her pussy sucked the come straight out of his balls.

Who could resist that kind of dirty talk, honestly?

Neither of them, apparently.

Shari quit first. She began to quake beneath him, begging Ben to let her show Ryan how much she appreciated his performance and, of course, his equipment.

Ben sealed their fates. "Yes, you may."

The first ripple of her pussy around Ryan's shuttling cock put him right there with her.

"Oh, God. I'm gonna come." He looked to Ben for permission.

Granted.

"Do it. But make sure you save a little to spread on her pussy with mine. Then I want you to clean her off. Taste us all. Together."

That thought alone was guaranteed to set him off, and Ben knew it.

His devious grin as he watched Ryan throw back his head, slide balls-deep, and surrender proved it. What he didn't expect was Ben softly urging Shari, "You're still right there with him, aren't you? Keep coming. Milk him dry."

Then he dipped his head and bit Shari's taut nipple while his fingers pinched the other.

The instant clamping of her pussy on Ryan's cock as he came and came enhanced his already epic orgasm. Had anything ever felt as good as sex with these two people?

No.

Definitely not.

It kept getting better. Every time. Every moment.

His ass clenched and released as he thrust into Shari's welcoming body for as long as possible.

Then, at the last second, he pulled out so that a few drops of his semen splattered over her mound, mixing with Ben's.

Since his cock was still hard, at least for a little while longer, Ryan used two fingers to press it down and reinsert it so he could keep riding out her climax. It felt so good when she massaged him with her pussy like that.

If her groan and the clawing of her nails down Ben's arm were clear enough signals, she liked it as much as he did.

To his surprise, she shrieked then shuddered, climaxing on him again. Or still. He couldn't quite tell. If his body had been able, he would have kept going, but the contractions of her pussy squeezed him from paradise along with a trickle of fluid.

He wasn't about to leave her wanting.

"Don't you dare stop now, boy." Ben had paused whatever he was doing to her breasts to shoot him a glare. "Clean her off and keep her going until she's had enough. No one's leaving her unsatisfied today. We're not leaving her alone. Not horny or otherwise. Ever again."

As if Ben's words alone tripped Shari's circuits, she screamed their names, her hips moving in small, reflexive arcs. Hell, yes.

Ryan had seen a lot in his sexual lifetime. Shari topped it all.

He slipped his fingers inside her, spreading them to make sure she was full enough. From time to time he withdrew them to taste the silky secretions he could feel saturating her. In the meantime he ate, and ate, and ate.

After a sequence of softer orgasms, she went limp.

"Mercy, Ben."

"Stop," he commanded Ryan.

Exhausted and replete, the three of them arranged themselves in front of the space heater in a tangle of limbs and bodies. They kissed and stroked, complimented, and shared amiable silence.

Ryan knew they'd been away far longer than they'd bargained for. They'd have to go soon.

So he began to look around, trying to commit every tiny detail to memory so that he could relive this afternoon in his dreams forever. That was when he started noticing things.

Things that probably wouldn't seem important to anyone else.

"Hey, Shari?"

"Hmm?"

"Is that a propane hookup over there?" Ryan asked. "Next to the two-twenty electrical and the plumbing rough-ins?"

"You've got an armful of naked woman and you're worried about the utilities?" Ben smacked him upside the head. "What the hell is wrong with you, boy? We must not have fucked you hard enough."

As he lay there, staring at the gorgeous beams overhead and the open floor space, he was getting some ideas. The tack areas of the old stable would make a pretty decent-sized kitchen. He shrugged. "Just thinking."

"Yes, Ry. My mom and dad had plans for this place. They talked about when he retired from the military, maybe making this into one of those boutique farm-to-table restaurants. They'd grow their own ingredients, raise the animals, that kind of stuff. My dad played around with a few improvements when he was here on leave, but they never got the chance to do it for real. He was killed overseas on duty. She died of cancer and never knew about his fate at least."

"Damn, Shari." He hugged her tighter. "That sucks. But what an awesome idea."

His brain began to dust off the cobwebs and imagine what this space might look like converted into an upscale, exclusive establishment that blended quality with small-batch artisanal elements.

It had potential. Lots of it.

"You know what? Fuck this." Ben startled them both from their reverie with his overly loud outburst. "The three of us know pretty damn well that life can toss you a wildcard at any time. Like your parents. Like John. Like April. Like whatever the fuck craziness this is that we're in the middle of again. I don't ever want to lose the chance I have right now to tell you both..."

He swallowed hard.

"How much I love you," Ben swore to Shari before turning to Ryan. "And you. So in love with you."

Well, shit.

Ryan hadn't expected that kind of breakthrough today. But he would gladly take it.

He glanced at Shari to find her wearing as big of a grin as he must be right then. They smiled at each other, then turned to Ben as one.

Together they piled on top of him, smothering him with laughter, kisses, and the same precious words in return.

"I love you too," Ryan swore. "I have since we met and you told me what you'd gone through to save your sister. You're like me. Except totally different, too. You are my counterpart."

Shari sighed, her lower lip trembling.

"You too, Shari." He took her hand in his, brushing her knuckles with the pad of his thumb. "You make us work. Without you, we nearly fucked everything up. You're patient and steady. Everything we need to stay grounded. You keep us from getting jammed up in our past."

"Did you just call me relationship lube?" she laughed.

"I'll probably get better at this stuff the more I practice." He shrugged, embarrassed. "I've never been in love with someone before you two."

"Me either." She set her palms on his cheeks and kissed him softly. "So I know how rare this is, and how precious. I will never stop loving you guys."

They each leaned forward, pressing their mouths together in their first ever three-way kiss.

It would certainly not be the last.

Unless, of course, Ryan dropped dead on the spot, his heart bursting as he tasted them both simultaneously. Lips, tongues. He couldn't tell whose were whose. Nor did it matter, because they were one. They instantly became his new favorite dessert.

Never to be surpassed.

TWENTY-SIX

When they arrived back at the main house, Shari's hackles went up. Lucas was tense. Ellie sat too close to Julie, hovering. Ben and Ryan must have sensed the change in the atmosphere, too.

"What happened?" Ben asked.

"Take a look at Julie's drawings. She's unusually prolific today." Lucas jerked his head toward the kitchen table. So they trundled over there. Shari wondered if Ben and Ryan's feet felt as heavy as hers. Like they were trying to keep her from finding out something that would ruin the high the guys had given her.

The first thing that caught her attention was how many sheets of paper littered the tabletop. They hadn't been gone *that* long.

Ellie focused entirely on Julie, handing her whatever she asked for as she worked furiously.

"What's all this?" Ben asked.

Julie hardly acknowledged him. When Shari picked up one of the drawings, she realized it was a self-portrait. Julie was trying on princess dresses with the kidnapper in the background. His face was accurate enough to be recognizable compared to the surveillance footage.

"I think you'd better call Dr. Epstein," Shari said. "Maybe the Men in Blue, too."

Ellie nodded. "It might be my fault. After I was rescued, art would calm me. She was a little worried after you guys left, afraid something might happen to you. I encouraged her to use her drawings to help work out her nervous energy. I've never seen something like this before. It's like her memories are pouring out. Damn, these are good work. Better than anything she's drawn before. Beyond her years and skill. It's like some other part of her brain has taken over."

Shari watched in awe as Julie completed another image and reached for a blank piece of paper.

While she did, Ryan jogged to the bedroom and returned, handing Ben his tablet. They'd Skyped with Julie's therapist a few times already since they'd arrived and she'd told them to call anytime.

She hoped the doctor had meant it.

After just a few rings, the doctor answered. "Everything okay?"

"I'm not sure. Take a look at this." Ben flipped the camera setting so that it showed Julie hard at work.

"Wow, she did all of those?" The doctor squinted as she studied the pictures.

"Yes. In the past couple hours." He explained the situation and let Julie speak with the doctor for as long as they could distract her from drawing.

After about a half hour of observation Ben stepped away from the table. Dr. Epstein told him, "I think it's okay. We knew the day would come when her memories resurfaced while she was awake. You should let it happen naturally and encourage her to talk about whatever she's ready to discuss. Don't push beyond that, though. Let her keep drawing as often as she likes. It's a good thing. A positive step. And she shows real talent here, too."

"Okay." He ran a hand through his dark hair. "Great, I really appreciate you taking the time for us."

"It's no trouble. I'm glad to see progress."

"Me too." Ben nodded. "Thank you."

"You're welcome. Ben?" Dr. Epstein had him stopped short before disconnecting their call.

"Yes?"

"I realize things are happening quickly, but I did want to mention one other thing to you." Dr. Epstein lowered her voice. "I think part of this behavior is stemming from how safe she feels there. I don't think it's wise for you to bring her back too soon."

"Don't worry about that." He shook his head. "I don't want to make her—or myself—live among those ghosts. Not at the apartment and definitely not at that school, no way. I think it's best if I homeschool her. I'm thinking I'd like to make a lifestyle change. Something pretty big. Move out of the city, away from the insanity. I..."

He looked up at Shari then as if she might be upset when he was saying everything she'd dreamed of hearing, him clearing one of the last hurdles to a long-term relationship with her. So she extended the offer she would have made regardless of today's developments. "I would love it if you'd consider staying here."

His entire posture changed, relaxing as his shoulders sank and he exhaled in a rush. "Thank you. Yes, I was hoping. This could work for us."

Whether he was speaking about him and Julie or him, Ryan, and Shari, she approved.

"I'm happy for you, Ben. Though Julie has been my patient, that doesn't mean I haven't noticed your own struggles. You deserve to be happy."

"Uh, thanks."

Ryan was grinning like a fool as Ben wrapped up his call. Shari figured she was also.

Except they didn't get to discuss it. No sooner had Ben hung up then Lucas's phone rang. "It's JRad." He connected the call with a quick, "Yo," then listened.

"I'm going to put you on speakerphone and connect the video feed. There's something you should see. Record this. Ready?" Lucas punched a few buttons, then held his phone over the table and the drawings Julie had done.

"I am now. Go ahead." JRad gave Lucas the green light.

Shari tried not to interrupt as Ben sat beside his niece and asked her some gentle questions. "Can you tell me about your drawings, honey?"

Her gaze dropped to the one Shari had picked up, the one where Julie had a princess dress on. She pitched her voice low and said, "Your fans like the purple dress best. Put that one on again."

Then she took another, one that showed her marker tattoos and the kidnapper frowning in the background. "After dinner, we're going to have to wash them off. I don't think that's what your fans will pay for. Besides, it's too much information."

It went on like that for a while. A lot of what Julie remembered the kidnapper saying to her had to do with fans. Shari didn't quite understand what that meant.

Apparently, Jeremy did.

"Ho-ly..." Jeremy drew Shari's attention to the screen of Lucas's phone. "I don't think you guys understand what a huge breakthrough this is."

"Yeah, we had her therapist on the phone. Seemed like a big deal." Lucas nodded.

"That's great," Jeremy said. "But I meant for the case. I think you just gave us the proof we need for a warrant."

"What? You've got the guy tracked down?" Lucas moved away from the table again so Julie didn't overhear. Shari, Ben, and Ryan followed.

"Sort of. There's a guy who has been under investigation for a while. He sells a streaming service. A disgusting gray area. Kids doing stuff. It's obviously aimed at pedophiles, but there's no sex on tape. It seems like he's been trying to find a particular model based on some videos online of a very popular little girl."

"Julie..." Shari whispered, horrified.

"Yeah. They had her on tapes from the Sex Offender scandal. I haven't had a chance to go through them all yet. The most popular one is of her trying to protect her mom. Then April..." He shook his head. "I don't want to tell you everything. *Can't*, really, given the secondary investigation.

It's bad. I think that's how they found Julie. Why this guy went after her."

When she peeked over at Ben to see how he took the news, his jaw clenched and his hands balled into fists. "So what do we do now?"

"The video I just recorded of her, and the drawings, are the missing link to prove the kidnapper is the same guy that was speaking off camera on the streaming stuff. He was careful never to be onscreen. We found that movie of her trying on the princess dresses online—on that site—a couple hours ago. With her ID, and Special Agent Salinas using the schoolyard audio to confirm the voice of the kidnapper is a match to the streaming guy, we have layers of proof to bust him for something exceptionally criminal. In case the court throws out one or the other, he's still going to be on the hook. Taken together, this stuff is pretty damn incriminating. The kidnapping, intent to harm a minor, the list goes on. He's going away. For good."

Sickness and relief warred within Shari.

"I need to go. Have to brief the chief and the rest of the guys. I've got his location. He's not even bothering to hide since he's gotten away with this shit for so long. We'll be moving on him within the hour. I'll call you when it's done." JRad nodded, then ended the video chat.

"Uncle Ben?" Julie reached out toward him, her voice soft. "I'm tired. Too much drawing."

"Okay, honey."

Shari's heart cracked a little when he went to collect her. He lifted her as carefully as possible and started to carry her to the room she'd claimed as her own. "Wait, will you hold me for a while?"

"Anytime." Ben kissed her hair, then brought her near Ryan and Shari, who took turns hugging her too.

Then Shari couldn't bite her tongue a moment longer. "Can we go back to what you said before, to Dr. Epstein?" She feared raising her hopes too high before they'd locked in a plan. Better to be direct than to assume, she figured. "About staying here. Do you mean you'd like to move in? Because you know I'd love to have you two. But what about everything else? Your job. Ryan..."

"I have a plan." Ben shifted. He took a deep breath as he looked between her and Ryan. "I didn't want to say anything before. There's enough to worry about. But when I called into work yesterday, they gave me shit about taking time off to come up here. So I had a screw-it-just-do-it kind of moment. I quit."

"What?" Shari gasped.

He shrugged. "To be honest, it was just a job. When I look at the Men in Blue and their passion for justice, or Ellie and Lucas and their commitment to improving prosthetics through their new company, or Ryan making people happy by serving them the best meals of their lives, it makes me feel like maximizing profits for a faceless corporation isn't really how I want to spend so much of my life. I'd rather use my talents to build something I actually give two shits about. So, tell me if this is dumb. I was wondering if you'd consider letting me manage this place. I found some hospitality service courses I can take online to learn about the industry specifics. As for the rest, my experience and education will help me analyze the business and get things running smoothly for you again."

Shari didn't say anything. She couldn't.

"Oh, shit. Is that too much? Am I butting in?" He frowned. "I mean, you can say no. I won't be pissed or anything."

"You idiot." Ryan was grinning. "She's about to pee her pants, she's so excited. Just overwhelmed."

Shari nodded vehemently.

It was obvious now that Julie couldn't return to the city. Not until she was older. They may have shut down the kidnapper, but those videos of her from the Sex Offender ring were out in cyberspace and there was no getting them back under wraps.

Here, they could give her a fresh start.

Selfishly, Shari wanted to shout and dance around. She would get to stay here, in the place that she loved, except finally she wouldn't have to do it by herself. Be alone.

"No, no. I don't want to say no." Shari laughed and clapped. "It's...so much more than I hoped. Are you sure? If you get bored in a month or two or whatever, you can tell me."

"I think there is plenty of potential here to keep me busy for...well, forever, I hope." His shrug in no way came off as casually as he'd probably hoped. That only thrilled her more.

"Speaking of big ideas—" Ryan took one of each of their hands in his. "I have some of my own. How do you think an exclusive restaurant would fit into your business plan? Shari's parents were on the right track. That barn would make an excellent facility. When we were there, together, I could picture it. Clearly."

"That would make them so happy." Shari sniffled. "It's like it was always meant to be."

Ben nodded. "Kind of makes you wonder sometimes what the universe has in store for us. Yes, I think it would be awesome. A critically acclaimed chef and his signature restaurant would drive traffic to the resort because people from the city aren't going to haul their stuffed and probably liquored-up asses all the way back to the city after you ply them with a thousand delicious courses and fine wine. We could offer stay and dine packages for a bundle price. Maybe eventually add a spa, too."

"Free for sisters of the cook, though, right?" Ellie had returned to Lucas's side and was practically bouncing in place. Maybe this could work if it sounded half as good to them as it did to Shari.

"Does this mean we get to move here?" Julie's eyes were huge when she lifted her head from Ben's shoulder to look at them. "That we can stay with Aunt Shari? You, me, and Uncle Ryan? Could I have a cat? And ride the horses every day?"

"What's everyone say? Should we vote on it?" Ben asked, though Shari already knew the result would be unanimous.

"Yes!" Julie shouted.

Ben grinned. "On the count of three...who wants to live here, run the best resort and restaurant in the state, and live happily ever after?"

Julie shrieked and threw both of her hands in the air.

Ryan, Ben, and Shari put their hands up too. They met in the middle in a three-sided high five and clasped each other's hands, which made it easy to lean in for a matching kiss.

Julie pulled a face and said, "Blech."

When they broke apart, laughing, Ben said, "I don't have rings or anything fancy, but I hope you both know this is a promise from me to you. The forever sort."

Shari wasn't sure how the pieces had clicked into place so quickly. All she could say for sure was that her dreams had come true and then some.

Now she had two men, and a child, to share her happiness with.

She had plenty to go around.

With them by her sides, she would never run out.

Lucas cleared his throat then showed them a picture on his phone. The kidnapper, cuffed, in the back of a patrol car. "It's official, boys and girls. The Men in Blue made their arrest. It's done."

"The new bad man is going to jail?" Julie asked.

"For a long, long time," Ben promised.

∽ TWENTY-SEVEN ∽

Ben checked the monitor beside the bed to make sure it was on before locking the door to Shari's room. If Julie needed them, they'd know right away. Still, he figured extra insurance didn't hurt. She didn't need to be disturbed any more than she already was.

Keeping quiet was going to be a challenge for them. He was up to it.

Besides, Ryan would probably enjoy being gagged.

"What'd you do that for?" Ryan asked from where he'd taken a clean T-shirt from the dresser. Somehow it made things more real to see their stuff beside Shari's instead of in their duffle bags.

"Drop that. You won't be needing it for a while." He couldn't believe how much he wanted Ryan and Shari. No matter how many times a day they managed to sneak in some loving either together or in pairs while one of them was busy with a math lesson, or resort stuff, he still needed them.

Both of them. Together like this.

Shari glanced up from her ereader and caught the look on his face. She tossed it onto her nightstand without question.

"Remember that box that came today?" He hoped his smile wasn't as wolfish as it felt.

"I'm guessing it didn't really have your new planner in it, huh?" The sparkle in Shari's eyes said she couldn't wait to find out what he'd had delivered.

"Nope." He rummaged around in the bottom of the cedar chest at the foot of her enormous bed, then showed them his purchases.

"Fuck me." Ryan's murmur was followed by the man shucking the sweats he'd recently donned.

"That's the plan, boy."

Ryan practically leapt onto the bed without having to be told, assuming a classic position on his back, arms and legs spread. Ben had noticed he almost always closed his eyes when they played like this, so he gave Ryan his first present.

Ben handed Shari the blindfold he'd bought. It was black leather with faux fur on the inside.

She ran her fingers over it, humming at the softness as it glided over her fingertips. "You're going to like this, aren't you, Ryan?"

"Yes, Shari. Put it on me, please?"

She slipped it over his damp hair. As Ben watched his lovers prepare themselves for him, he took note of Ryan's stiffening cock and the tight discs of his nipples. Then he looked at Shari.

"You're wearing too many clothes."

Not for long. Eager as Ryan, she shimmied out of the satin babydoll nighty before tossing it over the edge of the bed.

"She's so beautiful, Ryan. You're missing a pretty view."

"I can picture it," he murmured. "I know every curve by heart."

They had spent an inordinate amount of time lately getting to know each other in every possible carnal sense. She rewarded his sweet talk by petting his chest. He rose to meet her touch.

"When I can't see, I can feel it more. So good." Ryan panted, already fully erect.

"That's right." Ben wandered closer so he could drag his hand from Ryan's foot up his leg to his hip.

The other man shuddered.

"So you'll be that much more turned on when we use you to pleasure ourselves tonight, won't you, boy?"

"Fuck, yes."

Ben brought his other hand from behind his back so that Shari could see what he had in mind. Her pupils dilated and she gestured for him to hurry.

High quality wrist and ankle restraints that matched Ryan's blindfold would be necessary to keep the man still when they dished out exactly what he craved.

Shari held up her cupped hands. So Ben tossed her the wrist restraints while he kept the ankle shackles for himself. As one, they fastened them around Ryan's limbs, making him moan and shiver as they buckled the cuffs.

"Thank you," he breathed.

But it wasn't until Ben grabbed the restraint and used it to stretch Ryan unbelievably wide open that he really understood what was about to happen. Shari attached the cuffs to the carabineers dangling from the hardware he'd installed in her mammoth wooden bed.

In less than a minute, they had their partner splayed, spread-eagled, on the bed between them.

That would definitely do.

Shari knelt close to Ryan's head, running her fingers through his hair then along his arms to test the fit of the restraints, in no hurry to rush to the next attraction. They let Ryan soak in his new bondage, knowing the act of being bound alone was foreplay for him.

Though they were topping the shit out of Ryan, the sense of desperation Ben had felt in the dungeons or when someone else had used him, had vanished. Instead, Ben felt like they could relax into their roles, take their time, and play only to their desires.

There was something genuine and unhurried about the exchange as compared to the scenes he'd witnessed before. He supposed that was because it wasn't a show. It was their life.

This was how they fit together.

Perfectly.

Without speaking, Shari pointed to herself, then Ryan's face. Ben nodded. When she straddled Ryan's head, facing his feet so that she could see everything Ben was about to do to their man, Ryan moaned.

"I can smell you, Shari. Please let me eat you. Sit on my face and use my mouth to get off. Please."

It was a good thing Ben hadn't planned to torture them with denial tonight. There was no way she could resist when Ryan begged so prettily. He meant every word too. It wasn't something he said because he knew it turned them on. He was honestly expressing his desires.

They just so happened to be Ben's as well. Shari's too, judging by the sublime look in her eyes as she settled on Ryan, leaning forward and planting her hands on his abdomen as she situated herself precisely where it felt best then began to fuck his face.

Ben had to join them then. His balls ached with the need for release despite having bent Shari over his desk in the office earlier that afternoon and the spectacular blowjob Ryan had given him in the woods after their run that morning.

It didn't matter how many times he came in them, he always wanted more of that rush.

Restless, Ryan tugged at his new bonds. They didn't relent. He was well and truly caught.

Theirs. To do with whatever they pleased.

Ben tickled the sole of Ryan's foot to prove his point. The man jerked, yet couldn't evade the contact. He cried out. With a sharp slap to his inner thigh, Ben silenced him. "Quiet."

Ryan obeyed, though his chest heaved and his cock twitched on his abdomen, spreading glistening pre-come across those lean muscles. Shari reached out, her fingers hovering above Ryan's dick as she looked to Ben for permission.

He nodded again.

When her fingers wrapped around Ryan's shaft, he must have increased whatever wonderful techniques his talented lips and tongue were applying to Shari's pussy. Her eyes fluttered shut as she worked Ryan's cock gently. Too slowly to end their fun so soon.

"You're such a good girl," Ben crooned to her as he climbed onto the bed and kissed her. "So generous. There's no need for you to wait for us. If he's doing a good job eating that pretty pussy, come on his face. Show him how much you love what he's doing. As often as you want, okay?"

"Thank you," she whispered, then craned her neck, requesting a kiss.

Ben obliged. He felt the moment she stiffened, and her mouth paused its motions on his. Her moan filled his mouth and his mind.

A sound he'd never get tired of hearing.

When she'd finished coming and focused on rebuilding her semi-slaked desire, Ben couldn't wait any longer to get in on the fun. He ran his hands along Ryan's displayed body, absorbing the man's groans and the way he tried to lean in to the touches.

Then Ben coated his cock with lube and took his place between Ryan's spread thighs.

He cursed when Ryan's ass kissed the head of his cock, trying to draw him inside already. Eager and unbelievably tight, he was temptation incarnate.

They didn't help his stamina any when Shari sat up straighter so she could reclaim his mouth as he advanced within Ryan. They made out, with her hand pumping Ryan's erection, while he stuffed Ryan full of his own stiff cock.

They both knew his responses well enough by now that when he began to rock his hips and his cock took on a purplish hue, Shari let go.

Ryan's ass eased its clamp on Ben's cock a tiny bit, allowing him to tunnel deeper. Though Ben didn't increase his pace, he extended his strokes, pulling nearly all the way out before burying himself balls-deep in his partner with his relentless fucking.

It was only fair that he tormented himself as much as Ryan with the slow, steady thrusts.

Observing their restraint and enjoyment, Shari came again, showering Ryan with her arousal. He never once stopped manipulating her flesh with his mouth, his chin bobbing and throat flexing as he swallowed every bit of her pleasure.

When she recovered, she took up where she left off, bringing Ryan back to the edge with her soft hands on his hard-on. Eventually, Shari stared into Ben's eyes as they made out, then backed away enough to say, "I can't hold myself up anymore."

Her thighs were trembling around Ryan's face.

"Lay back," Ben ordered, and she did. Reclining against the pile of pillows, she rubbed Ryan's jaw and told him how well he'd done.

While she cared for Ryan, Ben unhooked all four of his cuffs, leaving the carabineers dangling from the head and footboards. A permanent reminder of their interludes.

He didn't give Ryan much of a reprieve, though. "Roll over, boy."

Despite any aches in his muscles, he did, gracefully. Ben had his legs reshackled in seconds.

Then he wrapped his hands around Ryan's trim waist and lifted so he rose to his hands. Though he didn't reconnect the cuffs on his wrists to the headboard, he left them decorating Ryan's arms. They looked right there. Like they belonged.

Because they did.

"Let me know when you're ready for your intermission to be over," he told Shari before climbing back onto the bed and smacking Ryan's bubble butt a few times, because he could. "Until then, I'm going to take this boy for one hell of a ride."

Hopefully Shari would get so horny watching them that she'd want in on the action before he lost control and pumped Ryan's ass full of come.

With that end game in mind, he took his cock in hand and pressed it back into Ryan's hot hole with a groan. He leaned forward enough that he could bite the side of Ryan's neck as he fucked. "That's right, boy, push back against me. Show me how much you love my dick in your ass."

He talked dirty to Ryan while he ramped up the pounding of his hips until his pelvis slapped Ryan's bottom with every lunge. When he began to push the man forward, he reached out and took hold of Ryan's hair in his fist, arching his neck and spine as he pulled back, using the grip to anchor Ryan against his hammering.

When he met Shari's glance, her entire face was flushed, her lips parted, and her hands had wandered to her breasts. Oh yeah, it was almost time.

"Let him suck your tits," Ben rasped.

Shari scurried to do his bidding. She positioned herself so Ryan could latch onto her and suckle as Ben continued to ride him from behind.

Just to make sure he was sufficiently rewarded, Ben leaned down and cupped Ryan's rigid cock. He let his fingers form a loose fist around Ryan's hard-on. Every time he bottomed out in Ry's ass, the other man pushed forward, through his fingers.

Before long, Shari said, "Ben, I'm ready. I want in on this. Let him fuck me, please. Give me his cock so I can come all over it."

Ryan moaned his agreement.

Who was he to argue?

"Slide under him," he told Shari.

She did as he told, scooting between Ryan's arms so she lay face up on the bed beneath him. Then she wrapped her arms around Ryan's neck and tugged while Ben sank lower, bearing Ryan down to the mattress, and Shari, in the process.

Since his hand was already in place, he used it to align his lovers. They both moaned when Ryan's cock hit its mark and began to drill into Shari's pussy.

Ben knew Ryan would try his best to resist so they could take as much rapture from his body as possible, but the truth was they were on borrowed time now.

Linked, nothing had ever felt as good as this.

"You in there?" Ben growled.

"Yes, sir," Ryan gasped.

"Every bit of that hard-on?" he double checked.

"Fuck, yes." This time it was Shari who responded. "It feels so good having that long, thick shaft in me. I love your cock, Ryan."

He jerked at that.

"I love all of you," Ben promised him. "Both of you."

Then he began to fuck in earnest.

He loved knowing that as he slammed into Ryan, the motion would transfer to Shari. He used Ryan's body to fuck her. No complaints from them either.

Shari's hands came up to hug him as best she could before allowing them to slip lower and her nails to rake Ryan's exposed shoulders. He responded by kissing her. Ben adored watching their tongues parrying while he rode them both.

When her breathing turned to panting and her moans escalated to whines, he knew they were about to reach the pinnacle together.

"Who's with me?" he asked.

"Me," Shari answered.

"Me too. Always," Ryan grunted. "I'm going to come. Please let me."

Ben gripped Ryan's hips and frantically drove into him, finally allowing himself to fuck unconstrained. When Ryan climaxed, he would wring the come straight out of Ben's dick as he always did. "Yes."

He sealed their fates with that one word.

Ryan buried his face in the crook of Shari's neck and allowed his unimaginable control to unravel. He began to flood their woman. Every pump of come that left him made his ass squeeze Ben's cock impossibly tighter. Ben fought to penetrate the stubborn muscles as he too began to shoot.

Shari turned her head into the pillow to muffle her scream. She writhed on the bed, joining them in ecstasy.

It seemed as if their orgasms lasted forever, each one delivering more pleasure to their partners. Eventually the ecstasy faded and a bone-deep satisfaction replaced it.

Ben withdrew, watching his come trickle from Ryan's ass and down his sac with a possessive thrill coursing through him. He tended to the wrecked man, unhooking him and cleaning him before allowing Ryan to do the same for Shari.

Finally, they snuggled together in Shari's bed, with her in the center, where she preferred to sleep between them. He realized they were forming a routine, and couldn't be happier.

Their new normal was the one he wanted to keep for the rest of his life.

He could grow old and die content, just like this.

∽ TWENTY-EIGHT ∾

Shari smiled as their whole gang packed a waiting room at St. Ann's Hospital yet again...this time for much happier reasons than usual. Well, Jambrea, who was in hour twenty of labor, might not exactly agree with that assessment. Lacey was also missing, since she was assisting in the delivery.

When the exterior door opened and a man in a dark trench coat entered, Shari's stomach flip-flopped. Everything from his short, slicked-back hair, to his dark sunglasses, to his non-descript yet expensive clothes reminded her of men who had visited her brother at their compound, when it had still been more fortress than resort.

Whoever he was, he clearly belonged to an elite, well-funded organization. Friend or foe? Military or civilian? That, she couldn't say. Frankly, she hoped he kept right on walking. They'd had enough of that kind of shit to last a lifetime. Boring, that's what she wanted.

He glanced discreetly around the room, then strode to her with enough purpose that JRad and Mason stepped closer, about the same time Ben and Ryan angled themselves in front of her.

"Ms. Shari David?" he asked, though he obviously already knew who she was.

Which put her at a severe disadvantage.

"Who wants to know?" Ben demanded.

"I'm a representative of the Banks Fund," he replied, as if they should know what that meant.

"Oh!" Izzy hopped up from where she'd been keeping Ezra and Julie entertained at a low table with a wooden train set on top of it.

"Sweetheart, you know this guy?" Razor asked his wife.

"Not exactly," she responded. "But I grew up with Archer Banks."

"You must be Isabella." The man smiled at her and extended a black leather-gloved hand. "So nice to meet you. Your family is lovely. Archer sends his congratulations."

"Likewise. I'm so proud of what he's accomplishing." She held herself more formally, as if etiquette instinctively threw her back to her socialite days. It was easy for Shari to forget sometimes where they'd each come from. The only thing that mattered was that they'd ended up here, together, as if they'd been intended to find each other from the start. "If you're here, does that mean…?"

The man nodded once, then returned his attention to Shari, Ben, and Ryan. Specifically, he stared down at the two-piece set Shari wore on her left ring finger. "That's very beautiful. Unique."

"Thank you." She didn't plan to pretend it was anything other than a pair of precious promises, given to her by the loves of her life. "My men gave them to me to symbolize our partnership."

"I see. I believe this is my favorite delivery yet." The man cracked the hint of a smile. "I'm honored to give you this on behalf of the Banks Fund."

From his breast pocket, he withdrew an ornately embossed envelope which didn't have a single dinged corner or smudged bit on the parchment. He presented it to her with the front facing her, so she could clearly make out her own name, Ben's, and Ryan's in astonishing handwriting that probably took a skilled calligrapher hours to perfect.

"I, uh, thank you?" Shari wasn't sure how to respond.

"You are so very welcome." As soon as she accepted the envelope, the man turned to leave. He was out the door before she could think of what to ask him next. Right before he stepped out into the chilly afternoon, he gave Izzy a subtle tip of his head, then left without another word.

"What. The. Fu—"

"Fudge." Jeremy cut off Special Agent Salinas, who had officially accepted his new job with the OSPD, before he could owe the kids more money for the curse jar.

Everyone turned to stare at Izzy.

She gave them a coy shrug. "It's a good thing, I promise. Go ahead. Open it."

Shari looked up at her guys. "Do you know about this?"

"No clue." Ben eyed the envelope suspiciously while Ryan shrugged, shaking his head.

The stationery was so thick it might as well have been cardstock. It felt extravagant between her fingers. With the utmost care, she slid her finger beneath the flap in the back, sad to break the royal blue wax seal with an ornate D stamped into it.

Odd for something from the Banks Foundation, wasn't it? Why not a B?

She didn't have long to wonder.

From within the gold foil lined envelope, she withdrew what turned out to be an invitation.

"What is it?" Ellie wondered from where she perched on Lucas's lap.

Shari read it aloud, hardly able to form the sentences when they seemed so surreal. "'You and the guests listed below have been selected for an all-expenses-paid luxury cruise on Archer Banks' mega-yacht, the *Divemaster*. We would like to thank you for your courageousness in maintaining the home front for some of the bravest men and women to have served our country. In addition, we would like to show our appreciation of the valor you and your friends, who have each made major contributions to your community in their own ways, have demonstrated. It is our hope that by offering you and your life partners the chance to celebrate a commitment ceremony at sea, in whatever location you select in the world, some of your selfless actions will be rewarded. Nothing would please us more than if happy memories could replace a few of the dark ones we understand each of you carry.

"'Please contact us at your earliest convenience to arrange the dates that work best for you and your party so we can schedule our private jet to pick you up and transport you to the *Divemaster*. A month of leave for each of the Men in Blue members has been prearranged and secured with a generous donation from the Banks Foundation. These funds will be used for the expansion of the technology department of the OSPD and significant raises for each man and woman employed there who is included in this missive. We're sure you will have many questions, which we are glad to answer. We look forward to welcoming you aboard! Sincerely, Banks, and the Divemasters.'"

By the signature line, her mouth had gone dry and her hands were trembling so hard she thought she might drop the beautiful letter.

"Is this for real?" Shari looked to Izzy, blinking rapidly.

Her friend nodded, too emotional to speak.

Tyler did it for her. "Damn, that's like getting a golden ticket to Willy Wonka's factory. But better. I heard about this on the news. They've been sending these things out to notable people across the world. Who would have thought we counted?"

"I can't believe it." Detective Tran, who'd stopped by for a bit to add her support, said, "You guys are so lucky! And the department! So much good can be done as a result of that funding. This is amazing. Congratulations."

"Raya," Shari said softly. "You're coming too."

"*What?*" For the first time since they'd started hanging out with her following the kidnapping, she forgot to wear her stone-cold bitch face. "Are you kidding me?"

"Nope. Gregory's also on the list. You all are."

"Hell, yes!" The Special Agent broke decorum to shout.

Julie looked up from the train set only long enough to shake her finger at him. "That'll be a quarter, please."

Razor whooped, then said, "Bathing suits are optional in international waters, right?"

"Your cheeks are too white for skinny dipping." Lily gave them a solid spank.

Lucas spun Ellie around, while Shari watched Ben and Ryan share a deep kiss before turning toward her. "I guess we're getting hitched."

She bounced up and down. "I'm finally going to see the ocean! Tropical blue water, palm trees, and a romantic destination wedding with our friends. It's a dream come true. You guys are my dream come true."

"All I need is for you two to be happy," Ben said softly to her and Ryan before hugging them both so tight they almost merged into one person.

They would have continued their celebrations, except just then Clint burst through the door. "They're here. Come quick. We want you to meet our kids before Jambrea uses up the favors the other nurses owe her."

"Uncle Clint! Don't mess around. Are they *girls*?" Julie demanded as she ran to his side and grabbed his hand.

"Why don't you see for yourself?" He picked her up and carried her into the main area of the hospital. The rest of their bunch followed close behind.

Razor tackle hugged Clint from behind. "Congratulations, Daddy."

The rest of the guys who could reach took turns slapping him on the back.

"When you're ready for a break, I've got a box of cigars out in the car," Jeremy told him. "Good ones."

As they squished themselves into Jambrea's room, Shari thought about a scene not so different from this one. Ezra had only been days old, Lucas a mess after his amputation. She'd only recently met Jambrea, though she'd known right away they'd be friends for life.

Shari had stumbled into this eclectic blend of people. Friends with a complex web of ties between them. Somehow she'd become one of them.

Grateful and weepy, she couldn't hold back her happy tears anymore when she spied Jambrea, exhausted yet radiant. She nursed a tiny, perfect human with a pink hat while Clint rocked an equally itty-bitty baby with a blue hat.

"One out of two isn't bad. Good job, Uncle Matt." Julie patted his hand, then abandoned him in favor of gawking at her new besties.

Shari laughed and cried at the same time.

She'd never been happier in her life. Each morning she kept shattering her personal best record from the day before.

And she had a feeling that they would continue that streak for many years to come.

Don't Miss Divemasters

A Brand-New Trilogy Coming From Jayne Rylon This Summer. Pre-Orders Available Now, Sneak Peek Excerpt Below

Going Down – Coming May 10th, 2016
Going Deep – Coming June 14th, 2016
Going Hard – Coming July 12th, 2016

Three SCUBA instructors, who happen to be sexual dominants, are about to take the ultimate plunge. If you're extraordinarily lucky, you'll be invited to join them on the Divemaster, where work and pleasure go hand in hand. Welcome aboard!

Archer Banks relishes his carefree lifestyle. Together with friends and fellow divemasters Miguel Torrez and Tosin Ellis, he travels the world, SCUBA diving by day, entertaining lonely female tourists by night. Until his father dies, instantly transforming Archer from a beach bum to a billionaire by shackling him with an enormous, undesired inheritance.

With the help of his family's longtime butler, Archer is determined to turn his new golden handcuffs into a golden opportunity. He prays Miguel and Tosin will come along for the ride when he repurposes his family's mega-yacht into a vessel well-suited for both work and hardcore play.

Never in his worst nightmares does he expect their maiden voyage to be such rough sailing. Not only is Archer's old crush, Waverly Adams, among their passengers, but the men have also stumbled upon a vast sunken treasure—one worth killing for.

Waverly surprises Archer with an alluring naughtiness he never got the chance to experience in their younger days. Busy accepting the challenge she issues his dominant side in the Divemaster's onboard club every night, he might be distracted and short on sleep. But could he also be blind to more dangerous facets of her personality?

When the divemasters can no longer deny there's foul play at hand, will Archer be going down with the ship, cursed by his family's fortune, or will Waverly turn out to be the woman of his most wicked dreams?

Sneak Peek – Going Down, Divemasters, Book 1

Prologue

Archer's ringing cell trampled the tropical night symphony composed of lulling waves, chirping bugs, and rustling palms. He would have fumbled around on the nightstand to silence the racket if an armful of bronzed, slender woman hadn't stopped him. After rolling the beach bunny off his chest, he settled her quickly yet gently on the edge of his double bed. Refusing to be distracted by her wild, sun-bleached mane, or the way the moonlight steaming in the window highlighted her damn-near-perfect ass, he forced his dick's attention from the adorable snuffle she surrendered as she burrowed into his lumpy pillow.

Archer turned his back on all that natural beauty. He rebelled against everything in his soul by lunging for one of the only remnants of offensive technology he allowed to intrude in his life. He didn't have a choice, really, since the hunk of plastic threatened the integrity of his eardrums by refusing to shut the fuck up.

Only one person in the entire world had been programmed with that specific God-awful, completely unnatural racket that now blared from his phone. The man who was instructed only to interrupt his solitude in a life-or-death emergency.

Fuck. Fuck. Fuck.

Archer launched himself from the freshly laundered sheets, which smelled of sunshine and salty ocean spray.

"Don't expect me to rush to that bastard's side for some kind of deathbed confessional." Archer figured he maybe should have said hello first. His bitterness rushed out before he could manage anything else.

"No need. He's gone." The familiar voice on the other end of the line, thousands of miles away, made Archer more homesick than the news of his own loss. "It was fast. Painless. Though probably traumatizing for the two young ladies your father was attempting to have sex with when the stroke hit."

"Jesus." Archer stumbled across the room. He slipped out the sliding glass door that led to a half-rotten deck, barely big enough for two plastic chairs, then down the three stairs to the beach. Naked, he sank onto his knees in the sand. He glanced over his shoulder toward the woman whose name wasn't nearly as memorable as the way she'd sucked him off before getting him hard again, then riding him with thighs powerful enough to cling to a breaching humpback.

Brittany! That was it. He was almost sure.

Was he turning into everything he'd spent his entire adult life trying to distance himself from? Had his father remembered the names associated with the pussies that had killed him?

Archer's stomach churned at the thought. Acid seared his esophagus. Just like it had before he'd left that world he'd never belonged in. He hadn't looked back since.

This was definitely going to be the worst night of Archer's life.

"Sir?"

He shook his head when the question came softly—kindly, even—from his family's butler, who'd been more like a true relative than any he shared filthy blue blood with. It was the reason he'd borrowed the guy's name when he'd fled. "Come on, Banks. You changed my shitty diapers plenty of times. Don't you think formality's a little uncalled for? I've never been that person. Much to my father's disappointment—"

"Archer." A soft chuckle warmed Banks' tone this time. "That might have been true once. But not always. Over time I think he might have envied your escape. Admired it, though he was too proud to admit such things. Or maybe he respected you too much to go against your wishes and contact you."

"I highly doubt that." Archer swallowed hard against the feelings he'd thought he'd buried long ago. He might be a thirty-year-old man, but part of him would always regret that he hadn't been able to be the son his father wanted.

"Well, this is for certain. He didn't truly disown you. You were never cut out of his will. In fact, despite your wishes, he left you everything."

"Everything?"

"His entire holdings. All of it, down to the last cent." Banks delivered the most devastating news of the night.

Everything Archer had never wanted had finally caught up with him. Golden chains ensnared his wrists and ankles, keeping him from imagining he could ever move freely again. He'd seen firsthand what it took to run an empire.

Just like that, Archer had gone from beach bum to billionaire.

Fuck him, life as he knew it—and loved it—was over.

He scrubbed his hands through his hair and caught sight of the woman he'd left in his bed dressing hurriedly by the light of the wall-mounted lamp before blowing him a kiss and heading for the door.

At least he'd gone out with a hell of a bang.

Literally.

"It's not exactly a death sentence, Sir."

"Banks," he growled.

"I mean...Archie."

The shock of hearing that long lost nickname, right now, had Archer blinking fiercely. Somehow he didn't think there was enough salt spray in the air to blame his reaction on that. "It feels like it. I'm proud of who I am these days. I don't want it. I don't want to be like him."

He scrunched his eyes closed. It was as if he were a recovering alcoholic who'd been offered an entire chain of distilleries. Archer knew how easy it would be to be corrupted by unimaginable wealth. It hadn't been easy to sacrifice everything once, but he'd quit superfluous material possessions cold turkey and had never been happier than he was here. With next to nothing.

"So we'll give it away." Banks' solution seemed genius. Simple yet complicated at the same time.

"Really? Will you help me?"

"Of course. If that's still what you want, after you've really thought about it some," Banks promised. "I am the estate's executor. It will take some time to settle things. Let me see to the legalities, and you start dreaming about who you'd like to help. This fortune can do so much good in the world."

"I...uh... Okay, thanks." Archer couldn't believe this was happening. "Pay yourself. A shit-ton. Ten times whatever you think is an outrageous salary. You deserve a hazard bonus for the decades you've put up with my family's shit. God knows I couldn't do it. As if that wasn't obvious when I bailed."

"I will." Banks laughed, then said warmly, "For the record, I'm proud of you too. Dream big, Archie."

ABOUT THE AUTHOR

Jayne Rylon is a *New York Times* and *USA Today* bestselling author. She received the 2011 RomanticTimes Reviewers' Choice Award for Best Indie Erotic Romance.

Her stories used to begin as daydreams in seemingly endless business meetings, but now she is a full-time author, who employs the skills she learned from her straight-laced corporate existence in the business of writing. She lives in Ohio with two cats and her husband, the infamous Mr. Rylon.

When she can escape her purple office, Jayne loves to travel the world, SCUBA dive, take pictures, avoid speeding tickets in her beloved Sky and—of course—read.

Made in the USA
San Bernardino, CA
04 November 2016